FOR SALE —

Wedding dress,
size 20,
never worn.

A COLLECTION OF STORIES BY
Sophie Slade

ISBN 978-1-66783-277-7 (Print)
ISBN 978-1-66783-278-4 (eBook)

Welcome to My Readers

Welcome to *"For Sale: Wedding Dress, Size 20, Never Worn"*. This is a compilation of 23 short stories each written in a different genre. The first story describes how the book came about. The stories range from fact to fiction to pure fantasy. Some have elements of autobiography woven with fiction and others are purely the outpourings of my, at times weird, imagination. They are all about relationships in one way or another. As a couples' therapist for 30 years and as a person who has been through the many ups and downs that relationship challenges have brought my way, I have long been fascinated by this topic. None of the stories are about my clients or any members of my family.

Following each short story is an invitation to readers who are interested to write something of your own. I hope that it will inspire you to plumb the depths of your own imagination and discover yourself more deeply through writing. However, many readers may want to ignore these invitations and just read the stories.

I offer my stories with trepidation about what people who know me will think of me. It takes courage to reveal who I am through my writing. It has been a joy, a surprise and at times a shock to discover myself as the stories unfolded in front of me.

I hope you enjoy them, are moved by them, relate to them, react or respond to them.

Comments from Readers

"*For Sale: Wedding Dress, Size 20, Never Worn* by Sophie Slade is a delightful book. In this multi-genre collection of diverse kinds of short stories, the author moves us from mythology to poetry to mystery to tragedy, each time answering the intriguing question—who is selling an unworn wedding gown in the local paper, and why? Readers are sure to devour—and be inspired by—this fun, imaginative, and insightful short-story collection."

NIKKI ALI, NOVELIST, EDITOR & HISTORIAN
(@mistressmwriter)

"The stories in this book are poignant, funny, imaginative and psychologically true. Sophie Slade is a great writer with creativity and wit.

CHERYL DOLINGER BROWN, LCSW, PSYCHOTHERAPIST, NYC

Table of Contents

The Start of It All—Part 1

"Do you remember me telling you about that ad in the *Malone Free Trader* that I saw a few years ago?" asked David as they sat in a restaurant together having dinner. "The one that said, 'For sale: Wedding dress, size 20. Never worn'".

"Vaguely," said Sophie. "Why do you ask?"

"It made me feel so sad," said David. "It has stayed with me. There's a story behind that ad."

"Mm." said Sophie. "Yes, probably. But we'll never know it. What's the story you would make up?" They spent the rest of the evening making up stories which became ever more fanciful and elaborate. David's was about a couple who loved each other very much. The guy was a lumberjack and was killed when a tree fell on him. David had had an unfulfilled desire to become a forest ranger. Sophie's tale started to become more and more elaborate and detailed. She couldn't wait to start writing it down. In all her excitement an idea started to form.

"I bet every person would make up a very different story, come at it from a different angle. I think it would make a great book of short stories to gather a bunch of different people's writings. The title of the book could be "For Sale: Wedding Dress. Size 20. Never worn," said Sophie, getting increasingly excited by her own idea. She had recently been enjoying a compilation of mystery stories by well-known and new writers, so had that format in her mind.

"Wouldn't it be neat! I'm going away on retreat with a group of my women friends next week. I'm going to ask them each to write a short story that comes out of that title. Then maybe I can somehow get them published. I'd love to have some men's writings in there also. Would you be willing to ask your guys when you go and meet up with them, if they would be willing to write something as well?" David was getting together with a couple of the husbands whilst Sophie was on retreat with her women's group. "Retreat" would not exactly describe the men's time together!

Sophie could see it all. She almost had the cover designed. Perhaps she could go wider and get submissions from other people she knew. Her brain was buzzing with possibilities.

The next day she began to elaborate in her mind on the story she had come up with the night before over dinner. She started to write it up on her computer. She could not keep up with her own thoughts, they were flowing so fast. She felt a huge creative surge. Her whole body felt vibrantly alive and full of energy. One idea after another zapped through her brain as she typed, and the story flowed of its own accord onto the paper.

Sophie was convinced her women friends would get excited about the idea of the book and jump on board with her. She couldn't wait to tell them.

It didn't happen quite that way. When she proposed it to them they were intrigued by the idea and started to play with one- or two-story lines, but when it came to actually writing something none of them came through for her. There always seemed to be something else to do that felt perhaps easier or more appealing—yoga, meditation, conversation, walks, cooking together, crafts. The time flew by.

However, whilst she was on retreat with them Sophie's ideas kept coming and coming and she kept writing and writing during their free times. She was surprised at what was pouring out of her almost unheeded. The first story she wrote, The Police Report, was quite edgy and raw, with an ending that startled her. It was like the material was flowing effortlessly from her own shadow, the untapped, partly repressed parts of her that would have been totally unacceptable in the very proper environment she grew up in. At the same time, she felt so alive and generative, so connected with her own creative source.

When she read the story she had written to her friends, they gave her lots of very positive feedback, but still no-one got down to writing something themselves.

"OK," thought Sophie. "I'm going to have to rethink this. I'm having so many ideas myself, perhaps I can come up with several stories each in a different genre—a murder mystery, a torrid erotic bodice-ripper, a sci-fi story, and so on. They don't have to all be about the same dress. Each story might be about a different *dress, in a different genre just as if different people were writing them. And then I could put them all together and publish them. It would be a lot more work but I'm loving writing. The main challenge would be to find the time in my already overloaded schedule, especially given the other two professional books I'm currently not finding time to work on. Maybe this is a doable project to get me going and would help me find a way to complete the other two."*

So, Sophie kept writing and writing. For several months the stories kept pouring out of her, some just spontaneously and effortlessly, others she had to work on writing and rewriting. What follows are the 23 stories that she produced. However, she never gave up on the hope of getting other people's ideas.

The Invitation

I invite you to jot down your ideas for scenarios that are prompted by the ad "For Sale: Wedding Dress, Size 20, Never Worn", just an outline of the characters and the story line. Who placed the ad? Why? What happened before or after the ad was placed? Just go with whatever comes up for you.

Or write a whole short story yourself. See what it feels like to come up with your own ideas. Start with one question such as Who placed the ad? Who responded? And go from there. Try not to censor what comes or to overthink your plot. Just let it come, let it emerge by itself. You can always go back and edit it later but see what emerges spontaneously from your own psyche.

If you start to hear some old childhood messages telling you all the things you can't do or aren't good at or should/

shouldn't be doing, it may be helpful to just acknowledge them but let them know clearly that they are not needed right now. They may just be the voices of your parents or teachers trying to protect you or keep you safe in the ways they knew. But you are an adult now and you have other ways to keep yourself safe, other choices. It's time to grow beyond the old restrictions and discover for yourself what lies inside you.

Maybe stories sometimes come from the same places in us that our dreams come from. When we dream we have endless creativity. Stories and scenarios emerge with great detail without any conscious effort on our part. Perhaps dreams are the psyche doing its inner work, resolving unfinished business. And no-one can really tell you not to dream or how you "should" or "shouldn't" be dreaming. Perhaps stories written this way are also ways of discovering ourselves, accessing those parts that were not allowed expression in childhood, our untapped or stunted inner selves. So, take a risk and open yourself up to this fascinating possibility of self-discovery through writing, even if your own internalized critical voices try their best to stop you.

After each story there will be an invitation to you to write something yourself with some hints and ideas about how to go about this or a topic for you to play with.

Please feel free to ignore these invitations if they don't speak to you. I hope that you will enjoy my stories anyway and share them with your friends or book group if you belong to one. My women's group have been so supportive of me throughout this even though they didn't write any stories of their own (yet).

If the invitations do inspire you to write, I hope you have as much fun as I did, discovering the weird and wonderful vagaries of your own mind.

And when you have written your own outline or story read on.

The Police Report

She's in a hotel room down the street from the church waiting to hear he's arrived. She's wearing one of those soft terry robes over her underwear which is silky, new, more lace than the practical style she usually wears, bought specially for the special day—and the night. She paces around getting increasingly anxious and puzzled. It's not like him. Her best friend and maid of honor, Joanne, tries to soothe her, reassure her, distract her as the minutes tick by, past the scheduled start time of the wedding. Finally, a knock at the door. Hopefully, Dianne goes towards the closet to get the dress as Joanne goes to open the door. Dianne's father is standing there. He enters and comes straight towards her. He puts his arm around her. She flinches, knowing instinctively that something really bad is about to happen.

"Di," he says, "You'd better sit down. I have some bad news." He pauses for breath as she sits on the bed. "There's been an accident. Jim and Ted—on their way to the church. A collision with a truck. I don't know how to say this. Both dead on impact. The minister will make an announcement in the church. The police dispatcher who took the call recognized Jim's name when the accident report came through and knew you were marrying him today. He called one of your colleagues. They checked it out. There's no mistake. A dreadful tragedy." He paused a few moments to let it start to sink in, then continued. "Come home with me. I'll take care of you, baby."

"No," was all Dianne said. Then turning to Joanne, "Take me back to my apartment."

Her father turned away. "I'll go and sort everything out," he said as he left the room. "Anything you need."

Dianne carefully put the dress back in the garment bag and zipped it up, then put her street clothes back on over her lacy underwear, aware of the incongruity. Joanne scurried around and put the rest of her stuff, make-up, hairbrush—all new—in her suitcase with her going-away outfit and new silky nightgown. Joanne drove the silent Dianne back to her flat, put the dress in the closet, the suitcase in the bedroom, then poured them both a stiff gin. Joanne sat with her in silence as day changed into evening and the light faded.

Finally, Dianne said, "Thanks, Jo. I'll be OK. I want to be alone. I'll try to get some sleep. I'll call you."

Reluctantly Joanne let herself out, feeling inadequate to say the right words to comfort, to make it hurt less. In her job as a policewoman she had on several occasions had to tell people bad news. She always felt totally inadequate to the task and knew that in the end all she could do was leave and let them handle it however they would.

Sitting there in the dark Dianne wondered if she had always secretly known that it was all an impossible dream, that it would never really come true, that she'd been kidding herself to think it would. After all she was 36 and Jim was the first real boyfriend she'd ever had. She'd met him at her church—at a bible study group they both attended. He was nice, caring, gentle, nurturing, not pushing her for things she wasn't ready to give like the rough and ready cops she mostly knew. They were always making sexual comments and jokes, probably because they knew it made her uncomfortable. She and Jim had, in accordance with the values of their shared faith, decided they would wait until after they were married to be fully sexual with each other. In their occasional kissing and fondling, Jim had taken it very slowly and she loved and respected him for this. She had told him, perhaps in rather vague terms, how after her mother died when she was 12, her father would come to her bed some nights for comfort. Sometimes he would just hold her in his arms and cry into her soft flesh, stroking her hair. Sometimes he sought other kinds of comfort. She never gave Jim any details—how she never turned him away—somehow she couldn't. She would lie there night after night while he did unspeakable things, things she never even hinted at to anyone, and thought about recipes she would make. She turned to the comfort of food to deal with the devastating loss of her mother and the nightly visits from her father.

She started by trying to recreate her mother's recipes, trying to bring her back perhaps through the familiar food. Then gradually she branched out and introduced new and more exotic foods. She knew her father didn't like the spicy, foreign foods she served him, beautifully presented, beyond reproach—Indian curries, Mexican dishes flavored with hot chilies, tangy pad Thai noodles. He liked the very basic, bland foods her mother had always dutifully prepared, exactly to his taste. For Dianne it was one very small way of protesting, of getting back at him. He didn't say anything about not liking what she served up to him. He took it "lying down" without complaint. Maybe his penance, his apology. She didn't know. They never spoke about it. She just sat and watched him as he chewed and swallowed the food she put in front of him.

She put on weight. Gradually over time a protective layer of fat grew up around her soul. She kept herself to herself. She didn't date. Her only friend was Joanne, also a loner, whom she met when they attended police academy together. During those teenage years her other comfort or distraction was cop shows—where predictably week after week, episode after episode, the police would catch the "bad guy" and put him away where he deserved. She found such comfort in the inevitability of this outcome. She never linked it directly with a secret hope that her own father would someday be caught and punished. *CSI—Special Victims Unit* was her favorite. She just watched the shows and tried to figure out how the police would unravel the clues to the certain conclusion.

So it made sense that when she finished school she signed up for the Police Academy. Over the years she made her slow progression through hard work, attention to detail, dedication, up to the rank of detective sergeant. She achieved results through solid, dogged police work rather than through flair and brilliant hunches as some of her earlier heroes and heroines had done. She was well enough liked although no-one except Joanne would really call her a friend. She kept her head down and did her work. She attended church regularly, and what little social life she had was through her connections there.

She sat in her chair through that night and all through the next day after the terrible news of Jim and Ted's deaths feeling a range of feelings—grief and sadness naturally, maybe some relief too because she could go back to her old life, keep doing what she'd always done and knew how to do, not have to face any new and frightening challenges of being with someone, being a wife. At times she felt disbelief, at times self-blame, at times resignation. Surprisingly, what she didn't feel was hunger, she didn't turn to food to deal with her grief, she didn't cook. She didn't pace. She just sat numb for the rest of Saturday and all through Sunday. On Sunday night she went and lay down on her bed and slept some. In the morning she got up, got dressed, and went to work. She was supposed to take 2 weeks off for her honeymoon but begged to be rescheduled into the roster. She needed to go back to work.

The first week was hard but it gradually got easier. She immersed herself in her work. She sold her wedding dress by placing an ad in the *Free Trader:* "For Sale: Wedding Dress, Size 20, Never Worn". She packed up the lacy underwear and put it in the poor box at church. She didn't talk with anyone about what had happened and her colleagues seemed as happy as she was to avoid the subject. A hush descended if it was ever referred to, even obliquely.

After a few months of numbing herself out, of trying not to think about it at all, of trying not to feel, she started to notice her natural curiosity returning. She didn't address the big, unanswerable question of why it had happened, but did feel she needed to know what had happened—to get the details of the accident so she could put it to rest and move on—who was driving, whose "fault" it was, although no charges had been laid. She couldn't believe it was Jim's. He was always such a good and careful driver, but it was his wedding day. Was he anxious, distracted? Had he had a drink to give him some Dutch courage? She was a details person and she wanted details so she could understand and file it away like an old, solved case.

But when she went to look up the case report the sergeant on duty seemed uncomfortable, looked away. "No, no, you don't want to go digging around in that. It was an accident. Let it be. Can't bring them back. No one's fault—just an accident."

So she walked away. But the itch to know stayed and would not let her be, with another layer of questions now—why didn't the sergeant want her to see the report? Were the injuries gruesome? Was it something else?

Her need to know increased and one evening when a new person who didn't know her was in charge of records, she returned. She stood in the records room, reading through the report—standard stuff, until the very end of the coroner's report. On Jim's body there were traces of semen—his own and someone else's—that of the other victim in the crash. The men had been engaged in a sexual interaction with each other shortly before the crash.

• • •

Jim got up on the day of his wedding full of anxiety and excitement. Finally, everything was going to be OK, thanks to Dianne. His marriage to her, his sacred vows would save him from his own past, save him from his own sin. He would finally be a normal man with a loving wife. Dianne was such a wonderful person—quiet, steadfast, chaste and such a wonderful cook. And kind—the way she had taken care of her father after her mother's death, cooking for him, comforting his tears—was saintly; a woman who had spent her days fighting evil and perversity. He knew she was the one who could save him from himself. He was almost 40 now. It was time. He was ready. It was now or never. Oh, to be free of the shame, the guilt, the secrets, the lies, the fears of being found out. Maybe he would even go to confession one day and be absolved in the eyes of God. He would live a pure clean life from here on, grow old with all that behind him, welcomed back fully into the flock, forgiven in the eyes of the Lord. For the Lord knew and had brought him Dianne to save him from sin. He was so grateful to her. He vowed to be a good husband and was looking forward to making those vows before God and the congregation this day.

He got out of bed, showered and shaved and called Ted. Ted was going to be beside him today, his best man—the irony did not escape him. He had known Ted so many years, since they were both altar boys together. They had found comfort in each other when the priest had done things to them they were not allowed to tell anyone else about. They had been chosen as special, as vessels to receive the special sacrament that only they could know about. They were warned that if they told anyone they would not be believed and would be seen as evil liars, as blaspheming against God's representative and would be condemned to burn in eternal fires of Hell. They kept their secret, even when they no longer believed in the rhetoric. They shared the same shame and guilt, the same sense of being somehow special and yet wrong and dirty.

During their adolescent years, as they became more aware of the ways things were in the world and started to understand, the forbidden nature of what they had experienced only increased the intensity of their excitement when they touched each other and continued where the priest had left off. Sometimes they tried to stop, they tried to be like other boys who were always talking about girls and tits and cunnies. Sometimes they pretended, making coarse jokes with the guys or kissing the girls in the dark, but the only way either of them was excited by this was if they imagined it was each other they were kissing, but roving hands quickly revealed the differences. They soon returned to each other filled with even more fear and inadequacy. By now they knew their Christian faith despised their sinful lusts and behaviors. They continued to be careful, secretive, split inside between who they pretended to be to the world and who they felt they really were. Even as more and more gays came out, they knew they could not and still be accepted within their faith community. They would be shunned and condemned.

They purposely chose to go to colleges on opposite sides of the country, hoping this would finally bring an end to their sinful bond. Jim studied law on the west coast and Ted went into architecture on the east. They didn't see each other for several years. Despite this separation, neither felt free to love another. Jim for a while engaged in many meaningless sexual encounters with men he didn't know, always feeling profound shame and self-loathing after the quick sexual release. Eventually he moved back to his hometown. He did not go back to his old church but sought out another church—his faith was still a strong part of who he was.

The first time he ran into Ted again he knew he had been waiting and looking each time he turned a corner, each time he entered a room, hoping to see him there. Ted was back in town for the Thanksgiving holidays, to celebrate with his family, when they ran into each other on the street. They went out for a drink together, as old friends do, to get "caught up." The tension and excitement between them were palpable from the first moment. Jim offered to drive Ted home. He parked in a dark spot at the end of Ted's street and before either of them could stop it they were in each other's passionate embrace. Jim drove Ted back to his apartment where they tore off each other's clothes, feasted on each other's bodies sating the hunger and thirst of the loveless years apart.

At the end of the holidays Ted returned to the east coast but they saw each other whenever they could, stealing moments secretly. Jim was terrified that if he were found out it would ruin his career and all his ambitions to become a judge. He would be rejected by his family and by his church. He knew his love for Ted was wrong, a thing to be cast out and yet try as he might he couldn't do it. When he was with Ted he felt alive, he felt himself.

When he met Dianne at bible study group, where he went to look for strength and guidance, he liked her immediately. They shared an interest in the law and in bringing the wrongdoers to justice. She was down-to-earth and real, he thought—no games, no subterfuge. She didn't make a lot of sexual demands on him that he couldn't meet. She represented all he longed to be. He told Ted about her. They argued and fought, said harsh things. Ted tried to convince Jim it would never work; he could never be the man he wanted to be no matter how much God was guiding him. Finally, Ted came around and supported Jim in his resolve to put the past behind. They had agreed that after Jim was married they would remain friends but there would never again be anything more. Ted agreed to be best man, to symbolically give Jim away to Dianne as the bride's father traditionally gave his daughter away to her new mate.

On the morning of his wedding Jim and Ted had arranged to have breakfast together and say a final goodbye to all that had been between them, burying it at last to leave Jim free for his new future. Ted went to pick Jim up at his apartment.

As soon as the doorbell rang Jim could feel the usual excitement rise within him. He resolved to fight it off. He opened the door. Ted was standing there already partly dressed in his wedding clothes for his role as best man. His dark grey suit pants fitted him perfectly. His brilliant, white, shirt was open at the neck and his grey waistcoat was unbuttoned. His jacket and tie hung over his arm. Jim took a deep breath in at the sight of him and let his breath out slowly, trying to calm himself. Jim had planned for them to go out for breakfast to some local café where they would be safe from temptation and say what needed to be said in a veiled and public way. Jim looked at Ted standing there for a long moment. Neither was aware who made the first move but soon they were again in each other's arms, carefully removing Ted's clothes, then kissing passionately, licking each other's bodies, sucking each other's cocks, penetrating, ejaculating on each other, crying out from love and lust and longing, the poignancy of this final lovemaking only adding to their desperation, until finally they dozed peacefully entwined together. Three hours later Jim stirred and looked over at the clock.

"Oh, my God," he cried, jumping out of bed. "Look at the time. We're supposed to be at the church by now. Throw on your clothes, quickly, we have to go."

Both dressed in great haste and were out the door, down the stairs and into Jim's car. He drove fast, exceeding the speed limit, frantic to reach the church, berating himself that he had let this happen again and on his wedding day.

"You know I will always love you until the day I die," said Ted softly. Jim turned towards him, looking deep into Ted's eyes, seeing the sadness and longing there. He held his gaze for a few moments. Maybe he was going to say something, maybe not. He never saw the stop sign or the truck coming towards them.

The Invitation

This was the first story which came out of me as I started to write—yes, Sophie is partly me and "The Start of It All, Part 1" is as it actually happened. I present the stories pretty much as they came through me, with some editing of the writing suggested by my wonderful editor, Maria Americo.

Regarding The Police Report, Maria has sensitized me to the prevalence of tragic queer characters who die in literature, especially that written by straight writers such as myself, a trend so common it has been referred to as "Bury Your Gays". (By the time you've read all my stories you might question just how "straight" I am—twisted might be a better descriptor). I took another look at the story and considered how I might change it but couldn't make it work and still keep the punch lines, so I have left it as it came.

I also looked inside to examine my own prejudices—to see if the story came from some personal biases. While I am sure I do have many biases and prejudices, as a couples' therapist I have worked with many straight, gay, lesbian, trans, queer + couples and I think I see a couple as a couple, no matter what their orientation, and work hard for all my couples to have happy endings, or at least to offer them the skills to make their lives full of joy and connection.

I invite you to write an "Unbury your Gays" story in which your queer characters get happy endings. If you have particular prejudices based on sexual orientation, I invite you to write this also into your story—you don't have to show it to anyone—but make sure the queer characters have happy endings. I invite you to write it with compassion for all your characters—the ones who are most like you but also, and perhaps especially, the ones whom you see as least like you.

Surprise, Surprise!

The next day I called the office of the *Free Trader* and told them to put a fucking ad in the paper "For Sale: Fucking wedding dress, size fucking 20, never fucking worn." She said that would be $5 plus 75c per word for 8 words for each day it was in. I counted 11 words, but I guessed the ones she was leaving out and didn't quibble. I placed the order to go in the next edition and told her to keep running it each week until I let her know it was sold. I gave her my credit card number.

I hadn't been feeling well the day before. I was definitely coming down with something—a flu bug was going round the office. My boss told me to take the rest of the day off. Thanks a lot! Would it have been better to not know, to get married and then find out what a fucking prick he was? Maybe I could have milked him for gobs of alimony plus damages—got him on breach of contract or something. Anyway, I straggled home feeling like shit, not knowing I was about to feel a hell of a lot worse in no time at all.

As I entered the apartment I could hear sounds coming from the bedroom. He was supposed to be at work. He'd said he had a big contract he was working on and that was why he was coming home late from the office so often recently. So at first I thought it must be burglars. My heart started to pound and my hands got all clammy. I didn't know whether to turn and run, to call the police, to look around for a weapon—a kitchen knife or baseball bat, although I knew we didn't have one of those handy as neither of us played baseball. With hindsight, I wish I'd called the fucking police but by the time they arrived it might have been too late to catch them in the act and that would have been a shame.

As I stood there deliberating what to do, I started to realize that these were not the kinds of sounds that a burglar was likely to make, unless he was going through my panty drawer and jerking off—yuck! But this was a duet not a solo—above the sound of male grunting and huffing, was a high-pitched squealing like a pig caught in barbed wire—a mounting crescendo of squeaks and squeals. I didn't linger long. I may have been blind and naïve but I'm not stupid. I caught on pretty fast to what was going on in there in our bed—our fucking bed. You'd think he'd at least have the decency to take the fucking whore to a hotel room—the cheap bastard. I didn't want to wait a second longer. I wanted to spoil their fucking orgasm in a way they wouldn't soon forget.

I thrust open the door loudly and ran into the bedroom at full speed, screaming at the top of my voice like a deranged banshee. I jumped up and down, I waved my arms, I screamed obscenities and then I threw up all over the bed and the two of them. I hadn't actually intended that bit ahead of time, it just sort of happened as the flu took full hold of me. I think it was the most satisfying part of all.

When I entered they were joined together in some kind of contortionists' position that I couldn't even figure out and that we had certainly never tried together. At my grand entrance they pulled apart immediately—I'm surprised I didn't hear the pop as he pulled out of her. And then I saw who she was—his fucking secretary! How fucking cliché! Couldn't he have been a bit more original and picked his hairdresser, or the haberdasher's wife? But no, his fucking secretary. And the fucking cunt can't have been any more than a size 8.

The Invitation

In this story it is so cliché that the guy is having it off with his secretary. I invite you to take a cliché that you find particularly irritating, trite or overused ("You can't judge a book by its cover", "One man's meat is another man's poison", "Every cloud has a silver lining", and write a short story with that as the central theme. You can beat it to death if you want or be as subtle as you like!

The Goddess Bride

I know I am going to die soon. I know my old body will give out before very long. I can feel the life energy ebbing out of me. I've had a good life, a long and fulfilling life. I have studied the sacred healing arts of women, the traditions, the rites and rituals handed down from times beyond remembered time. As I have aged and moved beyond my fertile years, crossing over into crone, into the post-menopausal years I have become a leader in this community of women who follow the teachings of the goddess. As a crone I carry much of the wisdom of the tribe. I have tried my best to pass it on to the younger women. I have sat with other crones of this community as we move closer and closer to joining the goddess in all the fullness of death. We talk about the wisdom we hold within. We argue at times with an ornery passion and conviction and yet with a willingness to listen and be informed by each other. Sometimes we bang our fists on the table to bring home a point of view and yet we listen to each other's different perspectives with deep respect. Together we struggle with the question of what our responsibility is towards the world which sometimes seems to be heading towards self-destruction and sometimes seems to be taking giant leaps of consciousness. We explore the meaning of being a crone, no longer maiden, no longer mother.

What is this wisdom that I hold within? I have seen so much, faced so much myself each day I have lived. Have I been able to share it with the young people in ways that are meaningful? Although we crones live now in seclusion to some degree in a sacred community of women, we still have faced the struggles of relationships in many of its forms: sisters, daughters, mothers, lovers—for the expression of our sexuality is an important aspect of our full aliveness and of our ways of being with each other. For certain festivals we also invite men into our midst to live out the ancient rituals of the joining of masculine and feminine. We have to face our jealousies and our rejections, our anger and our fears. I have interacted much with the outer world as a social worker and a teacher.

But now the time has come to let go of all things past and prepare myself to move on, knowing not what lies beyond the grave. I have done what I have done, lived out my destiny for better or for worse. At this point there is no undoing the fabric of the life I have woven. I must just finish off any loose ends left hanging.

I take the box out from the back of my cupboard. It is the only thing I have kept from my former life, my life before joining this community. I open the box and run my hand over the silky fabric of the dress within. I take it out and hold it to my chest. A tear rolls down my cheek. Is it a tear of sadness or regret? I don't think so. I would not have changed the path I chose could I go back and do it all again. It is perhaps a tear of loss for all the paths I chose not to walk across the many years of my life. With each path I chose there were many others I chose not to take. I lay the dress out on my bed—its whiteness a stark contrast to the midnight blue and gold of my bedspread. It is my wedding dress or was to be. It is the symbol of the life I chose not to live when I joined this sacred community of the goddess.

I ring the bell beside my bed and one of the young women charged with my care enters my room. She looks at the dress spread out on my bed and moves towards it. She gazes and strokes the fabric.

"It is so beautiful," she says, gently.

"I would like you to sell it," I say. "Perhaps you can put an ad in that *Free Trader* flyer we get through the door each week. 'For sale: Wedding dress. Size 20. Never worn.' I would like you to use the money to buy an iris to plant on my grave—a deep blue iris, the color of the night sky, with a center of brilliant gold. Will you do that for me?"

"Yes, crone woman," she answers me respectfully. "If you are sure this is what you want."

"Yes, take it away now, please. I have held onto it too long already. I don't know why I needed this symbol for so long of what was never to be lived but I did and now I must let all things go—the choices I made and those I did not, what I have accomplished and what I have not, what I have passed on and what I have not. It is all done now."

"Very well, crone woman. If that is your wish." She folded the dress with great care and put it back in the box, wrapped in the soft tissue paper. She left, taking the dress with her, and I lay down on the bed where the dress had been.

As a young woman I had followed a traditional path, training to have a "little" job in an office until I would get married and raise a family. I had come so close. There was a man. I had loved him deeply and he, I believe, loved me. We were engaged to be married. I had bought the dress. And then something stirred within me. I felt a need, my last menstrual period before my wedding, to go away somewhere, to be with other women, to bleed in a community of women. I had read of such communities, had even kept some clippings. I searched through my old file and found the one that had spoken to me most. It was in Glastonbury, England, an ancient place of legend and lore, a place where the ancient goddess wisdom had come into contact with the new Christianity many centuries before, a place where the mists of Avalon held and concealed the secrets of the ancient feminine divine.

I contacted the women's retreat center and booked a room. I had no idea what I would do when I got there but the pull was strong within me. I tried to explain it to my fiancé but had a very hard time finding the words to express the call I felt in my body to do this. He didn't understand any more than I did but said that if I felt I must do it then I should go. I packed my bag for a week's stay and left.

I never again returned to my old, prescribed life. I wrote to him and told him I would not be coming back but didn't tell him where I was or try to explain—there were no words that made sense. I had a few things sent to me by a friend I could trust, including my wedding dress. I wasn't sure at the time why I wanted it, or why I kept it but somehow I felt even then that I needed to, that it was right for me to hold on to this possibility of what might have been, the door I had chosen not to go through alongside the one I had. As I lie on my bed, I wonder what he has made of his life since I left. I hope he has found happiness. I imagine it hurt him deeply when I disappeared into the mists.

I found that a whole community of women existed behind the face of the retreat center, which welcomed and nurtured women who needed a time away from all the pressures of work and family, a place to come back to themselves. I immediately felt a strong sense of coming home, of belonging, of my body returning to some natural state that I hadn't even realized I had lost.

I discovered that the community embraced an alternative lifestyle of simple living, and study of the ancient goddess texts and mythologies. We usually rose with the sun, prepared ourselves for each day of service and manifestation of the goddess with meditation and a simple meal. Some of the women worked in the world outside as teachers, community organizers, health professionals—whatever they were trained for or best suited to. Property was shared. In the evenings we ate our meals together, prepared by the women who worked each day within the retreat. Most of our food was grown by us or bought from surrounding farms. Conversation was often lively as we related events from our day or challenges we were facing in our lives, in our relationships with each other and with the great divine mother. Conflicts, which sometimes arose, were talked through, held by the whole community. If a woman reacted from past pain in ways that were experienced as mean or selfish each of the other women shared with her a memory of a time when the woman had done something kind or caring for her. In this way she was welcomed back into her belonging in the community and her positive aspects were mirrored to her while her unkind actions were held without judgment. In the evenings we had time for solitary contemplation or for conversation, singing and dancing together in community as we chose.

Through our rituals we honored the cycles of our own bodies, the cycles of nature and the phases of the moon in ways that reflected the symbolic meaning of each. Spring was celebrated as a time of strong creative energy, summer as a time of ripening—we gathered many of our herbs at the summer solstice—, autumn as a time of letting go, winter as a time of quiet inner contemplation. Similarly, the new moon was welcomed as a time to start new projects, and to plant our seeds. During the waxing moon we nurtured that growth to help it come to it's fulness. Harvesting was done at the full moon. Waning moons were times of weeding out what was no longer needed and sometimes we fasted.

Each month at the bleeding time women could choose to withdraw into a special part of the retreat center. The irritations and dissatisfactions that emerged within us at these times were seen as important to contemplate so that we could make adjustments in our lives if needed. It was a time to notice what was out of alignment that could no longer be ignored. It was a time of solitude and journaling as well as deep explorative conversation. Living as we did in a community of women many of us menstruated in synchrony with each other. These times were both challenging and enriching, as we experienced our bodies cleansing themselves to make way for new life, new possibilities.

As a community of women our sexuality was honored and seen as an important part of the cycle of living. We lived it out in various ways. We took great care of each other's bodies as the vessels of our beings—bathing, massaging, oiling, brushing each other's hair. Both tender and erotic rituals were built into our lives. We bathed and frolicked in the red, iron rich waters that sprang out of the earth.

We developed special friendships, some of which lasted just a short time—simple infatuations—and some lasted many years. Full penetrative sex with men was mostly reserved for the annual Beltane fertility festivals and the winter Solstice celebrations, when young people, men and women from the surrounding communities, would join us for nights of feasting, music, dancing and of sexual joining to honor the coming together of the masculine and feminine energies of creation. The baby girls who were born of these couplings were raised by our community of women. The boys were raised lovingly by families in the surrounding villages, often the families of the young men who had sired them, if it was known who he was. Our community had a good relationship with the surrounding villages because of our reputation and all we contributed to helping the less fortunate and improving the lot of all who needed help—men and women. The children of the Beltane and Solstice rites were considered as special, sacred gifts from the goddess by us but also by the local villagers. They were much cherished and frequently visited by their birth mothers.

There was no real hierarchy in our community. Everyone's voice was considered equal, but the elders were honored for their great wisdom and experience. It was the calling of some to see to the smooth running of the community. All this I learned gradually after I asked to stay on when the week I had booked was over.

When I first arrived, being in the quiet retreat center among other women as I let my blood flow was very soothing. I had always menstruated heavily and suffered from migraines during my periods. Each month after my bleeding was over I felt as though I was clawing my way out of a dark underworld place back towards the light. The image of Persephone often came to my mind. The story, as I remembered it from my childhood, was that the maiden, Persephone, was stolen away from a sunny meadow where she was playing, by the god of the underworld, Hades, and taken down to his dark domain. He kept her hidden away there. Her mother, Demeter, Goddess of the harvest and fertility, searched throughout the world but could not find her daughter. She neglected her duties caring for the land and all the plants withered and died. Finally, Zeus intervened and told her where Persephone was being kept. Demeter went and pleaded with Hades for her daughter's return. Hades eventually agreed but stipulated that if Persephone looked backwards on her climb out of the underworld, then she would have to spend half the year with him and only half with her mother. Climbing out of the underworld, Persephone did indeed look back and so for half the year Demeter rejoices and cares for the corn and growing things and the other half she grieves and winter spreads across the land. Through the cycles of my own body I connected with this old tale of the cycles of nature. I felt a kinship with Persephone clawing her way up out of the darkness as I monthly struggled to regain some energy and life force.

I started to research this old myth and found several versions. Through my connection with Persephone I rediscovered her mother, Demeter. Perhaps today Demeter would be diagnosed as bi-polar and medicated out of her cyclical nature. Who knows?

As I moved in my own life from maiden to mother I connected more strongly with this goddess of fertility. I bore and raised my own two daughters, conceived during the Beltane fertility rites when men and women join together in sacred communion and Bacchanalian pleasure. I loved being a mother, from nursing my babies at my breast to seeing them grow and start to move away from me to school and colleges, returning with their wonderful, joyous discoveries. I raised them in this loving, sacred community that honored their femininity and launched them out into the world. They both chose to live outside the community as adults but they come back often to visit and renew their connections to us all.

I became passionate about our community garden and spent much time there tending the flowers and vegetables, taking an inordinate delight in harvesting the herbs, especially for the midsummer solstice festivals, as well as in gathering the vegetables we grew in abundance.

So, through my reading and research I came to Gaia and Sophia, to the great mother goddesses of Earth and Wisdom. Something shifted in me when I discovered the idea that for 30,000 years or more of human history the great divine creative energy of the universe was viewed by many to be female, embodied in statuettes such as Venus of Willendorf and Venus of Dolní Věstonice. These were usually amply proportioned, female figures with large breasts, rounded bellies, wide hips and curved buttocks. They were voluptuous, plump women I could relate to, being ample bodied myself. As a child I had been told of the Pantheon of Greek gods headed up by the male triumvirate of Zeus, Hades and Neptune. I had been told and was expected to believe in and worship the one male god of Christianity and Judaism, a judgmental old boy with a beard up in the sky somewhere, and his more compassionate and human son, Jesus, who got crucified after a short ministry—nothing much I could relate to there. But no-one ever gave me the alternative of a feminine divine to connect with. The Catholics, who at least had the figure of Mary—virgin, mother, Queen of Heaven—to turn to, were looked down upon and shunned in the circles I grew up in. In the Protestant and Anglican churches I attended, Mary only put in a brief appearance at Christmas, looking nothing like a woman who has just given birth in a stable after a long journey on a donkey, heavily pregnant.

When I discovered these voluptuous, ancient Earth Mother goddesses I suddenly felt connected in a way I hadn't ever experienced before, connected to the divine who flowed through me as woman. I felt connected to a Mother in a way I hadn't to my own mother, a good, caring woman but physically and psychologically corseted and constrained. I knew then that my intuitive pull to join this community in Glastonbury had been right for me. I knew that I wanted to live out my life manifesting the divine feminine through my own body and through my own works.

Sometime after I joined the community, I was visiting a women's retreat in Paris, France, and happened to go to a Catholic mass at l'Eglise St. Ignace. During the time of silent prayer that was a wonderful part of their ritual of worship, I realized more fully why I was so much more attracted to a feminine divine energy than to a masculine. I had a father who was warm and loving, welcoming of me, playful, joyous, gentle-manly, a much nicer character than the "spy in the sky" God, the judgmental old man who watched me all the time—not just my actions, but my very thoughts and what was in my heart, who could see me inside and out, who sat in critical judgment, a God who meted out punishment for my unrepented sins.

I am sure there have been many throughout history in many cultures around the world who needed the sense of an ever present father figure who cared about their every thought, word and deed and who guided them in their behavior. Many,

many cultures have suffered the consequences of absent or distant fathers who were present but uninvolved, dead, or gone off to fight a war or earn a living.

Not I. My need was much more for a warm cherishing mother who would hold me tenderly in her arms, support me from beneath rather than judge me from on high. My need was for a mother who was earthy and solid, who showed all her many faces. In the Christian church in which I grew up, through communion Jesus gives his own blood to be received into the bodies of his believers. I needed a mother who was willing to receive my blood, to receive the most primitive of the offerings of my own body without disgust or shame, my urine, my feces, my monthly flow. I needed a mother who was willing to receive the outpourings of my body, my heart, my mind, my soul, who could receive me and be enriched by me in her own capacity to give in return without appropriating what I gave and without rejecting it with ridicule whenever it didn't fit what she thought I should be putting forth into the world. I needed an earth mother whose own annual cycle of blood red leaves falling to earth mirrored my monthly cycle of menstrual blood. I needed a mother who could show the faces of her many seasons, her moist rotting fecundity, her winter barrenness, her frigidity and dark starkness, her glorious dress of fresh winter snow which quickly dirtied turning grey then black and filthy, a mother who could tolerate mess, without washing it away each day in the bath, or each week in the ritual of laundry. I needed a mother who could explode joyously into spring, from one day to the next, who could turn from muddy, sodden brown into a glorious green of fresh leaves and a riot of colorful budding flowers, who could show herself in all her rampant fertility, shout, dance, prance in wild abandon and who could quickly lose that freshness of youth and grow sere and dry in the hot summer sun. I needed a mother who could come full circle to the glory of her own menstrual time again. I needed a mother who could show herself in all her aspects unconstrained by her post-Victorian puritanism and constriction. I needed a mother at whose breast I could have suckled voluptuously or rapaciously, lazily taking my time or with desperate hunger, a mother who could have held me skin to skin and delighted in our bodily connection and sensuality without fear. No, it was a fecund, fully alive earth-mother goddess that I needed not a cold judgmental father or even a more gentle, compassionate brother god.

When I arrived in Glastonbury I intuitively knew this was where I belonged and that this was my path, the path I chose myself, the path that wasn't chosen for me by society or my parents. I studied to be a social worker to care for the people who needed to be held in the loving embrace of the Great Mother. I studied the ancient texts to immerse myself deeper and deeper in the ancient feminine wisdom. I studied what little is still known of the Eleusinian Mysteries, to understand the implications for today of the journey of descent, search and ascent. And so I moved from Mother to Crone, to elder of the tribe.

The wisdom that I hold within is about connectedness— connectedness to the earth, the Great Mother Earth that nourishes and sustains us all, to whom we must relate with respect;

connectedness to ourselves, our essence, our spirit, to our own life tapestry, to living each day in integrity with who we are and who we aspire to be, woman or man; connectedness with others, knowing that we co-create the future of the universe with each thought and deed. We are always impacting those around us positively or negatively with our look, our tone, our gestures of care or our ways of defending against our own pain. Through those we touch directly we ripple on outwards. I hold within me the knowledge of the responsibility of such connectedness. Just as acts of terror have ripple effects around the world, so too do each of my own words and actions, whether loving or judgmental, perhaps not so obviously but just as truly. Sadly, the great acts of kindness may not be as widely covered in the news but they impact the brains of all those who are touched by them just as truly. Just as each act of hatred and abuse ripples outward and forward through history, so too does each act of love, of understanding, of compassion. We are all inextricably connected in a web of energy out into the furthest reaches of the universe and beyond.

The wisdom I hold within me is that if we attack or criticize, shame or vilify those who, out of their own pain, their own beliefs and convictions, their own fears, have attacked us or sought to terrorize us, they will feel even more unsafe, misunderstood, marginalized, and will defend themselves against us with ever greater vehemence. I see that if we fail to hold to clear and firm boundaries we support them in acting out their pain in ways that hurt us. I also know that sometimes, miraculously, things of great beauty grow out of the worst circumstances.

We are sowers of seeds—we cannot know what will become of them. Yet still we must try to sow healthy seeds in fertile ground and then take care of them with sustained attention. Perhaps if we can work to increase our own sense of awareness and safety enough so that we can risk growing beyond our old ways of defending against our own fears, can search our own hearts for times when we have lashed out in pain and can simultaneously reach out to seek to listen to, understand and have empathy for those who attack us, then maybe we can find our way out of the darkness, can find the path of ascent and there will be some hope for the future. If we can hold others in our hearts as human beings who are responding to pain, fear, deprivation or whatever, then perhaps we can open a different door and take a step along a new path towards a different future. That is our choice.

This is the wisdom I hope I have lived increasingly in my own life. This is the wisdom I hope I have passed on to others. Marriage and committed intimate relationships in all their forms are a vehicle for living out these choices. The ways we treat each other each day in each interaction impacts us, our brains and our relationships. We can choose criticism, judgment, negation of the other's humanity, or we can choose compassion, understanding, empathy and the setting of clear boundaries. Marriage was not the path I chose, I never walked down the aisle in my beautiful white dress that I kept for so many years, but I have tried to live out the principles that create strong healthy, relationships in my community and with others outside. My dress is gone. I am ready to let go now.

We began as stardust you and I,
We are cosmic energy made manifest,
Each of us unique and yet connected,
So how can I hurt you and not hurt me.

The Invitation

I invite you to write a short story of your own spiritual journey, or that of someone else. It could be a famous person, such as Jesus, St. Theresa of Avila, Buddha, Mohammed, a prophet..., or someone you know personally that you interview—whoever you choose. Or you could imagine a fictional community—of women, or of men, or both. How do they live? Why do they live that way? Give it as much detail as you can.

Joseph was a Mensch*

*Note to Reader: *Mensch—a person of integrity and honour. From Early 20th Century Yiddish, originally from German Mensch—literally "person". Oxford English Dictionary on-line. While this is a Yiddish term the story is meant to be read with a British cockney accent.*

Joseph was a Mensch. I mean just consider the other possibility. Mary shows up one day and says:

"Guess what, Joseph. Some angel named Gabriel appeared from nowhere, wings and all, honest, and told me not to be frightened. He said that the Lord God really fancied me, that I'd found favour with him. He said I'd get pregnant and have a son. He even told me that I had to call the boy Jesus. What kind of a name is that? He told me that the Lord will acknowledge him as his legitimate heir, that he will be known officially as the Son of the Most High and that he will rule over you and all your descendants forever.

"So of course, I asked 'How is this going to happen? I'm still a virgin. Even though Joseph and I are engaged to be married, we never done it, I swear.' And this angel bloke said the Lord God would come on me and the power of the Most High would overshadow me. He seemed to know all about my cousin Elizabeth, too, that she's six months along, even though we kept it real quiet. She never thought she could get pregnant and she's really far too old to be having kids. It's disgusting at her age, although I didn't say that to him.

"Well, I didn't know what to say, so I just said 'Whatever. I dunno. I'm his servant but still, I don't think Joseph's going to like this.' Then this guy Gabriel told me again not to be frightened and he left, just like that. I don't remember anything after that. I was a bit gobsmacked. Perhaps he slipped something in the drink of water he gave me because I came over all kind of faint like. Anyway, now my period's late and my breasts feel sore."

What if Joseph had said "Right. Who are you trying to kid? Pull the other one, it's got bells on! If you expect me to believe that cock and bull story you must be dreaming in technicolour." (Well maybe he wouldn't have said 'technicolor' because it hadn't been invented yet, except by the Lord God in nature and all that). "Do you take me for a fool? Who have you been sleeping around with? Is it that Jacob guy from next door? You always did have a thing for him."

What if he'd called the whole thing off? Lots of guys would have. What if he'd cancelled the wedding and told her to put an ad up in the market square "For sale: Wedding dress. Size 20. Never worn".

The story might have had a very different outcome. Who knows what would have happened to Mary if Joseph hadn't stuck around—young woman, pregnant, no husband and her spouting off about angels and the father being the Lord God, the Most High? That probably wouldn't have gone down very well in Galilee back then. Religious lot they were. She might even have been stoned to death and nothing more would have come of it. It seems highly unlikely that two thousand years later anyone would know anything about some pregnant, schizophrenic girl with hallucinations and delusions of grandeur, no matter who had got her pregnant.

No, Joseph must have been a hell of a Mensch to stick around. I wonder if he ever looked back and wondered if it had all been worth it or if he'd been a complete chump, especially given all that chasing around on a donkey that they had to do to escape from people who wanted to kill them because the rumour got around that this kid was the Son of the Most High.

It sounds as though Jesus wasn't the easiest child to bring up either, wandering off all the time to hang about with old men in the temple, bit of a know-it-all, 'n all. Maybe he was a bit of a party-goer too, turning all that water into wine at weddings. Joseph must have wondered about him sometimes—hanging around with those twelve men all the time with only one woman among the lot of them, and her of decidedly dubious reputation. And then he went and got himself crucified with a bunch of robbers and other criminal types. Mary was right upset when that happened and poor old Joseph was probably the one who had to try to console her—pretty thankless job that, I should imagine. Maybe he did look back and wish he'd called it all off when he had a chance. Or perhaps he thought it was all in the kid's genes and therefore not his fault.

The Invitation

I invite you to take a religious figure or spiritual teacher from your own culture and see if you can write this figure from a different perspective—or not, if you are offended by this sort of thing.

Just a Kiss

I knew I shouldn't invite him over for dinner whilst my fiancé, Peter, was away but I made myself believe it was innocent enough. Simon had said he would take a look at some re-decorating work I had to do on the apartment and offered to come round one evening to assess the job. With a wink and a nudge, Peter had jokingly asked Simon to take good care of me whilst he was away—a comment I found rather insulting, as if I couldn't take care of myself, or I was his to pass around to his buddies.

They were good friends. Well, maybe not good friends but they hung around together with the same crowd from high school and it wasn't unusual for a few of them to come over to our place a couple of evenings a week to play cards, watch a game on our big screen television, or listen to music on our top-of-the-line equipment. Peter liked to have all the best electronic gadgets. His car even talked to him, for God's sake. I thought it was all a bit silly and shallow but didn't complain when they all came by. I liked the company. We had a lot of good laughs together. So there didn't seem to be any harm in Simon coming over by himself to look at the job and me cooking him a bit of dinner. I'd be cooking anyway.

I did notice that I put more time than usual into choosing a recipe that I thought he might particularly like. When I'd prepared it all and set the table I noticed the excitement I felt as I took a quick shower and got dressed. I even blow-dried my hair, something I never normally bother doing. I chose a blouse that was silky and accentuated my breasts, whilst not looking too dressy or sexy. I dabbed on some Chanel No. 5—just a very little. As I waited for him to arrive the excitement mounted. I felt more alive in my body than I had for a long time, tingly all over. I even had a fantasy of Simon taking me into his arms and kissing me passionately and realized I longed for that to happen. I didn't take it any further than that—just a kiss.

Simon was a good-looking man with reddish-brown curly hair and green eyes. He was tall, well built, strong. He owned a small company that did home renovations and had a lot of practical skills. There was nothing pretentious about him. He was recently divorced. He had a son who was 4 years old who adored him. His son stayed with him every other weekend and he was a very involved and loving dad. I liked that a lot about him.

When the doorbell rang, I jumped a little and ran down the hallway to let him in. I felt very happy to see him and I must have shown that on my face. He seemed a little surprised.

"Were you expecting me?" he asked as if he was surprised at the warmth of my greeting and thought it was someone else I had expected to see at the door.

"Oh, yes," I said. "I thought you might be a little hungry coming straight from work. I hoped you'd be able to join me for some dinner before we look at the job."

"That sounds great. I'm starving. I didn't have time for lunch today and I came straight here from the job. Something smells wonderful," he said as he moved past me into the hallway. I felt a shiver as he almost touched me.

He was wearing jeans and a work shirt. I got a whiff of a slightly musky, man-sweat smell as he moved past me—the smell of a man who does real man work for a living. Peter was an accountant and worked in an office. He always smelt of deodorant and the colognes I had given him as gifts. I thought Simon smelt wonderful!

In the kitchen I served him a beer, which he drank whilst I put the last touches to the dinner. Before we ate he went to the washroom and came back looking as though he had had more of a wash than just rinsing his hands. I asked him to open a bottle of wine whilst I put the food on the table and served it up. We both seemed to be feeling the tension. We had never been alone together before—always with a group of friends so conversation was a little awkward and stilted at first. I laughed a little too much like some silly teenage girl, but he didn't seem to mind. He complimented me a lot on the meal and had a large second helping. We probably drank a little too much wine. We talked about mutual friends, music, TV shows and the job I wanted him to do. Neither of us mentioned Peter.

After we had eaten and I had cleared away the dishes—he actually helped me, something Peter never did without being asked—we went to see the job I wanted done. It was some work in one of the bedrooms. I was very aware of the bed looming large in the middle of the room. I had never been in the bedroom with him before, or with any other man besides Peter since we started dating. Not that I was imagining Simon and I doing anything on the bed. I just kept having this yearning that he would take me in his arms and kiss me—just a kiss. He didn't.

After he had finished looking at what needed to be done, I asked him if he would like to stay and have a coffee or another glass of wine. He chose the wine and we went into the den. I put on a new CD I had purchased a couple of days before, some husky, raunchy love songs, and flicked on the gas fireplace—very cozy and intimate. I never thought about what I was doing, that I was seducing him shamelessly with every trick in my book. I never thought about where it would lead and what the implications would be on my life and my relationship with Peter. I just knew I wanted to melt into his arms and be kissed by this musky-smelling man. My body was in charge and my brain was nowhere to be found.

We clinked glasses and I looked deeply into his green eyes. We each leant forward a little and the next moment we were kissing, hungrily, passionately as if we would devour each other. His lips were soft on mine and then his tongue was in my mouth exploring, thrusting, withdrawing, inviting my tongue into his mouth. I used my tongue to explore his mouth, his lips, his face, his ears and then back to his mouth again. I felt myself become engorged and hot—my juices flowing wet. I could feel the pulsating of my vulva as it swelled with desire. We kissed for a long time till finally I could bear it no longer and I took his hand and put it on my breast. His workman's hands were a little rough on my silk blouse but it felt so good. I wanted more and more and more. I unbuttoned my blouse, taking the lead each step, took my breasts out of my bra and put his hand back on my left breast. He caressed it slowly at first as we continued to kiss and then pulled away a little, gazed into my eyes and then down at my breast. I shivered but not from cold. We both watched his hand as he started to play with my nipple, the slight roughness adding a little friction to the exquisite sensation that started in my nipple and travelled straight to my vagina. I let out a little sigh as though this was what I had been waiting for all my life, this moment, this touch, this knowing of pure physical joy. He then brought his other hand to play with my other nipple, to caress my right breast, rolling both nipples between his fingers, pulling gently and then harder till it hurt just enough to be delicious. I wanted it to last forever, to never stop, and at the same time felt I couldn't bear it to go on another moment. It was too intense, too beautiful to bear. And then he put his mouth to my left breast and started to lick it. He flicked first one nipple then the other with the hard tip of his tongue and then he sucked. He sucked my breasts gently and hard, hard and gently, varying his pace until I felt I would come into his mouth through my nipples, great gushing fountains of ejaculate, into his mouth and down his throat, but of course I didn't, I couldn't have that release which heightened my need, my longing to have his cock inside me.

I pulled him to a standing position and slowly undid his shirt button by button. I caressed his nipples, pulling and rolling. Then I unbuckled his belt—a leather belt. I pulled it off and ran the leather across my breasts, loving the feel of it on my nipples. The intensity of my desire made me brazen and shameless. He watched me turn myself on with the feel of it, my nipples so sensitive now and standing out sharply from my round voluptuous mounds. I liked him watching me. I felt daring and reckless. I knelt down and removed his socks and shoes, trousers and underpants.

I sat back and looked at his erection, taking it in with my eyes first, then I took it in my hand and gently caressed my cheek, my eye lids, my lips with the tip of his hard cock. The skin was so soft on my face it felt like velvet and silk blended together to be the most sensual fabric the world would ever know. Slowly, oh, so slowly, I started to take him into my mouth. I used my tongue to lick and moisten so he started to slide easily into my mouth. I thrust my tongue into the slit and he groaned with pleasure. I could feel a little bit of sticky fluid which I smoothed around the head of his penis with my tongue. He leant forward and continued to play with my nipples, caressing and pulling, twisting and flicking with his thumb and finger until I wanted to scream with pleasure. I moaned and the vibration flowed into his erect dick and up his body. I sucked him deep into my throat but after a couple of thrusts he said, "Stop, I'm too excited. I'll come." I moved and placed my vagina where my mouth had been and thrust hard, with all the intensity of my need, my longing, my sense of finally finding what I had been searching for all my life. He held my breasts in his hands as I thrust down on him, once, twice, maybe four times at the most. Then we both came with a seismic shuddering that felt as though every atom in my body had blown apart and might never reassemble the same way again. He stayed inside me as the aftershocks continued and I squeezed his shrinking member with my vaginal muscles. Each squeeze would send another shock wave through him, until we started to giggle.

We lay in each other's arms for a long time and then I took him by the hand and led him to the bedroom. We woke in the night and made love again and then again in the bleary morning light before he left to go home and get ready for work.

I spent every moment I could with him that week. We made love over and over again. I couldn't seem to get enough of him.

We were doing it on the dining room table when Peter walked in, back early from his business trip. He found us like that. Sadly perhaps, I didn't even have the grace to feel bad. As I said, my brain had disappeared somewhere and some other creature who was pure raw sexual passion had been unleashed and taken over. Peter was angry and bitter, especially because he had considered Simon a friend. Obviously he was deeply hurt. Who wouldn't be?

I packed up my things and moved in with a friend for a while. I realized that my relationship with Peter had felt empty for a long time. I just hadn't seen it, hadn't stopped to question it—I'd been asleep. We'd stayed together mostly out of convenience and habit. Both of us had been focused on our careers, but some essential element had been missing—there was no raunchy passion in our feelings for each other or our love making. Simon made me see how much I needed that. I could have had a good life with Peter, enough money to do the things we wanted, success, material possessions. What Simon awoke in me was my lust for life, to live fully, juicily, edgily even. I am so grateful to him for that.

I put an ad in the *Free Trader*, "For Sale: Wedding Dress. Size 20. Never worn," and sold it to a lovely young woman. I wished her well.

Simon and I continued to have torrid sex whenever his son wasn't staying with him, which probably gave us both a needed break.

Forty years later Simon and I are still enjoying passionate, mind-blowing, deeply satisfying lovemaking together—not three times a night, like we did at first, but the excitement is still alive between us and we wallow in the joy of sleeping each night in each other's arms—life partners and lovers. Even today, all these years later, just the thought of his kisses still excites me and sends vibrations through my body.

The Invitation

Do you remember your own erotic awakening or moments of particularly intense arousal or seduction by you or your partner(s)? How would you write a seduction scene? How would you write a sex scene in an on-going story? How explicit or not would you make the sexual elements? Does your story turn you on as you write it? Would you read it to a lover or friend? Would sharing it turn you on or stretch you too far out of your comfort zone? I invite you to put your "feather" pen to paper, metaphorically speaking, and start to write. Don't censor yourself. Enjoy.

A Pair of Queens

"So, I'll see you. What have you got?" asked Cassandra.

"A pair of queens, ace high," responded Roberta. "You?"

Cassandra threw his cards on the table, a tear in his eye. "That beats my pair of Jacks," he said. "You win—the dress is yours."

"Oh, Darling, I'm so sorry, but I do love it so much and I know I'll be such a hit in it. It fits my body so perfectly, with my figure. I'm sure you'll find another dress that's just right for you."

Cassandra glowered. He had really wanted the dress. He loved every inch of it—the strapless, sweetheart bodice covered in seed pearls and silver beads, tightly laced at the back to accentuate his cleavage; the yards and yards of cascading organza ruffles that flowed into a graceful train at the back; the beaded roses just below the waistline. Everything about it was exquisite and feminine. He knew he would have felt beautiful wearing it and would have been able to carry it off. Maybe with the black wig. The contrast of the long black hair and the white dress would be stunning. He knew he would have been able to weave it into his act as the "piece de resistance". It wasn't just A dress, it seemed to him it was The dress. From the moment he saw it he pinned all his hopes of reviving his sagging career to this dress, his hopes of being up there in lights like the big names—Divine, Dame Edna, or Toronto legend Michelle DuBarry.

And now he never would. All for a lousy pair of queens. He had lost it to that strumped up bitch, Roberta.

Roberta couldn't believe his luck. He rarely won at cards or any other game of chance. The dress was his! He couldn't wait to put it on, get all dressed-up with a wig and make-up and see himself in full splendor. He could already see the audiences clapping and cheering—the standing ovations he would receive. He could already see his name up in lights. He would prove to everyone that he mattered, that all his choices had been worthwhile. He had seen Suzanna perform in the dress and had envied him from the depths of his soul. This was it. This was what it was all about—this level of artistry and showmanship was what took drag acts out of the ordinary into the extraordinary. Perhaps now his parents would see him and be proud of him as a true performer, an artist to be respected, instead of speaking about him in hushed or mocking tones or oblique euphemisms.

Their friend, Suzanna, had bought the dress three years previously from an ad, "For Sale: Wedding dress. Size 20. Never worn," in a *Free Trader* magazine in upstate New York whilst performing in a cabaret show in Lake Placid. He had created a stunning finale to his act with drag king Vesta Shields. Night after night there was barely a dry eye in the house when the two pledged their vows and sang their final number together— the Joe Cocker classic "You Are So Beautiful to Me". It was a triumph.

Vesta had trained with Diane Torr and would have done the greats, like Stormé DeLarivierie and Hetty King, proud. She felt certain that she would even have been good enough, had she been around in the 50s and 60s, to have performed in the renowned Jewel Box Revue.

Suzanna and Vesta were destined for great things until Suzanna had his accident. He had been wearing a pair of amazing, red, kinky boots with two-inch platforms and ten-inch heels, in glittering vinyl right up his long legs almost to the crotch. He had had them made specially for him by the renowned Price's in Northumberland, England.

A collective gasp went up in the audience when he missed his step during a dance number and crashed down off the catwalk into the audience, hitting his head on the arm of a chair and landing in someone's lap. He would never be the same again, whether due to the injury or the embarrassment no-one could tell. As a result, he was selling all his gowns and moving back to live with his parents on a farm in Arkansas—a fate that Roberta couldn't even begin to imagine! How ghastly!

At the sale of all his costumes Roberta had Cassandra had started fighting over the wedding dress and would have ended up tearing it in two if Suzanna hadn't stepped in and stopped them. He proposed they play cards for it. Reluctantly they had both agreed.

"A pair of queens—how ironic" thought Roberta as he packed the dress up in a bag.

The Invitation

What do you think might be the motivations of these characters in desiring this dress? I touched on them lightly. I invite you to pick a performing artist—singer, dancer, actor, drag queen or king, circus acrobat—and write a story about them. In your story elaborate on their motivations for doing what they do. You can explore several different levels of motivation. For example, an actor might, on one level, want to be rich and famous, on another level they may want to be seen, be in the spotlight, without ever having to show their true self, they may not even know who that is.

Or, think about writing: what are the many levels of motivation behind your writing? I think part of my motivation for writing these stories is to discover myself more deeply in ways I never would in therapy, and writing is, I believe, a great way to do that—to find what lives and lurks within you. As a child I loved fantasy games and pretending to be people I wasn't— Robin Hood, a buccaneer, a cowboy—the list was endless. As an adult I love to read, immersing myself in the characters, and to travel, visiting different cultures. Is part of my motivation in writing these stories a continuation of that desire to travel into the inner worlds of people different from myself, to explore and experience beyond the limitations imposed by one life, one gender, one personality? But I am also hoping to publish this collection of stories. Is part of my motivation to finally be seen as I am—to come out and stand up and show myself as I am in all my colors and be accepted or rejected on the basis of showing my deepest self—"warts and all," as they say? As a child I often thought I'd get into trouble if I spoke up with my ideas or my wishes—so much seemed to be forbidden and unacceptable. I learned to hide a lot of myself to protect myself from criticism and ridicule. My adult life has been about growing beyond that. Might this be my next step on that journey? I invite you to write a story exploring motivation.

The Long Goodbye

"The doctor said 'metastasized' but I must have got the word wrong," my sister, Linda, said to me on the phone one Saturday towards the end of November. Denial is a very useful strategy when dealing with the unacceptable.

"Why did you go to see him?" I asked.

"I've been burping a lot, but not like food burps. And I've been very tired. But I've been working really late every night and not sleeping well. We're in the middle of a take-over and I'm leaving on holiday for a week."

She worked as a human resources manager and take-overs were a nightmare with lots of additional work sorting out pensions and goodness knows what else. I didn't really understand what she did.

"I thought the doctor could give me a pick-me-up or something to help me sleep. I'm sure it's nothing that a week of sun and relaxation won't cure. I'll call you when we get back."

She was going to the Caribbean with her partner, Brad. They were getting married in February—a Valentine's wedding.

Her husband had died in a car accident when her two boys were young and she had raised them by herself, devoting herself to them and her work. Finally, now the boys were off at university, she had met someone at the health club she had started going to—a lawyer, a really nice guy, caring, considerate, and as passionate about his work as my sister was.

'Metastasized' swam around in the back of my mind all week, but never made it to shore. Denial is a useful strategy when dealing with the unacceptable. I bought into the idea that sun and rest would do the trick. Many of my therapy clients find November is a difficult month, feeling more tired and depressed than usual.

On her return from vacation she called me.

"How was your trip?" I asked.

"Ghastly," she said. "I couldn't keep any food down. I lost 10 pounds in a week. I felt awful the whole time. We were at this all-inclusive resort and the food looked amazing. Brad said it was fabulous, but every time I tried to eat anything I threw up. I will call the doctor tomorrow and try to see him straight away." Her doctor had been her GP throughout her years of raising her family and they were on very good terms. I knew he would see her quickly.

"Let me know immediately what he says."

That was the beginning of our dance with cancer. She called me back the next day after she had seen the doctor.

"He thinks it's pancreatic cancer," she said. "He wants me to have more tests and I'm going into hospital tomorrow to have a stent put in so that I can eat."

"What does that mean—pancreatic cancer? What does the pancreas do?" I asked.

"I don't know any more than that right now. I'll call you as soon as I know anything."

I looked up 'pancreas' on-line and found out it had something to do with producing the enzymes to digest food. I didn't look up 'pancreatic cancer'. Denial is a useful strategy when dealing with the unacceptable. I still couldn't get my mind around the possibility that my big sister, who had always seemed so strong and capable, could be sick.

She had the stent put in that week and it certainly helped. She started to feel much better and could eat without throwing up. However, being right before Christmas, it was hard to get other tests scheduled. Departments were closing and the earliest appointments were for after January 6th, which seemed an age away. I couldn't wait to get down to be with her. I felt an urgency to be beside her, be with her. She lived about a 7-hour drive away.

Somehow I got through Christmas and my husband, Dan, and I left at the crack of dawn on Boxing Day. My anxiety was mounting with every mile.

She looked better than I'd expected. She'd lost some weight which she had always wanted to do. She was eating well and the sleeping pills were helping her too. The next day we moved into high gear to try to get to see some doctors, get some answers to all our questions, start some treatment as soon as possible. Brad had some contacts through his law firm and we were able to get some appointments between Christmas and New Year's.

She wanted me, Brad and her sons with her for all the appointments, so we trooped in en masse whilst the doctors scurried
around trying to find extra chairs. However, the doctors who
saw us seemed puzzled as to why we were in their offices. The
oncology surgeon assured us there was nothing he could do.
From the test results he had so far he said it was clear there was
no specific site of a tumor that could be surgically removed.
Similarly, the radiologist said that she could only use radiology
when there was a specific site she could hit, which wasn't the
case with Linda. They talked about quality of life, making the
most of the time she had. It didn't sound good. They seemed to
be suggesting, without actually saying it too directly, that she
had a few weeks to live, a couple of months at most.

It all seemed to be taking forever and meanwhile we
could all imagine the cancer spreading unchecked, taking over
her whole body, whilst no-one did anything to stop it. Not
knowing anything for sure was awful.

"What can I do to help?" I asked.

Always the practical sort, she said "We'll go through all
my stuff and get rid of things. I don't want the boys to have to
cope with that after I'm dead."

So that's what we did whilst we waited to be able to see
the doctors and get the test results. In the stoic style of our
British upbringing, we seemed to go straight from shock and
denial to acceptance without a glance at anger, bargaining, guilt
or depression—the stages of grief mentioned by Kubler-Ross.
Illness was never something we talked about or dwelt on in our
family. Our mother didn't even tell us when she broke her hip

on a vacation in Scotland when she was 90 years old. She just "got on with it", as she had her own stomach cancer three years later. "What's the point of making a fuss and drawing attention to yourself," she said. Keep calm and carry on was a national value and so we kept busy.

Together my sister and I went through her dresser drawers one by one, throwing everything away that was not absolutely essential, thinking she only had a couple of months to live. We had a lot of laughs together as we came across hordes of stuff she'd stashed away—every free shoe cleaner cloth from every hotel she'd stayed in, every toothbrush and miniature toothpaste kit from every overnight flight, every wet wipe from every restaurant, all her Remembrance Day poppies, (did she think she was going to re-use them and save the expense of a new one each year?), and much more. My sister had a lot of funny ways. She gave me purses she wouldn't need any more, and anything else I wanted—her little black evening bag, her beaded shawl.

When she was tired she lay down on the bed and sometimes I lay beside her. In those moments as we lay there together, body touching body, we experienced a level of physical intimacy we had never had—precious and tender. Sometimes as she slept I would go for long walks in the cold to clear my head and be with myself. I knew I had to be with her as much as I could given how little time we thought she had. I cancelled my sessions with the few clients I still saw for therapy or met with them by Skype, where possible. I wanted to be as fully present as I could to my sister. It was a very special time, having an intensity and poignancy that was sorrowful and sweet.

She said she didn't want anyone getting all emotional, so we talked in practical ways about her death and how to dispose of her body. At times we shared black jokes with each other, much to Brad's distress. He didn't see anything amusing in the situation, but Linda and I shared a sick sense of humor along with other genetic similarities. We weren't above "playing the cancer card" ("I'm dying of cancer and only have a few weeks to live") to get faster service on things we were trying to get done, like transferring airline points to me to help me with my trips down to be with her.

So, the days went by, one by one. After we had turned out her dresser, we turned our attention to her closet. We went through each of her outfits, laughed as I tried them on—her very professional dress style of business suits and silk blouses was not at all my more casual, off-beat style, so we giggled a lot seeing me dressed like her. Then at the end of the closet we came to her wedding dress. That's what undid us both. That's when the tears started to flow and we held each other tight and sobbed. We imagined what it would be like for Brad after she was gone—this devastated my sister much more than her own situation. That's the kind of person she was. We talked about all the trips we had planned to take together and other things that would never be, seeing her boys marry and have her grandchildren. We cried together and held each other close.

"Enough of this," she said eventually, when it seemed there could be no more tears for now. "I can't possibly marry him now. I probably won't even be alive by February. Get rid of it for me. I don't want Brad to see it. Get it out of here when he's not around and sell it. Give the money to the pancreatic cancer charity." So I took the dress. I wrapped it up carefully and when my husband drove down to fetch me and spend a few days with us, I bundled it into the car. When I got home I put it into the back of my closet.

The second week in January things started to move more quickly and we went from one medical appointment to another. We finally got to see the right doctor, a lovely young woman with a professional and compassionate manner. She confirmed it was pancreatic cancer which had metastasized to other sites throughout her body—stage 4. Initially she said that there was no point in having treatment. The doctor made it clear she should put her affairs in order as she didn't have long to live. At some point in the conversation she mentioned there was a new drug—it wouldn't cure her, nothing would do that—but at best it might slow it down so that she might have perhaps up to as much as a year, but the quality of life would be compromised by the chemo treatments.

Never one to give up easily, my sister decided to go for the chemo treatments. They started the next Monday—once every two weeks. I went with her to the first appointment and stayed whilst they hooked her up to the poison that would, we hoped, at least discourage the further growth of the cancer for a while.

I stayed with her through to mid-January when I had to leave to teach a course on couple therapy in Europe that I had committed to several months before knowing my sister was sick. People had booked their flights and accommodations from around Europe to attend. I teach a particular approach to couple therapy in many countries and still see a few clients. I was going to be away for a month. It was so hard to leave not knowing how much time we had together, believing it was very little. I toyed with the idea of cancelling but Linda insisted I go and carry on with my life. She still looked so strong and healthy it was hard to believe she would be dead in a month or two.

She responded well to the chemo. She usually had three bad days out of each two-week period. She became able to predict the days and would go to bed and stay there. The rest of the time she lived her life fully. She had not been back to work since she came back from her vacation in December. Now she took on cancer treatment with the same dedication and determination she had used in her career. She changed her diet completely, eliminating red meats and other cancer encouraging substances. (She had never drunk alcohol or coffee or smoked which was part of the irony of the situation.) She joined a wonderful center for cancer patients that was a short drive from her home and took healthy-cooking lessons. She volunteered there and made a lot of new friends. She joined an exercise class and made friends there too. She also had more time to meet up with other people she had known before and went to a weekly coffee afternoon with women friends from the yacht club. She lived each precious day to the max, learning how to manage her energy. She inspired so many people and enriched their lives with her positive attitude. Death receded.

She continued the chemo treatment for about a year and a half, amazing everyone, defying all the statistics. Like many other cancer patients and their families, we lived from test results to test results, holding our breath, crossing our fingers. Miracle of miracles the CT scans showed that the cancer hadn't grown and, in some places, had even receded. Hope crept back in and denial that she would die from this disease crept back in—a very useful strategy when dealing with the unacceptable. The 5-year survival rate at that time was about 1 percent. We started to believe she could be part of that very small percentage of people who survive pancreatic cancer. During that time she made two trips to Australia with Brad—one of her sons was doing a study program there—wonderful trips that she raved about and enjoyed every moment of.

I visited her whenever I could, flying down for the weekend or taking the train to be with her for a few days or a week. Each moment with her had become so precious.

The funny thing is that as kids we had hated each other. She told me she would lie in bed every night and try to figure out a way to kill me without getting caught. To me she always seemed so miserable and bad tempered, I could never figure out why my parents didn't just send her away, especially as they often threatened to put her in a boarding school if she didn't behave better. We fought and argued constantly and it seemed to me that her bad temper spoilt every family outing or fun event we ever went on. She never seemed to want to play dolls or board games with me and if she did she would never let me win or do things my way. To this day, I hate *"Monopoly"*.

I imagine like many older siblings she didn't want me in the first place, the precious, demanding, adorable new baby taking away all the attention that had been hers previously, without consultation or explanation to her 3-year-old self of why she alone was not enough for her parents, why they needed another child. As I grew older, I imagine I annoyed her even more, wanting to play with her toys, her friends, and being more outgoing and confident than she seemed to be, always drawing the positive attention.

The first time she was ever nice to me, in my recollection, was when she went away to Sweden at age 14 and brought me back a jade necklace. I was so surprised. After she moved into a flat at the age of 19 and I went off to live in France for a year as an au pair, things changed and we started to become friends. I emigrated to Canada when I was 19 and she came and stayed with me when I was pregnant with my first child. We sat for hours knitting baby clothes together and talking—more than we ever had before and got to know each other in new ways. She married a friend of my husband's and so ended up staying in Canada, although they moved away to another city soon after their marriage and we settled into our separate lives, only seeing each other at Christmas or Easter when one of us was willing to make the long trek. Then she had children of her own and got busy with all their sports activities in addition to the stresses of her work. After her husband died, she was even more busy, burying herself completely in her children and her work. I was busy in those years also. I had gone back to school to get a doctorate. Although we cared about each other and talked on the phone regularly we didn't see much of each other and our lives chugged along on separate paths. We never questioned that we had plenty of time remaining.

It's funny how the specter of death changes everything—how all of sudden distances don't seem to matter and I found the time to be at her side. Perhaps sad is more the word—nothing funny about it. Priorities take precedence, urgent trumps important. We treasured each moment together. Each time I left her I feared it would be the last time I saw her. The sort of stoic acceptance with which we had both initially dealt with it gave way to a range of emotions. However, the pragmatic coping strategies from growing up in post-war London, where above all things you must carry on and not make a fuss, were always close at hand. Shows of strong emotion were strongly frowned upon and met with the instruction to "Go to your room until you can get over it and can behave properly." Behaving properly was the overarching principle of life, which for us as children meant emulating the royal princesses who were always neatly dressed and well-behaved. And so we dealt with this also with a certain unemotional stoicism. Until the pain got bad.

Our mother's final month and then death from stomach cancer had already brought us closer. We stayed in her apartment and visited her in the hospital each day, each of us away from our otherwise busy lives in Canada. Together we went through her stuff and made the arrangements for her funeral (I wore traditional black; my sister wore bright pink in a reversal of our usual roles where I had been the rebellious one.)

We never had a fight or argument about who would get what or how things should be done. And every year after our mother's death we had gone away together for a week on our own—just the two of us—such precious times. We had had some wonderful holidays in Greece, at a spa, traveling around New Mexico and other places. The cancer stopped us from walking El Camino or going to Tuscany as we had planned before she got sick, but Niagara on the Lake was close by and doable. That was early September, almost two years after her diagnosis.

Don't believe them when they say they can medicate the pain away—at least they couldn't for my sister. Perhaps she was too stubborn and wanted to have her wits about her, so didn't make full use initially of what was available. But even later on when she did max up the dosage, she was still in a lot of pain. There comes a point in pain where stoic fails you, where denial no longer works and all there is is pain—constant, unremitting, unrelenting, unforgettable pain. It eats away at your mind, your character, your resolve, your will to live.

The journey from then on was downhill. The following February they did an eight-hour operation on her back and put metal rods in so that the cancer that had spread to her spine would not so weaken her back that it would break. I was on holiday in Venice whilst that was happening and was constantly trying to find a good signal on my cell phone to get news. I felt very far away. She had hoped that after that the pain would lessen and maybe it did for a brief moment but then it showed up again with renewed force in her hip. In May they did an experimental ablation on her hip, but the pain continued unabated.

After that they decided to stop all further treatment. That was a pivotal moment—when there was no more hope, no more possibility of denial, when nothing but an increasingly painful existence loomed before her, ending with an inglorious death. She felt abandoned by her treatment team whom she had become close to over the past two and a half years. We talked of assisted suicide and I promised to be there with her and help her in whatever ways I could. Dear Brad couldn't deal with that at all, it went against his moral and religious beliefs. Assisted suicide was still illegal in Canada. That's where her anger finally hit. A bill was under discussion in parliament to allow it in certain very restricted circumstances, such as hers—unbearable pain, terminal illness with no hope of recovery. Arguments for and against were touted on the news daily. Linda would become incensed by the people who argued against it. She wanted them to suffer as she was suffering. She felt she was being treated worse than a dog that would be put down to release it from its misery. All the outrage of the unfairness of the cancer now had an outlet and a voice.

Over that summer the window of her ability to function got smaller and smaller. She would stay in bed dozing on sleeping pills until noon when the morphine and other pain killers had kicked in to the extent they were going to, from the morning dosages. She would then get up and I would help her shower, going into the shower with her to hold her up and wash her body and hair, then help her dry off. I rubbed lotions into her skin which was becoming dry and itchy. Our relationship changed again with this kind of skin-to-skin body connection, a new level of physicality and touch. She let me care for her in ways she never would as the big sister when she was well.

In the afternoons she would either have a friend over for tea or be picked up to visit with friends. She had gone from a stick to a walker to a wheelchair by now. But each day she would try to have something in her life to bring joy and some distraction. On my visits I would get together with her group of friends to play Mexican Train dominoes one day a week. We had a lot of fun and they all loved and admired Linda so much. I think it did her the world of good.

Our week together that summer was a 'virtual' trip to Tuscany, where the new patio she had finally had built in her back yard served as the courtyard of our imaginary Tuscan villa, and Brad took the role of our swarthy Italian manservant pouring the Prosecco into champagne flutes—not that she drank any. By 3 or 4 o'clock she was exhausted and would go back to bed until dinner time when she would try to join us for an hour, even though she wasn't eating much. She was trying to help Brad learn how to cook the way she did—from very elaborate recipes that took hours to prepare. It had always been one of her passions and her relaxation. I'm not sure how successful she was.

At the end of July she decided she wanted to have a "Celebration of Life" party whilst she was still alive, rather than a funeral after she was dead. She never liked to miss out on anything. She hired a room at a local golf club, a beautiful setting, and ordered lots of delicious food. The golf club manager's mother had died of cancer earlier in the year and engaged herself fully in making this a wonderful event for Linda. It was held in mid-August. Over 100 people came and celebrated her. One of her sons emceed it brilliantly, having put together a montage of photos from earliest childhood to present day. Her other son told funny stories that expressed his appreciation of the lessons she had taught him—like how embarrassed he had been as a kid that his lunch sandwiches had been wrapped in the lining from used cereal packets, whereas his friends' lunches came in purchased sandwich bags, but that it had taught him to reuse things and not be wasteful. Brad said some very loving words about her. I told a couple of funny stories and read a short poem I had written. Writing poetry had been my primary way of processing my own experience throughout the journey—a way of accessing and expressing whatever lived within me. It was brief but people seemed to be moved to tears by it.

There,
You were always there,
There somewhere,
Near or far, but there.
From the time of my birth
You were there.
So now, where will I be
If you're not there?

Then her former boss announced that a scholarship was being named after her. She had organized the award to support highly deserving children of employees of her company to continue to advanced education. I don't think there was a dry eye in the house at that announcement, certainly not mine, seeing my sister honored in this way for her many years of dedication and for her contribution. The whole day was a wonderful, joyous occasion, where so many people from different spheres of her life came together to show their love and respect for her.

It was the last day that it could possibly have been held when she would have been able to attend and enjoy it. We got a hospital bed moved into the den and the window of pain-managed time each day got smaller. The wonderful community nurses visited frequently, sometimes twice a day. They did their best to ease her pain but sadly with little success.

In October I was down visiting and to give a training in her city. I arrived on Wednesday and by Thursday night it became clear we could no longer care for her at home. She got up in the night to try to go to the bathroom, didn't make it and fell. I found her bent backwards over a chair and Brad and I had a terrible time trying to get her back in bed whilst she cried out in agony.

The hospice took her that day. It was a beautiful, peaceful place in lovely gardens with bird feeders on the windows. The staff and team of volunteers were amazing human beings with a dedication to caring for the dying. Mostly Linda was medicated into oblivion but sometimes the pain would break through and she would scream in agony and call out that she wanted to die. It was heartbreaking and awful to feel so powerless to help.

The only time I left her side for more than a walk was on the Saturday after she went into the hospice. I went into town to teach. I was scheduled to co-teach with a colleague, who had taken it over by herself, but she was not available that day and so I went in to do it. I took the train and by chance ended up by the finish line of the Marathon race that was being run that day. All of a sudden I was a blubbering mass of raw emotion, a weeping puddle on the sidewalk, as I watched friends and family members of the runners cheer their loved ones across the finish line.

"You're almost there," "It's almost over," "You've run a good race," "Not much farther," and suddenly I knew that that was my role with my sister—to cheer her on, to encourage her over the finish line, to give all the support I possibly could to help her bring her own race to an end.

I stayed with her pretty much round the clock from then on. I wanted to be with her. It felt right. It was the only place I could be. As my big sister she had been with me from the time of my coming into the world. I would be with her till the time of her leaving. I talked to her, explained all the procedures that the nursing staff were doing, rubbed cream into her dry skin, held her hand and sat by her side. Ironically, at night, as I lay on a cot beside her, I tried to figure out a way to kill her where I wouldn't be caught, just as she had done with me as a child, although for rather different reasons. Her pain was so bad when it broke through the fog of the medications it was agonizing to see.

And then it got worse. She went into an overdose reaction from the morphine that was constantly being pumped into a body that was no longer able to process it. She went into the most awful, excruciatingly painful muscle spasms in a body already racked with pain. Emergency measures were taken to deal with it, but it must have taken about seven horrendous hours to get control of it. I would have willingly killed her that night if I had had the courage and the willingness to face my own fear of being caught. I felt sure the staff were so familiar with death they would be able to distinguish the signs of being suffocated from that of a natural death and so I lacked the courage to help her.

Thankfully, mercifully, she died the next day. I was alone with her. She had been suffering from apnea for a couple of days so she would take a gasping breath, hold it for several seconds and then eventually let it go. As I sat with her at 9.38 on the Sunday morning finally the releasing breath failed to come and she was dead. I wept more from relief at that point than from sadness, from joy that she was finally released from the pain after over a year of it being her constant companion. Brad and her sons arrived shortly afterwards and we all sat with her body whilst we waited for the funeral company to come and take her away to be cremated. They wheeled her out on a gurney in a crimson body bag. Her body looked so frail and small within it. That was the last we saw of her.

That day, when I was out walking, I saw two, bright green, praying mantis standing to attention by the side of the road that the hearse would have taken when leaving the hospice. I also saw a mourning cloak butterfly, very unusual in Southern Ontario at that time of year. I don't know what greater power or connection exists in the universe, but it seemed to me that there was a synchronicity in these symbols of prayer and mourning showing up that day.

It has taken me a long time to be ready to let go of the wedding dress. Recently, I put an ad in the *Free Trader:* "For sale: Wedding dress. Size 20. Never worn." A young woman came and bought it. I didn't tell her the story. It broke my heart to let it go because of all that that meant. It was like a final goodbye to all she was, to all the life that she had hoped to live and never would, to the happiness she will never live out.

The experience has changed me in many ways. I live for two now. I grab each day and try to make the most of it. I cherish life more intensely. I try not to waste a single moment of this one and precious life being pissy-assed about inane irritations and mostly I succeed. I am careful about my health, no longer holding the illusion of invulnerability and yet still living the delusion that if I live my life right, if I eat well, exercise, get enough sleep and reduce my stress, I will be immune to the ravages of death. Denial is a useful strategy when dealing with the unacceptable.

When October comes
And the leaves are aflame
In shades of crimson and gold
When the light slants through the trees
With that special crisp brightness
Will I always think
Of these nine days?
Nine days and nights of vigil

By your hospice bed
Nine nights and days of watching
Pain or oblivion your only options
Written in the gaunt lines
Of your death's head face.
Nine days of waiting.
When October comes
And the leaves are aflame
In shades of gold and crimson
Will I go back there in my mind's eye?
Will I feel the fatigue and grief
All over again
Of these nine days?

The Invitation

Have you ever experienced a significant loss of someone or something that was precious to you? Most of us have at one point or another in our lives. I believe it can help us to process the experience to tell our story. For me telling the story over and over to people was important in helping my experience of loss become a chapter in the book of my life rather than seeming like the whole book. It then could take its place on the bookshelf of my experiences—an important, life-changing experience but one of many. Revisiting it and writing about it has helped me continue to process my grief. I invite you to write a short story about a significant loss.

The Man from Mobius

Many people believe that when aliens land on the earth there will be massive death and destruction as they try to annihilate or enslave humans. This is not in fact the case, at least not so far. When the beings from Mobius in the distant Andromeda galaxy arrived, they lay low and took time to observe human activity. They noticed that one of the most pleasurable seemed to be the coupling of two humans and that men in particular seemed to seek out, find release and delight in this rather bizarre activity.

Initially they were quite surprised to discover that this was the way that humans procreate. On planet Mobius the form their bodies took was more similar to that of a snake and reproduction did not involve anything resembling the sexual intercourse, or "bonking" that humans seemed to so enjoy. So, when they took on human form the prototype they settled on was that of a large, well-hung and rather attractive male. In order to fit in unobtrusively to the new culture they listened very carefully to everything humans said and adapted themselves accordingly.

The focus of their existence became to seek out sexual encounters wherever they could with the dual purpose of experiencing pleasure and ensuring the survival of their species. "Make Love, not War" was a motto from the '60s that would surely have well suited this invasion of alien beings. Because the nature of the invasion was so different from the "War of the Worlds" ideas humans had of what an alien invasion would involve, very few humans knew they had been invaded at all.

Claire was an exception. She met Monty, a Mobian, in a bar one evening when she was out having a drink with some girlfriends. She and another of the women were getting married in a few months, so much of the talk was of wedding plans. She couldn't help noticing him across the room as she sat chatting with her friends and when she went to the washroom she had to walk straight past him. He was a stud! He was tall and thin, and bald, extremely handsome in a slightly reptilian sort of a way. Her eyes were drawn to his and they made a connection that stirred something deep inside her. She was surprised. She had always been faithful to her fiancé, Jason, and never normally even looked at other men much, but there was something different about him that she couldn't quite put her finger on. She tried to pull herself together whilst in the bathroom, but when she came back out again he came up to her and introduced himself.

"Hi, I'm Monty. You are so beautiful I couldn't take my eyes off you all evening. Will you have a drink with me?"

"I couldn't possibly," said Claire immediately. "I'm here with my friends. And besides, I'm engaged to be married." At the same time she couldn't help feeling the urge to say "Yes."

She was a large, voluptuous woman, of a size not particularly fashionable in these days of skinny, anorexic models and movie stars. It was very unusual for a man to single her out like that and tell her she was beautiful. She could feel both the slight mistrust of his motives and the pleasure at the same time. There seemed to be a sort of naiveté to him that was very attractive, in addition to his good looks.

When she went back to sit with her friends she told them what had happened. They had all been drinking and were loosened up.

"Why not have a drink with him." "He's a real dish." "What harm can it do." "Last fling before you get married." "A guy would do it in a flash, given a chance like that," they all encouraged her. Intrigued and tempted though she was she laughed it off and left at the same time as her friends.

A couple of nights later she was back in the same bar to meet one of her girlfriends for dinner. They were going to discuss ideas for bridesmaids' dresses that would both highlight and complement the wedding dress she had bought. She arrived before her friend and ordered a glass of wine whilst she waited. The waiter had just brought the wine to her table when she received a message from her friend saying she was held up at the office but would get there as soon as she could. That was when Claire noticed Monty standing at the bar and looking right at her. As she put her phone away he walked towards her table. He gave her a drop-dead gorgeous smile and said,

"How nice to see you again. I came back here this evening because I hoped that you would be here. Are you meeting your friends again?"

"No," said Claire, "Just one friend and she is delayed at the office."

"May I sit with you until she comes?"

"I suppose there wouldn't be any harm in that," said Claire. "I hate sitting in a bar by myself. She probably won't be long."

Around 8.30 Claire received a call from her friend apologizing profusely. A crisis had come up at work. She had thought she would be able to get away a lot sooner, but it looked as though she would be there for a while yet. Claire felt both annoyed and delighted at the same time. She and Monty had already had a couple of glasses of wine and surprisingly the conversation had flowed very smoothly. He wasn't quite like anyone else she had ever met—extremely polite and considerate and he listened to her talk about herself like no-one else ever had in her whole life. She found herself being very open and vulnerable. Perhaps it was also because he was a stranger and she didn't expect to see him again.

After the call from her friend, he suggested they order some dinner and so they did and shared a bottle of wine. She was fascinated by the way he swallowed his chicken breast, bones and all.

He asked her if he could walk her home and she agreed.

When they arrived at her door it seemed very natural for her to invite him in for a cup of coffee before sending him home. He offered to help her make the coffee but as they were standing in the kitchen together he said to her,

"I think you are so beautiful. I would really like to have some intercourse with you. I think I would enjoy that a lot. Would you be willing to engage in bonking with me? I am sure it would be a great pleasure for both of us. My penis is quite large and I would take a lot of care to make sure you experience the maximum in enjoyment. I do like to experience pleasure. Do you?"

His smile was so open and genuine she felt quite disarmed. No-one had ever come on to her in quite that way before. In fact, not many people had ever come on to her, not even her fiancé. It was a new and intoxicating experience.

"Wow, what planet are you from?" she asked. "That's quite an invitation."

"Mobius, in the Andromeda Galaxy," he said without pausing to think. Claire giggled and then both of them were laughing and tearing off their clothes. Indeed, his long, rather snake-like member did bring her a great deal of pleasure and he seemed to enjoy himself so unabashedly there was something completely endearing about him. As they lay together afterwards, he told her about Mobius and the Andromeda Galaxy. He was so convincing, weirdly she found herself believing him.

"That must have been the strangest one-night stand anyone has ever had," thought Claire next morning after he had left and she was getting herself ready for work.

Three months later when Claire told Jason she was pregnant with the child of an alien from Mobius in the Andromeda Galaxy, Jason called off the wedding. When she realized he was serious, that this was not something he was going to get over, she put an ad in the *Free Trader* "For sale: Wedding dress. Size 20. Never worn."

The Invitation

How do you imagine aliens? Your imagination can go completely wild here—no limits, no boundaries. I invite you to write a short story about an alien being. You can draw on your own experiences of feeling alienated to flesh it out (pun intended). Have fun or scare yourself to death!

Bonsoir, Madame

Madame Pascale saw the ad in the paper "For Sale: Wedding dress, size 20. Never worn." She responded immediately and bought the dress for $25. She was the owner of a brothel, the madam of a house of pleasure. It was a very special brothel that catered to particular tastes. It specialized in wedding scenarios. She always looked for deals in second-hand wedding dresses and bridesmaid outfits and snapped them up as soon as she found them.

She had offered a wide range of wedding scenarios to a diverse clientele over the years she had been in business. Some were standard scenarios and some were made to order in response to particular needs. She advertised discreetly in the "trade" magazines—the soft porn, erotica press. There are a lot of people with wedding fantasies and fetishes.

Many of her male customers liked to pretend to be the groom. In some scenarios they would start out hidden behind a screen or curtain, watching as the maids of honour prepared the bride for the wedding. They would get aroused seeing the young women, dressed in skimpy undergarments, help the bride wash and shave her private parts, clip her pubic hair, sponge-wash her breasts, comb and dress her hair, perfume her, get her into her very lacy undies and then put on her gown. For many of the men, the voyeurism of watching this foreplay was enough to bring them to ejaculation which often resulted in them being "discovered" and "shamed" or "punished" by the bevy of bridesmaids.

Some of her customers were men who love to ravish virgin brides. Madame Pascale had her ways of helping the girls simulate the breaking of the hymen and the blood that comes from first penetration. She also schooled her girls well in the role of the sexually naive "virgin," who shyly and submissively lets her eager and dominant new "husband" tear her wedding dress from her body and ravish her "virginity," often with little or no thought for the blushing "bride's" enjoyment or pleasure. As whores they expected no more. Madame Pascale always charged more to cover the cost of the damage to the wedding dresses. But the men thought they were great studs, initiating their virgin brides to the joys of carnal pleasure. They often left the establishment leaving big tips and feeling like the cock of the roost.

Another scenario that Madame offered was where the "best man" stands outside the French doors and spies on the "bridesmaids" in a bacchanalian romp. Madame knew that a lot of men have a strong voyeuristic streak and like nothing more than watching beautiful young women pleasure each other. So the best man watches from outside as the bridesmaids undress each other, suck on each other's breasts, play with each other's nipples, caress and lick each other's pussies, at which point many of the men burst in through the French doors and engage in a sexual frenzy where the bridesmaids turn their attention and energy to bring him to climax.

It surprised Madame Pascale only a little the number of clergymen (whether real or imagined) who had fantasies of feeling up the bride and bridesmaids surreptitiously before, during and after the service. The forbidden is always a wonderful turn on, as Madame well knew. One clergy in particular was a regular visitor and he always liked to bang the bride's mother in the vestry, just before he presided over the vows.

However, men were not Madame's only customers. There were a surprising number of women who availed themselves of her services and so she had male prostitutes available as well as female. Some of her women customers, often well into their 40s or 50s, wanted to pretend they were virgins again—never been kissed, sweet, pure, unsullied by life's harsh experiences—treated like queens for a day and goddesses for a night. Her boys were well schooled in the tender deflowering of these aging "virgins", treating them with just the right amount of deference and dominance to meet their fantasies.

Another popular scenario, especially among women whose adult children were getting married, was of being the cougar woman, the mother of the bride or groom, who in turn seduces each of the ushers, pulling them behind the shrubbery on the patio, following them into the washroom and sucking them off or giving them a hand job in the back of the church, emerging with a satisfied grin with which to cruise through the rest of the harrowing ordeal of their child's wedding.

And then there were the cross-dressers who loved nothing more than to dress up in wedding gowns with all the frills and flounces and then surprise the "naive" groom with an unsuspected body part on the wedding night. The customers never failed to be delighted when the well-taught boys, acted shocked and horrified when the offending member was revealed in the marital bed.

Many and varied were the desires of her clientele and Madame Pascale responded to each request with flair, style and attention to detail, no matter whether her clients were straight or gay, young or old, male, female or non-binary. She met the diversity of human sexual desire with openness and without judgment, except if it involved children. That she drew a definite and clear line at.

The size 20 wedding dress was bought for a special order—for a man we'll call Hank, although that wasn't his real name. His wife had died recently after 40 years of marriage. They'd had a good and loving relationship, raised two children, but their sex life had been bleak. Hank blamed himself. When he had got married he knew nothing of sex and so to prepare himself he had watched a few porn videos his friend had procured for him. Pretty basic stuff of the "slam-bam-thank-you-ma'am" variety. The males were very forceful and inconsiderate lovers, with no preparation, no tenderness. Just in out, in out until they came. Sometimes they shot their spunk all over the women's bodies or faces. So this was how he thought it should be done.

Hank was a small man and his wife was a large woman. He was small in stature and in personality. He didn't take up much space, was generally willing to go along with whatever she wanted. She seemed to know so much more about everything than he did, be more competent, more in charge. But in the bedroom on that first night he imagined himself as mighty and as monumentally hung like the men in the video. The sight of her in her white lacy nightgown, the ample mounds of her large breasts excited him. The memories of the porn videos and of jerking off as he watched them made him hard. Without further ado he climbed on top of her, lifted her nightgown and shoved his engorged penis inside her. He came quickly, then rolled off her, not feeling as fulfilled as he had hoped, turned over and went to sleep. It had been a long and tiring day.

She lay beside him in a state of deep disappointment. Being a big, strong woman she had developed the habit of taking charge. However, she had hoped that in their lovemaking he would treat her gently, as a fragile thing, girlish perhaps. She had hoped to feel delicate and precious at least in this one area of her life. She hadn't known how much she wanted it until she didn't get it, certainly hadn't known how to tell him this. She would have felt too foolish.

This was the start of their sex life and it continued in this vein with neither of them feeling emotionally satisfied or connected. Never seeing her experience pleasure, he felt he was being a bother to her and tried to make himself as small and insignificant as possible in this area of their relationship also, except when his physical needs grew to fever pitch and he would repeat the embarrassing scenario of their wedding night. They never spoke about it, not knowing how. Despite this they were genuinely fond of each other and their relationship worked well in other ways. They raised two children together, saw them off to college.

As information about sex became more available in the general population and more broadly depicted in films, coupled with a more romantic presentation of sexually intimate couples, he realized more and more what an inadequate lover he had been on his wedding night and the impact this had had on her. It was like he had flicked a switch to "off" as far as her sexuality was concerned on that fateful wedding night and no matter what he tried later, she submitted to his need but never joined him with her own arousal. He lived with a lot of shame and regret. He so wished he could go back and do it over, but no matter how hard he tried, he never could.

When she died Hank felt his loneliness as a deep hole inside. Even though the lovemaking had been completely absent for some years he missed the sense of her body beside him. He thought often of their wedding night and his regret grew and grew. He continued to buy magazines and to watch porn to satisfy his need for sexual release and one day he saw the ad for the house of pleasure specializing in wedding scenarios. Slowly the idea came to him that somehow he could undo his regret if only he could undo that wedding night, could do it again but this time differently. He clipped it out of the magazine and kept it in his drawer for several months, but the idea had taken root and would not go away. So one day he called the number and spoke to a very kind lady who listened to his wish to re-enact his wedding night and this time to do it differently, to be a loving partner to his bride. He felt that this would heal the pain he carried deep within. He felt sure that he could finally do it better given half a chance.

The kind lady was very reassuring—she was sure that they could help him out—this was exactly the kind of service they could offer. She took some details, his wife's size at the time of their wedding—size 20—her approximate height, age and hair colouring. They scheduled a date for a two-hour rendezvous, and she took his credit card information. She suggested that he come dressed in clothes like those he had worn for his wedding and then hung up. It was all done and settled in minutes. He got off the phone a little shaken and surprised that it had all been so easy and that the lady had seemed so nice. He realized he had expected to be judged or ridiculed. He was also anxious and scared and almost called back to cancel, but something stopped him.

Hank's anxiety increased as the date drew near. He went ahead and rented a tuxedo, like the one he had worn so many years ago. He was rather pleased with the way he looked in it. He practiced over and over in his mind how he would be as a lover this time around. He would be gentle, take his time, pay attention to pleasing and arousing her. He would enter her gently, respectfully, with the utmost tenderness, only after she was ready. In his mind he became the gentlest, most adequate and sensitive lover any woman had ever had.

He arrived at the house of pleasure and was greeted by the woman he had talked to on the phone. She was a short, grey-haired woman, probably in her late fifties, who introduced herself as Madame Pascale. She was smartly attired in an elegant pale blue dress with matching jacket, as if she were one of the wedding guests. She welcomed him warmly, putting him more at ease. They were then joined by a buxom young woman in a beautiful white wedding dress. She didn't really look much like his wife, as he had imagined she would when he had prepared for this day in his mind, but Hank figured he had come this far and he could always close his eyes and pretend it was her.

Madame Pascale then took him up the very elegant wooden staircase to one of the rooms, congratulated them on their nuptials and left them there. There was a bottle of champagne and two glasses on a dresser, a large bed and a chair. Hank and the young woman—he called her Betty, his wife's name—seemed rather awkward and uncomfortable with each other at first as if neither of them really knew what to do. He poured some champagne for both of them and they sat on the bed to drink it. After a couple of sips he took her glass away and very gently asked her to stand up and turn around. He then slowly undid all the buttons down the back of the dress, fumbling rather as he did so. He slid the dress off her shoulders and let it fall to the floor. He was surprised to see her standing there naked. He had expected her to be wearing lacy under-garments that he would also slowly remove. He picked the dress up and laid it gently on the chair.

Hank did his best, poor soul. He took his own clothes off and then he tried to arouse the girl very tenderly in a variety of ways. He gently stroked her breasts, sucked on them sweetly, caressed her buttocks, played with her clitoris, told her she was beautiful but none of it seemed to be doing it for either of them.

Irony of ironies the girl, whose name was actually Bettina and had always hated it when people called her Betty, just didn't seem to be into it any more than his wife had been, even though she made a few attempts to pretend that she was. Hank remained limp and flaccid. She gave him a hand job in an effort to get some life into the member, but without any success. The blow job she gave him was no more effective. She just wasn't a very enthusiastic participant, and he was finely tuned to sense it.

The problem was the cake. Bettina had baked a cake just before the man's arrival and the cake was all she could think about. Her stomach grumbled as she thought about the cake and longed to go back down to the basement and have a piece. She loved to bake. It was what she loved most in the world. She was passionate about it. The cake she had just baked was a new recipe. It had smelled divinely of apples and cinnamon when she took it out of the oven. She was worried the other young men and women who worked there would get to it and eat it all up before she had a chance to even sample it, so she just wanted Hank to get it over with as soon as possible so she could get back to the kitchen. She was getting more and more discouraged and frustrated by his unresponsiveness. Why couldn't he just get it up, do what he had to do with her and go home? The longer he took the less and less likely it would be that there would be any cake left for her. All she really wanted to take into her body was a slice of that sweet, delicious cake, not the horrid little penis of this diminutive man who almost disappeared under her mounds of flesh.

Eventually Hank saw it was going nowhere and this was not going to be the healing experience that was going to repair his 40 years of marriage. He suggested that they give up on it, finish up their glasses of champagne and call it a night. He apologized profusely for his inability to be a better lover and thanked her repeatedly for her willingness to try, and then he left.

Madame Pascale was waiting for him at the bottom of the stairs. She enquired as to his experience and whether he was satisfied with the service he had received. He responded that although the sexual experience was less than satisfactory, he had got something much more important out of it. He said he realized that his wedding night and what happened subsequently wasn't all his fault. He understood that his wife wasn't very into it either and he had realized that it takes two to make things happen. He left feeling greatly relieved of the heavy burden of believing it was all his responsibility.

"Bonsoir, Madame," he said as he walked away.

Madame Pascale went upstairs and fired Bettina on the spot. She was running a brothel, not a therapy service, and couldn't afford to keep girls who couldn't at least pretend with some degree of conviction to be enjoying their work. However, because she liked the girl, she gave her the wedding dress suggesting she sell it and start herself up as a baker specializing in wedding cakes, which seemed to be a métier to which she would be much better suited.

The Invitation

How are you doing with your own writing? Are you doing any of it either in response to my invitations or in whatever way comes for you? If so, good for you. If not, no pressure—just enjoy the stories. Some of us just need a little nudge or support to express the writer within and some of us don't have any interest in living out that part of ourselves or are already doing it in our own way. I'll try to keep the invitations coming after each story for those of you who want to make use of them.

So, this story's invitation is to develop one of the other characters—Madame Pascale, Hank's wife, Bettina—the girl who thought about her cake. Who are they, how did they come to be who they are in their particular situation? How do they experience it? Have fun developing their character and their history.

Rosebuds from Paris

She was nineteen when she went to Paris.
From a sheltered life, virgin still,
An all-girls school. Good student. Good girl.
Dull life.

Then Paris—a job, a little money.
A garret flat in the Faubourg.
Reflected lights. The sparkling Seine. Bateaux mouches.
The Eiffel tower a-twinkle in the night sky.
The faded glory of the Moulin Rouge.
Freedom. Romance.

She fell in love.
Not with anyone in particular
But with Life, with Joy, with herself as a free young woman.
Freshly released from the prison of childhood.

When she wasn't working,
She walked the streets, explored the quartiers, the cafés,
the sights, the smells.
And then one day she saw it.

The dress.

In a shop window. The most beautiful dress she had ever seen.
A confection of white, with soft netting
and tiny silk rosebuds all over.
And she knew, knew absolutely without a doubt,
that this was the dress she wanted to be married in.
One day, when she met the right man.
She knew not when.
She knew she must have it. Could not live another day
without owning it.
She went into the shop and bought it.
She took it home to her garret.

Often in the evening she would take it out and gaze in wonder,
Fondle the soft gauzy feel,
Imagine herself the beautiful bride, radiant, fresh, innocent,
totally in love with her husband to be, who awaited her at the
altar, whose eyes teared up with love and awe when he saw her
come towards him, who loved her as totally as she loved him.
The perfect start to a perfect life of happiness together.
The dream kept her warm on many a lonely night
in the garret flat.

When she left Paris and went back home,
she packed the dress up carefully.
When she left again for a new job in New York this time,
she left the dress in the wardrobe of her room
in her parents' house,
Waiting, waiting, waiting for her,
waiting for the day she would come to fetch it,
As she waited for the husband-man—the one.

She loved New York.
The vibrant pulse of life,
the loud brashness of the people,
the round-the-clock energy,
the theatres, the clubs.
The people hurrying this way and that.
Walkers, joggers, runners, line-skaters speeding by.
Cars, taxis honking, buses sighing.
The hustle and bustle, the pushing and shoving.
The broad smiles and open-heartedness
The "couldn't care less", "let them die in the gutter" attitudes,
So different from the sleepy, nothing-ever-happens,
everyone-knows-what-you're-doing village she grew up in.

She dated a bit, even went steady for a while,
but always knew he wasn't the one—
The one to walk down the aisle towards
Wearing the dress.

Another job. A year in Perth, Australia.

Sun-drenched, dry, sere.

Kangaroos and koalas, kookaburras, gum trees,

boabs, spiders, snakes, jelly fish—

Poisonous, dangerous. Iconic.

Strange birds, strange animals, strange plants,

Red soil. Endless beach. Blue sea.

Summer temperatures rising to mid 40s.

A slower pace.

Strange men. Australian men, a different breed.

Pioneer and outback in the blood.

A hint of convict, escapee from death or incarceration.

Glad to be alive,

Survivor in a harsh and beauteous land.

Rough, unapologetic.

One man, a possibility,

But both of them too scared to be trapped,

tied down, enclosed in boundaries too small,

Marked out by the circumference of a gold ring.

Not ready yet to commit to one,

to say goodbye to freedom found.

The dress would never fit in this harsh land.

Rosebuds and lace too delicate to survive,

Her petals would be crushed before she bloomed.

A posting to Dubai.

All expats, pulled up from their roots like her. Ruptured ties.

Yet slaves all—to OIL.

Nothing sustainable. Desalinated water.

The ever-encroaching desert trying to reclaim her own.

Sandstorms.

False lawns watered endlessly in an arid land.

A ski-hill in a modern shopping-mall.

False wealth, false lives.

Affairs.

No buy-in to a culture struggling to find itself.

Sex without love, to pass the time, to simulate connection.

Innocence lost.

Masks and facades.

Undeserved wealth.

No, this would never be her home.

A needed transfer back to somewhere lushly green.

Montreal, Canada. Arriving in early summer.

An island in the great St. Lawrence seaway,

with a "mountain" in the middle, a cross on top.

Surrounded on all sides by mile upon mile

of green, lush countryside.

Unending miles of trees. Evergreens.

Mountains to the north, mountains to the south.

Great crashing thunderstorms, torrential rain and sudden sun.

Days of glory. A month of black flies and mosquitoes.

A too-short summer.

A stunning, crimson Fall—maples!

A world aflame with red, vermillion, ruby, orange, yellow, gold

Presaging the long months of unimaginable cold.
Too long the winter months—the icy sidewalks,
the slushy melts, the bitter winds.
Too long, too long "ce maudit hiver."
The two cultures, French and English living side by side,
And all the others from around the globe.
A blended family with all the tensions and challenges,
with all the joys and richness.
At times an uneasy peace, but mostly a spirit of reasonable
accommodation to difference, a learning to live
with "otherness" in some kind of harmony.
Like any marriage.

A relationship with a Quebecois, Guy.
A man from Trois-Rivières.
Montréal, his big move, his Great Escape from small town life.
Returning home whenever he could.
Belonging in Québec but not the world beyond,
which seemed alien, unwelcoming, even hostile at times.
A romance, a love of sorts.
Passion turned to conflict.
No shared mother-tongue to build a bridge
between two solitudes.
Everything needed to be explained, translated, to move
beyond the misinterpretations that so often clouded
the space between.
They came apart in anger and in sorrow. Unraveled.
Each licking their own wounds, unable to soothe each other.

And so back home to England. A job in London.
Throbbing heart of the civilized world—or so they thought
through the Empire years and maybe far beyond.
Somehow familiar to her, yet alive, vibrant,
pulsing with a raw, raunchy beat.
Theatres, concerts, museums, lectures, clubs,
restaurants and food a-plenty for the mind.
A flat in Notting Hill—old and new, trendy and Victorian.

"Ancient, beautiful, historic,
These are my roots. From this I came.
But the acorn and the oak are not the same"
she thought as she settled into her new life
back in the country of her birth.

Surrounded by parks,
Never far from bright green field, majestic tree,
from grazing sheep and cattle,
Never far from forest, wood and hilly down,
Never far from village green and welcoming pub,
Never far from country home or castle ruin,
Never far from salty sea, from pebble beach and seaside town,
Never far from "home"—from that feeling of belonging.

A man.
A meeting at a pub.
Eyes that met and there it was—
A spark that grew rapidly into flame.

It burned bright and sure. Steady. Strong.
A love from deep inside.

Similar and different they were.
Explorers both—he of the mind, she of the world around.
A love that grew and flourished, watered by the English rains,
Growing in a rich English soil.
Bridges large and small across the space between.

A proposal. Accepted immediately. No hesitation, no doubt.
An engagement ring, plans—the church,
the guest list, flowers, hall, the band.
A dress needed for the day.

And so returning to the carefully wrapped package
in the wardrobe of her parents' home.
Holding it up before the mirror. Looking this way and that.
Trying it on.
No longer her. No longer the young,
innocent maid of netting and rosebuds.
No longer the innocent maid with dreams of the perfect man,
of perfect wedded bliss.
Wiser now. Older. Worldly-wise.
Full of life experiences. Knowledge. Learnings. Scars.
A wisdom gleaned from suffering as well as joy. Hard-earned.
Wrought in the fires of life and love and quarrel.

No—the dress no longer expresses who she is—today as woman.
An ad in the *Free Trader* "For Sale: Wedding dress. Size 20.
Never worn".
A new dress, simpler, sleeker,
Cleavage showing her woman's form.

In marrying this man she must go forth from who
she is today—riper, sager, bruised and mellowed.
Ready still to evolve and change, to be forged
in the fires of marriage and maybe motherhood,
into new shapes, new possibilities.
A woman on the cusp of her fullest potential.
Solid yet flexible.
No longer bud but rose, opening,
unfurling, showing its emergent beauty
For all the world to see.

The Invitation

This story flowed from me as I sat in a café in Paris. I invite you to go to a café and start to write. The story is a love poem to various cities I have visited or lived in. You can follow this lead if you choose and write a story about a city or write a poem about a city you have visited—whatever comes to you as you sit in a café and look around you, look inside you.

But He's a Man

I thought I could do it. I thought I could marry James Turner, become Mrs. Sharon Turner and be happy. He's a good man, kind, intelligent, gentle even. But he's a man. I like him a lot. Marrying him would make my life so much easier, solve all my problems. I'd be accepted. I might even feel like I fit in, or maybe that's too much to ask. I'd also have some financial security where I'd have someone to fall back on if I lost my job, if someone found out about me. He has a good job at the bank, but he's not dull. He loves theatre and the arts, he has even travelled abroad—taken vacations in France and Italy. Not everyone does that even though we're already well into the 1950s. It shows a balance in his personality between his stability and his sense of adventure. He's a sharp dresser and good looking. We might have children one day.

No, that's where it all breaks down, where it becomes impossible to imagine. The idea of his penis, any penis, inside me, of his hairy male body on top of me disgusts me. I thought I could close my eyes and "think of Queen and country" as they used to say in Victorian medical texts, but I know I can't. I can't put myself through it or subject him to a marriage with a wife who despises the most intimate acts of love with him for years and years till death do us part. He doesn't deserve that.

I've imagined submitting to intercourse with him just often enough so I can give him children, and encouraging him to take a mistress for the rest, but I don't think he ever would, or if he did he'd feel horribly guilty. He's too decent a man to be unfaithful once he'd made his vows, no matter how much I subtly encouraged him. No, I'd be killing him slowly day by day if I married him just as surely as if I put arsenic in his morning tea. I'd probably be killing myself too, but maybe I deserve it.

You see, I always thought there was something wrong with me. It is women I am attracted to, not men. That is my secret, that is my deepest shame. I should have grown out of the adolescent crushes that all girls have at boarding school, but I haven't. I love women. It's women's bodies that excite me. Something in me must have got stuck. If anyone found out I'd lose my job and no-one else would ever hire me without a reference. My family would reject me. It would kill my father. My sister would never let me near her children ever again. I might even be imprisoned—I am sure there are still some laws on the books that mean I am a criminal because I have loved a women, because I have touched her wonderful, soft, round breasts, sucked on her nipples, licked her swollen, moist labia, been brought to the heights of ecstasy by her delicious attentions to my body, because I lust only for women and not men.

Love of this kind is a crime in London in 1957. And a sin. I am a Catholic and go to church each Sunday. My faith is important to me, it always has been, but I cannot go to confession and be absolved of this sin that lives within me. I am told I will burn in hell for all eternity for the love I have felt. How can my love be so wrong in the eyes of God when there are so many marriages where husband and wife treat each other with contempt and even violence? Yet this is ignored, or even condoned by a church that blesses their union because they can bring forth unwanted, unloved, children to live in the misery of this hostile environment, subjected to the withering chill of their parents' disappointments and dead love. Because my love cannot lead to children it is vilified, shamed, rejected, banned, seen as unnatural, sinful, criminal.

I grew up in such a loveless marriage. My father was distant, cold, judgmental, relieved but also bitter that he couldn't serve in the army, an engineer needed at home to run a munitions factory. My mother took out all her misery and frustration on me, the elder of her two daughters, the one who looked just like my father. It was a relief when I was sent to boarding school at age seven to get me away from the bombing in London and out of sight of my mother, I suspect. There was a nun, Mere d'Isère, from France, warmer and livelier than the rest of the nuns. She would take me on her lap, brush my hair tenderly, give me special attention. Perhaps she saw my pain, my feelings of being unlovable and alone in a hostile world, perhaps it resonated with something in her. With her, for the first time in my life I felt liked and special. I was happy there. I liked the daily routines, the concern of the sisters and mother superior. I did well at my lessons and got on with most of the other girls, finding my place in the group—neither the most popular—nor one of those who seemed to invite rejection. I had a sense of belonging in this all-female world of school and couldn't wait to get back there at the end of the holidays, much of which I spent reading books about girls' boarding schools. I loved Enid Blyton's *"The Naughtiest Girl in the School"* best.

When I was 11 my body started to change. I was surprised and excited by the budding of my breasts and the new sensations that I experienced when I touched them secretly lying in my bed at night. I started to furtively glance at the other girls in the dormitory to see if they too were developing breasts but many of them were still as flat as a boy. I was a big girl for my age and seemed to be developing faster than the others, so I would look at the older girls, trying whenever I could to glimpse their breasts under their shapeless school uniforms. Gym class was the best.

One day I had pains in my tummy and when I went to the toilet I found I had a brown, blood-like stain in my underwear. I was terrified. I thought I had some horrid disease inside me and was going to die. After two days of it continuing to get worse, I plucked up my courage and went to see the nurse. I told her I was dying. I was at first too ashamed to tell her of the blood coming from between my legs, but she didn't seem to be taking my tummy ache very seriously so in the end I had to. She just laughed and said "Sharon, it's nothing to worry about. Hasn't anyone told you about this? It happens to all girls when they become women. It's your body getting ready every month so you can have children." I didn't feel like I was becoming a woman—a woman was someone my mother's age—and I certainly wasn't ready to have children. I was horrified.

"You're young to start your periods, Sharon," she said. "The first in your class—probably because you are such a big girl. You'd better read this."

She gave me a little booklet and a packet of sanitary pads wrapped in brown paper. I left feeling very alone and still scared but at the same time a little reassured. At least I wasn't dying. I read the booklet in secret and tried to keep the pads hidden in my locker so none of the other girls would know. The next week the science mistress gave us a talk about the ways our bodies were changing but all the other girls just giggled. I became very secretive about this shameful thing that was happening in my body. I wasn't ready to be a woman.

Over the next couple of years other girls in my class started to have their periods but it still seemed like something shameful that must be hidden. We didn't talk about it even with each other.

The first day back at school after the summer holidays, the year I turned 13, my best friend, Hilary, came up to me as soon as we spotted each other and said,

"Sharon, I have so much to tell you. Let's escape after school and go to our secret place in the woods."

I noticed she had changed a lot over the summer. She must have grown six inches and her breasts were beginning to fill out under her school blouse. I could tell she was wearing a bra.

"Guess what," she said as soon as we were away from the school. "I got my period finally." She almost sounded proud.

"Me too," I confessed. Even though she was my best friend I hadn't told her I'd already started. I had been too ashamed to tell anyone.

"Oh," she said with surprise. "I was sure you'd started ages ago. I thought I was the only one who hadn't. I was so worried I never would, that there was something wrong with me."

When we got to our secret hiding place in the woods, a little clearing in the middle of a large rhododendron bush that we had been using for a couple of years as our special hideaway, Hilary pulled a packet of cigarettes out of her blazer pocket. She was always a bit of a rebel but still I was quite shocked. She took one out of the pack and lit it. She took a couple of hauls then handed it to me. I took it and puffed on it, drawing in deeply as I had seen her do. It was horrid. I started coughing and spluttering. I tried a couple more times but very quickly felt horribly sick and my head started to spin. I hate throwing up—absolutely hate it—so I stopped and told her I didn't want any more. I have never smoked again. But I did pull a chocolate bar out of my pocket. It was from the secret stash I had brought back with me from the holidays. I often stole chocolates at home, or even from the store and ate them in secret. I knew I shouldn't and I felt ashamed both that I ate them and that I did it secretly, but I couldn't seem to stop no matter how often I told myself I would. It seemed like the only time my dad paid any attention to me was when he told me I was fat and I must lose weight or no-one would love me, so I tried really hard but that just seemed to make it worse. Looking back I think shame was probably the most pervasive emotion I felt as a child and it hasn't gone away as I have got older.

After Hilary had finished her cigarette and very carefully put it out, burying the butt in a little hole she dug in the ground, she said to me,

"Sharon, did you notice I also got my breasts over the summer? They're not very big yet but I hope they keep growing. Would you like to see them?"

I knew immediately I very much did but didn't want to show her how eager I was.

"Alright. If you want me to see them," I said. I watched as she took off her blazer and undid the buttons of her blouse. I thought she'd just give me a peek by flashing open her blouse, but she took off her blouse and then her little bra.

"You can touch them if you like. They feel really nice."

I looked around to make sure no-one had sneaked up on us and was spying in the bushes. Then she took my hand and put it on her left breast. It was very small and firm with a little nub of a nipple sticking out.

"Touch the other one too," she said and put my other hand on her other breast.

"Oooh, that feels nice," she cooed. "Me and my cousin did this over the summer holidays when she came to stay. She's 15. I like to pull on my nipples. I keep hoping it'll make them grow faster. You do it. Like this." She showed me how she pulled her nipples, so I did it too. As I did I had the strangest feeling down between my legs. It suddenly felt very hot and swollen and the area below my tummy felt all queer. I was going to pull away, but she said, "Don't stop. I like it. It makes me feel all squirmy in my knickers."

After a little while she said, "Now you have to show me yours. It's only fair."

"No," I said. "Mine are so much bigger than yours."

"I know," she said, "I kept thinking about them this summer. They're so gorgeous. I've looked at you when you were putting your nightie on, even though the nuns are so strict about stopping us seeing each other's bodies. I hope mine will be big like yours one day."

I couldn't believe what she was telling me, even though she seemed very genuine. The idea that anyone would like any part of my body and want to be like me was such a new thought I couldn't get my head around it. So I undid some of the buttons on my blouse. I didn't take it right off and I kept my bra on, but I pulled my breasts out of it and the bra held them up so that they looked even bigger than usual, big, round mounds of white flesh. It was like I was seeing them for the first time, through Hilary's eyes, and they looked different to me—almost beautiful, voluptuous, like Diana Dors' or some other movie star's—the way they stuck up out of the top of her tight dresses, two round mounds.

She reached out and touched them, weighing them in her hands.

"Oooh," she said, "I think they've got even bigger over the summer. You're so lucky. Can I pull on your nipples?" and she did even before I answered. I knew what she meant about being squirmy in her knickers—I felt it too.

I was feeling really weird so I said, "I think we'd better get back or we'll be late for tea and they'll send someone to look for us."

We giggled at that thought although I think we both felt really scared about being caught because we knew that what we were doing was really naughty and we'd probably be expelled immediately and sent home in disgrace.

That was how it all started. Over the next year and a half, whenever we could, we would sneak away to our secret place. Because we didn't have much free time, our school days being so structured and full, we couldn't escape very often, but when we could we did. At first we just touched each other's breasts, then one day she put her head on my chest and licked my nipple. I gasped with pleasure and thought that the area between my legs would explode so I put her hand there on my knickers and rubbed it a little until something happened like an explosion inside me. I got scared even though I really liked it. I didn't want to let her do it again, although I did. One day I started to suck on her nipple, like babies do with their mothers and she seemed to like it a lot. She took my finger and put it inside her underwear and it was all wet and gooey. I thought she must have her period but when I took my finger away there was no blood, so I put it back and rubbed gently between her lips, which seemed very swollen and big. She cried out and looked like she was in pain, but then she kissed me on my lips and I liked that too. This is how we got to know each other's bodies and our own also, what we liked, what made us most excited.

Of course, we never told any of the other girls what we were doing, we let them believe we were going off to talk about our boyfriends, but some would tease us, calling us a couple of 'lesbos' because we sneaked away together. I don't think any of them had a clue how close to the truth they were, although I didn't think of myself as a "lesbo". I'm sure they would have been scandalized and immediately reported us to the nuns if they had known. Perhaps the danger of being caught, and the high stakes if we were, made it even more exciting.

Then suddenly Hilary wasn't there anymore. She never came back to school after the Easter holidays and the nun who was our house teacher said she had been moved to another school. I was desolate. I didn't understand what could have happened. I was sure her parents must have found out about us and I expected to be called into the mother superior's office at any moment to be told what an awful, hateful person I was. After a while, when that didn't happen, I asked the house nun for Hilary's address and wrote to her, but the letter was returned unopened marked "No longer at this address." I haven't seen her since.

I coped with the loss by eating to stuff down my sadness and fear, and by concentrating on my studies. I did well in my GCE "O" levels and went on to get three good "A" levels, which got me into university in Bristol.

That was where I met Allie. There weren't many girls at the university in 1952 so we were rather thrown together. I knew there was something special about Allie as soon as I met her. Perhaps she reminded me a bit of Hilary, with the same rebellious streak. I think we both felt the attraction, but we were both too scared to make any open moves. Then one night on the way home from the pub where we had been drinking with a bunch of other students, we were walking through the park and she pulled me into the bushes and kissed me.

"I've been wanting to do that for a while," she said when we came up for air, "and I think you've wanted me to also." I didn't deny it.

We fell madly in love. We were very, very careful not to let anybody know how we felt about each other. Fortunately, we could get away with seeming to be just good friends. Girls can go to each other's rooms without causing too much suspicion, although people did comment that neither of us ever had any dates with boys. We were teased a lot about that.

"Too busy studying," we'd reply. "Plenty of time for that when we've got our degrees."

It was hard the first year because both of us were sharing rooms with other girls so we could only grab odd moments here and there when we were sure that our roommates wouldn't burst in. We had a few close calls, so we always kept our clothes on. We would kiss passionately for minutes at a time and feel each other's breasts. Sometimes I would reach up under her skirt and caress the wet place between her legs but she wouldn't let me do it very long. We were both too scared of being caught and yet we couldn't stop ourselves.

My second year at university was the happiest of my life. Allie and I managed to arrange to share a room together in the dorm. Allie taught me so much about love and about how to pleasure each other most intensely. She taught me the words to tell each other what we wanted. "Stroke my clitoris," she would say to me, showing me where and how to touch her. "I want you to fuck me with your fingers—harder," she would moan. I got very turned on by her ability to express what she wanted. "Sharon," she'd say, "tell me how you like me to touch you. I want to know."

Sometimes I would wake up early in the morning and I would lie in bed and watch her sleep. Then I would make her tea and bring it to her in bed, waking her up with a kiss. I loved to watch her getting dressed and undressed each day. Best of all I loved to make love to her, caressing her breasts and licking her sweet, wet lips, kissing, flicking my tongue against her clitoris as I played with her nipples, until she came in a silent scream of pleasure. I loved it when she would climb into bed with me in the night, undo the front of my nightdress, take out my breast and start sucking on it. Sometimes I would wake up in the night to find her sucking at my breast. I wanted to lie there forever with her sucking on me like that. I wished at those times I had milk to give her and wondered if it would arouse me to nurse a child or if that was different. It must be. We still had to be really careful as there was no lock on the door. Anyone could burst in at any time to borrow some shampoo or some Ovaltine. We let it be known that we didn't like to be disturbed when we were studying but this didn't always keep them away. Some nights we did actually take the risk of trying to sleep in the same bed but they were single beds and it wasn't very comfortable. Usually, after we had brought each other to a silent, stifled orgasm, we went back to our own separate beds, still longing for each other's bodies. I never knew I could be so happy. It was the first time in my life I felt so loved and wanted. I couldn't understand how our love could be so wrong.

During the summer holidays we went camping together for a week before starting our summer jobs. We pitched Allie's brother's tent in a secluded spot near a stream out of sight of the farmhouse on whose land we were camping. It rained a lot that week, but we didn't care. We lay naked, our sleeping bags zipped together, skin to skin, breast to breast. I loved the feel of her breasts against my body. I loved to stroke the soft curls of her pubic hair. I loved the many ways we made each other feel loved and wonderful with our bodies and in many other ways besides. We felt free and happy. We laughed so much together. It was wrenching when we had to pack up and say goodbye.

Our third year of university we weren't able to share a room. It was terrible. The system had changed and despite all our efforts and complaints we couldn't get them to change the room allocations. We were devastated. Neither of us could afford to live off campus. We were also under a lot of pressure academically, especially as women. We had to do well to prove something. We longed for each other but when we were together we fought out of frustration and misery. It was so different from the passionate yet leisurely lovemaking we had experienced during our week of camping. I started to believe she didn't love me anymore, didn't want me, that she must have feelings for someone else. I became insanely jealous any time I saw her with someone else—a boy or a girl. So when we were able to see each other I was horrid to her, accusing her of being unfaithful or begging her to love me. That drove Allie crazy and she'd tell me to stop but I couldn't. I could see I was driving her away. Occasionally we found an uneasy peace, but it never seemed to last very long.

After I came down from university with a degree in modern languages, specializing in French and Italian, I had to look for a job. I got one working for a firm of translators. They wanted me to start immediately so the plans that Allie and I had been tentatively making to go camping, in hopes of recapturing something irrevocably lost, fell through. The firm had a big contract with a national bank to translate documents concerning a deal it was negotiating with a bank in France. That's where I met James Turner. He worked for the bank.

Allie got a job as a French teacher at a grammar school in Manchester. She wouldn't be starting work properly until September. She got a summer job working at a holiday camp and was always busy on weekends when I was free. I went up to see her a couple of times but she couldn't spend any time with me and waiting around to grab a few minutes together was worse than staying home. We thought it would be better when she started teaching, but it wasn't. She always had papers to mark or lessons to prepare.

Somehow I wasn't surprised when I got her letter just after Christmas saying she had got engaged to a fellow teacher and would be getting married the following summer. In some ways it was a relief that the frustration was over, and I could tell myself that she'd always really wanted a man even though she'd never shown any signs of being interested in men.

When I went back to work in January I accepted James' offer to take me out to dinner. We dated for a few months and then he asked me to marry him. I was still on the rebound from the loss of my relationship with Allie, and I thought I could do it. I went ahead with the wedding plans, bought myself a dress. I really did think I could do it—marry him and be happy eventually. But he's a man and I realize now I can't. My parents will be furious. I'm sure they'll think he dumped me and blame me. I'll have to face up to it and tell James I can't marry him and then tell them. Of course I won't tell them why, just say I don't love him enough or something. I'll have to cancel all the wedding plans, put an ad for my dress in the local paper, "For sale: Wedding dress. Size 20. Never worn." It sounds so sad. I wonder what the people who read the ad will make of it, whether they will wonder why, what's the story behind it.

Even though I won't be marrying James, I am hopeful about my future. Things do seem to be changing a little—at least I hope they are. There are a couple of girls at the place I work. I'm sure they are having an affair with each other, if that's even the right word. I know they live together. I see them giving each other little looks like I used to exchange with Allie. There's a young woman I'm really attracted to who has coffee at the same coffee shop I go to a lot. I never see her with a man. There's something about her that makes me think that she likes women more than men. The look she gave me the other day felt like a definite come on. Perhaps I could suggest we have a coffee together some time and get to know her.

Most importantly I know now that I can love with my whole heart and body and be loved as well. I know I can have a very fulfilling sexual relationship with a woman even if a lot of people think it's wrong. I just know it feels so right—so much more right than sex with James ever could be. I'm accepting more and more that this is the way I am and perhaps that's OK. I don't have to marry a man to feel OK about myself. I just need to find more people who have the courage, like me perhaps, to live outside the moral constraints imposed by church and family and be willing to be fully who we are, even if we don't acknowledge it to the people who might reject us. It took a lot of courage to decide not to marry James. It will take courage to live life on my terms, but I know I must. And I know there are others who will accept me, who are like me, a community where I will belong. Yes, I'm hopeful.

The Invitation

What do you think it was like, or what do you know from your own experience it was like, growing up in a culture and a time when it was not OK to be gay, lesbian, trans, bi, queer? It may still not be OK in your culture today. There may still be attitudes, limitations if not actual laws, that tell people this is not fully accepted. If you are straight, put yourself in the shoes of a GLBTQ+ person and write a short story about what this is like for you. Are you hopeful about the future? Or not? What makes you feel the way you do about the future? If you are GLBTQ+ write your story or that of someone you know.

Giant Deceptions—a Fairy Tale

Once upon a time in a land far away over the mountains, there lived a beautiful princess. She had jet black hair and eyes of a blue deeper than the ocean on a cloudless day. Her skin was flawless and as smooth and soft as baker's dough when left to rise. She was quite delicate and petite for the race of minor giants she belonged to, a mere size 20, almost a dwarf by giant standards. Being their only child, she was the apple of her parents' eye, and was given whatever she wanted, but as she grew she saw the poverty and devastation all around her and felt very sad and guilty that she had so much when others had so little.

She mixed little with the humans who lived near the castle. For many generations her family had struck fear in the hearts of the inhabitants of the area. Old tales lingered of the terrible goings-on in the neighbourhood, dating from times when these diminutive giants were thought to steal children from their beds to eat for breakfast. Even today occasionally there were stories of children disappearing suddenly, never to be seen again. People always assumed it was due to the dietary predilections of the giants. The people were wary and scared and kept away from the castle as much as possible. As a result, few of the people knew much about the giants who lived behind the high walls or knew what they lived on.

Despite being doted on by her parents and having everything she could possibly ask for in terms of clothes and toys, the princess was lonely and sad. Her parents were always busy with affairs of their small kingdom and there were no other young giants around. Now that she was an adolescent on the cusp of womanhood, her longing for companionship was even more acute.

Sometimes, however, she was able to escape the castle walls and go off into the forest to visit an old witch who had taken care of her when she was a young child. Like all the people around she was very poor and eked out a living any way she was able. The princess tried to bring her little treats whenever she could, but she feared being found out and stopped from leaving the castle. The old witch had helped her find and make alterations to some old peasant clothes, which were dirty and torn. She kept them hidden and wore them whenever she left the castle. Thus, she no longer looked like the giant princess but like a rather large, very ragged beggar who didn't warrant a second glance. Over the years the local peasants had got used to seeing her around and paid her no heed, assuming she was the witch's granddaughter.

When she visited the old witch she liked to help her scratch around in the stony soil where the witch tried to grow a few scrawny vegetables to put in her cooking pot, along with any toads or bugs she could find in the forest. She loved feeding the hens on which the witch depended for the occasional egg. The old woman lived a very meagre existence and so her witch-powers were diminished to almost nothing.

One day when the princess was poking around in the patch of ground behind the witch's cottage, a young man, with hair the colour of burnished gold and eyes of an emerald green like the forest at break of day, rode by on a fine black stallion. When he saw the young woman working in the garden he stopped to ask where he was and to see if he could purchase some food because he was very hungry. He was immediately struck by her great beauty and the majesty of her stature, despite her ragged clothes and impoverished appearance.

He had ridden many days from far away and had eaten all the food he had managed to bring with him from his castle. He was, in fact, a young prince, the son of the king and queen of the land he had fled from in such haste. He had finally ridden away because he could bear his life no longer. At court it was nothing but lies and intrigues, plots and counterplots. It seemed to him that whenever he asked his parents to tell him what was going on they just made up more stories which turned out to be untrue. He always felt uncertain, unsafe, never knowing what to believe and what not to. So finally on his 18th birthday he took enough food for several days' ride and some gold coins from his parents' treasury and rode away, looking for a simpler, truer, more authentic life.

When he spied the beautiful maiden with jet black hair and eyes of a deeper blue than the ocean on a cloudless day, he fell instantly in love. Here, he thought, was a vision of all that was simple and true in the world, a maiden who lived a simple life, eking out a living from the soil.

The princess was also immediately smitten with love for the handsome young prince, with hair the colour of burnished gold and eyes of an emerald green like the forest at break of day. She was so astonished and delighted when he paid attention to her despite her ragged, disheveled appearance. Attention and companionship were the only things her parents didn't give her and that she longed for most. She certainly didn't want to scare him away by telling him she was the daughter of the king and queen of the giants with a reputation for eating the local children. She thought he would reject her immediately and ride off into the sunset, never to be seen again. So she kept the deception going through the months of summer as he courted her. She escaped from the castle as often as she dared, to wander with him in the forest or sit beside the stream. They talked little, because neither wanted to share much of their lives so far with each other out of fear they would lose the other's precious love. So they walked and sat together in a magical cloak of silence where they felt connected heart to heart.

One brilliant, sunny day, toward the end of summer, just as the leaves were starting to turn to gold, the prince proposed.

"I don't have much to offer you," he said, "for I have left most of my wealth behind and I will not go back whence I came. But what I have will be yours and will surely be more than you have had so far. I will find a way for us to live in a simple luxury beyond the impoverished life you have now. Please say you will marry me or I shall die of sorrow."

"Yes, I will gladly marry you," said the princess immediately, but with much trepidation in her heart because she knew that somehow or other her secret would come out. However, she hoped that he loved her so much all would be well and perhaps he would even be happy with the news that she too was of royal blood, like him.

And so, in secret, she made plans for her wedding, neither telling her parents about the young prince, nor telling the prince about her background and her life in the castle. She found some beautiful rich fabric stashed away in one of the storerooms of the castle and with the help of the witch, she made a wedding dress fit for a princess. She kept it hidden away in a chest in the witch's house.

One day the witch said to her, "You are going to have to tell him and tell your parents. This deception cannot go on any longer." She knew the wise old woman was right.

The next day she told her parents that one day when she was out wandering in the castle grounds she had met a young prince and fallen in love. She told them she wanted to marry him. They were shocked and saddened. They felt they were losing their beloved child. They had been so busy they had not noticed her growing up. Hadn't they always given her everything she wanted? Hadn't they always loved her and cherished her? Why would she want to go off and marry some itinerant stranger, a nobody they didn't even know? It was unthinkable.

"Well," the princess thought to herself, *"that didn't go very well, but I am sure it will go better when I tell the prince and he will love me even more for being honest with him."*

The next day she sneaked out of the castle and went to meet him in their usual trysting place.

"I have deceived you," she said. "I am not the poor old witch's granddaughter as I have led you to believe. I am actually a princess, daughter of the king and queen who live in yonder castle. I didn't want to tell you because my family has rather a bad reputation in these parts and I didn't want to scare you so you would ride away into the sunset and I would never see you again. However, I couldn't go through with the wedding until I had told you," she finished at last.

"How could you deceive me so cruelly?" he cried aghast. "All that has happened between us is nothing but lies and deceptions. I cannot bear it!" said the devastated prince. "I thought I had escaped all that, and now I find myself lied to again by the woman I thought I loved, the one I thought was so simple and pure. It is too much. I cannot possibly marry you now." He climbed on his horse and rode off into the sunset sobbing piteously, all hope lost of finding honesty and authenticity in the world. He was never seen again in those parts.

The prince rode and he rode through many lands, until some years later he came to a land where everyone always told the truth. Whether it was something in the water or air, or whether lies had not been invented yet we do not know. He fell in love with the place and all the people. It was not until he had been married for a while to a rather unattractive and unpleasant woman who always told the truth no matter what, and had three obnoxiously honest children that he realized fully how awful it was to live in this way. Telling his wife frequently how much he longed for the beautiful princess did nothing to improve his marriage. He lived unhappily ever after.

Meanwhile the princess returned to her lonely life at the castle with the parents who thought they gave her everything she needed. She could often be heard on the ramparts at night howling into the emptiness. She too lived unhappily ever after. Her howling increased the rumours in the neighbourhood about the giants who lived in the castle and stole children out of their beds at night to eat for breakfast.

One day the witch removed the wedding dress from the chest and took it to a town some way away from the castle. There she placed it on consignment in a shop and put a notice in the window "For sale: Wedding dress. Size 20. Never worn." It sold very quickly, although it had to be cut down in size for the new bride. There was enough fabric left over to make a christening gown for the first-born child of the couple.

The witch took the money and bought a cow, a rooster and some seeds for pumpkins and squash. The cow grazed in the clearing behind the witch's cottage. The manure she collected from the cow enriched the soil so that her vegetable crops increased and she had enough pumpkins to sell at Hallowe'en. The rooster did his job with the hens so that some of the eggs hatched into little chicks and increased her flock. However, very occasionally, on the night of a new moon, she still would sneak into town and steal a child out of its crib and cook it up to eat for breakfast.

One moral that can be drawn from this tale: moderation in all things—too many lies and too much honesty will not bring you the happiness you seek.

The Invitation

My invitation to you is to write a fairy tale. Often fairy tales have some stock characters—witches, giants, ogres, princesses, princes, fairy godmothers. Often fairy tales have a moral or theme—goodness prevails over meanness, love wakes you up from your unconscious sleep, etc. One way to go about this is to pick a message you might want to convey to children, such as "honesty is the best policy," or "don't trust a frog" and build your fairy tale around this. In 1980 Robert Munsch's gender stereotype-breaking "The Paper Bag Princess" was published. It has become a classic feminist text that has been banned at times in some places. Is there some fairy tale archetype you would like to bust wide open? Witches are mean old hags, princesses wait around helplessly for their prince to come and wake them up, trolls lurk under bridges to prey on victims? What would you do with these?

Losses and Gains

Dawn was a big woman with low self-esteem. She didn't believe anyone would ever love her. Since she was a young child she had never felt loved or loveable. She mostly kept to herself but sometimes she tried too hard to be liked.

In her early 30s she met a man who took an interest in her and before very long he proposed. On some level she knew he was not very nice to her, he ignored her or criticized and insulted her whenever she did anything he didn't like, but she didn't expect people to be. In her family she'd taken the brunt of her father's drinking and her mother's frustration.

She had been a homely, fussy baby, born too soon after her brother, who had health problems. Her parents were overwhelmed and stressed and the last thing they wanted was another child to care for so soon. Her mother expressed her stress and unhappiness through constantly criticizing Dawn. It seemed that everything Dawn did was wrong.

At school she was shy and, being overweight, the other kids picked on her, called her names and ostracized her in the cruel ways children can. Paradoxically, she tried to make herself as small and invisible as possible whilst getting larger and larger because of the food she ate in an attempt to soothe herself and stuff down the loneliness and unworthiness she felt inside. However, the more she ate the worse she felt about herself.

When Bill proposed she figured he was her only chance to have the things that other people had—a marriage, maybe even a family—a chance to be "normal", to belong somewhere, to have people who loved her. She longed to feel like she fitted in, was part of the world rather than being a lonely outsider as she had always felt she was.

Bill was overweight also. His belly hung over his belt and he had a hard time bending over to tie his shoes. He waddled when he walked and was quickly out of breath. Moving was more challenging than sitting still so he spent a lot of time in his chair in front of the television. He hated to see his reflection in the mirror. He projected his self-loathing onto Dawn. He treated her with disrespect. He asked her to marry him so he'd have someone to look after him, to cook and clean, someone to kick around, someone to care for him when he got sick or old, an unpaid maid. Although he didn't think of it that way, he needed someone who would carry his own self-hatred. He too had been an overweight child. He'd had no friends. He was always chosen last for sports teams because he couldn't run fast. If anyone tried to come close he'd push them away.

Bill was the illegitimate child of a single mother in a world where the other kids had two parents, siblings, and people who wanted and cared about them. He was dyslexic and had trouble learning to read. His mother wasn't able to give him the help or the patience he needed and the teachers treated him as stupid and obstinate. The kids made fun of him and avoided him. He ate his way through his feelings of being unwanted, unlovable, illegitimate. The more he ate the more unlovable he felt. He convinced himself he wasn't accepted because everyone else was too stupid, too ugly, too mean for him to be worth wasting his time on.

When he proposed ("I suppose we might as well get married," he said, protecting himself from ever knowing he needed her to want and accept him), she accepted his proposal and went out that weekend to buy the wedding dress. She needed something concrete to convince herself it was true. There was only one shop in town that offered larger sizes and they did not have a wide range. She quickly picked a dress not really caring too much how she looked in it. She really should have got the size 22 but they only had the 20 and the 24. There was no way she was going to get the 24! To Dawn wearing a size 24 dress on her wedding day would have felt like another nail in the coffin of her self-esteem.

They hadn't set the date yet but it probably wouldn't take place for at least 6 months. She decided she would lose the weight before the wedding, so she could fit into the dress. If she could just lose 1 pound each month, the dress should fit her okay. That seemed doable—just 1 pound per month.

The first week she started to eat a little better. She had heard it wasn't good to eat after 8 p.m. because it was harder for the body to digest. She didn't know if it was true but she decided for the next month to cut out all the snacks she generally ate in the evenings sitting watching the television with him. When she saw Bill eating his way through bags of chips or bowls of popcorn and she wanted to reach across and just take a handful, she stopped herself. She was surprised how easy it was most of the time. She realized, when she was not herself so busy eating, that she even felt a bit disgusted by his crunching and chewing, the noises he made, the crumbs that dropped onto his protruding belly. She wondered how disgusting she must appear to others when she was munching away mindlessly on a bag of chips at work or on the bus. Did people look at her and despise her? She looked away from him, picked up her knitting and busied herself with that. By the end of the first week she started to think of herself in a new way.

"I'm the sort of woman who doesn't eat after 8 p.m.," she said to herself with a touch of pride, and that helped her stay her hand. She was starting to form a new sense of herself as a woman who had some kind of control over her choices, who could make positive choices for herself—the sort of woman she looked up to, aspired to be.

She also started going out for a walk at lunch time. One of her co-workers had a watch that counted steps and found it very motivating to help her make sure she walked ten thousand steps each day. Dawn walked to the store during her lunch hour to buy one and only had time to buy an apple and a banana for her lunch from a stall on her way back to work. She found she didn't die if she didn't have the sandwich, bag of chips, cookies and soda she usually had for lunch.

The first week she lost 3 lbs. She felt really good about that. "If I carry on like this I could end up being a woman of normal weight," she thought with surprise and disbelief. The phrase rang in her own inner ear. "A woman of normal weight." She tried it on. Somehow it seemed to take a hold on her in some new way. She had never really considered the possibility before. She had been on diets, many of them. She had lost a few pounds but always put them on again and a few extra for good measure. She had always tried to motivate herself by telling herself she was fat and ugly, and she should lose some weight but that just made her feel worse about herself and then she ate more to soothe herself. Some part of her always rebelled against that "should" word. It seemed to create some inner conflict between the parent part of her that told her what she "should" and "should not" be doing and the child part that just wanted to go ahead and do whatever she felt like without limits.

The idea of living her life as a woman of normal weight felt very different from going on a diet. It felt life-long—a way of being and living in the world so different from the way she saw herself now—a "fat cow", as he so often called her. It felt like something she wanted—a "bucket list" item. She held the phrase inside her like a precious seed and it started to grow into a wish, a desire and then an image of herself—"a woman of normal weight." She began to realize that ever since she was a young child she had longed to feel "normal"—feel that she fit in, belonged, would be included in games, would be chosen for teams, would be liked and accepted. But normal was something she had never felt. She had always felt like an outsider, different, less than, a misfit both at home and at school.

She started to imagine herself that way "a woman of normal weight", a woman who could purchase her clothes from the regular racks at any store, who had a wide selection of clothes in her size, a woman who could walk into a room with her head held high and feel she belonged, had as much right to be there as anyone, a woman who could sit on a chair and not wonder if it would collapse beneath her, a woman who would not worry on the bus or train that other people would not want to sit beside her because she took up too much space, a woman who might even wear the sexy underwear she saw in catalogues without feeling ridiculous.

"So how do I need to live my life", she pondered, "to be the woman I know I can be, that I want to be—the woman of normal weight?" She went online and figured out her BMI, her body mass index, and found she was bordering between overweight and obese at around 30. The normal range for her height was 18.5 to 25 on the BMI. She decided that if she lost just 1 pound per month for about 3 years she could get down to within sight of the normal range and maybe some months she could lose more. Initially three years seemed rather a long time but she wanted to make it doable. This was about who she was for the rest of her life and in that context it seemed to not matter if it took her a while.

Encouraged by her initial success Dawn continued. She decided that even though she had lost 3 pounds already she would still continue her efforts for the month and try to lose another quarter pound each week. No matter how much she had lost or not lost the previous month, she would aim to lose a pound in the subsequent month. For the rest of the month she continued to abstain from eating after 8 p.m. and to walk each day, measuring her steps, using her watch. She lost an additional 2 pounds.

Dawn came to love her daily walks. Sometimes she went to the park and walked beside the pond or through the wood. She found that being in nature calmed her. She started to experience her body in a different way, stronger, healthier. She got to spend time with her own thoughts instead of being assaulted by all the external input that came at her—TV, radio, newspapers, other people's chatter. She realized how little time she had spent just listening to herself before. Some days she ruminated on a mean thing that Bill had said to her and realized that she shouldn't be putting up with them. Sometimes she walked along the residential streets and looked at the houses, making up stories about who might live there, what their lives might be like, what she would like her own life to be like. She avoided the main street with all the food shops and restaurants.

The second month she decided she would set herself a new intention, whilst maintaining her walking and 8 p.m. deadline. She settled on reducing her portion size and eliminating all second helpings. She found this to be very challenging because whenever she ate something she liked she wanted more, and then more and more. Portion size too was a big challenge. She found it hard to serve herself small portions as she piled the food on Bill's plate. But she did what she could and lost another pound.

Within four months she had lost the weight she needed to lose to get into the dress. She knew she didn't want to stop there—she wanted to keep losing util she was in the "normal", healthy BMI range. Neither she nor Bill were bringing up the subject of their wedding. Their relationship seemed to be getting worse rather than better. With each pound she shed she felt better about herself and felt she needed him less. She became more and more aware of the disrespectful ways he treated her and at times less and less tolerant. It was inconsistent with her newly emerging sense of herself. Sometimes she was able to just walk away when he started to go on at her, although sometimes she still ended up in tears and heading towards the fridge.

As he saw the changes in her Bill became increasingly anxious she would leave him, because he too on some deep level saw himself as unlovable. Her leaving would be further proof of that. He dealt with it differently than her—whereas she took it on and despised herself, he protected himself by seeing others as unworthy of love. He managed his anxiety by criticizing and belittling others. Whenever he himself felt belittled he felt tremendous rage and turned on her.

One evening when she denied herself a second helping of the delicious lasagne she had made for dinner, whilst handing him another heaping plate full he turned on her venomously. "I suppose you think you're better than me," he spat at her. "Well, you're not. You're just a stupid, ugly cow. No-one will ever love no matter how much weight you lose." All the things that deep down he believed about himself he put onto her. He felt threatened by her weight loss and her newly emerging sense of self. He felt diminished by it as though her success was a commentary on his inability to take charge of his own life.

As Dawn was able to take increasing control of what she ate and stuck with her plan of exercising each day she felt a shift within her. She noticed how Bill seemed almost panicked by the changes she was making and felt sad for him more than scared of him as she had in the past. During her walks she thought a lot about her relationship with Bill, her childhood, and the way she felt about herself. That time to just be with herself and think was helping her to work some things out. She pondered on why Bill seemed so threatened by her changes and she finally realized it wasn't really about her and there wasn't much she could do to make him feel better, any more than she could have made her parents happy, even though she had put a lot of energy into trying and had thought for years it was her fault that they were overwhelmed and angry. She finally got that it wasn't her fault. She admitted there were things she did at times to provoke him, sometimes even on purpose. She became aware that sometimes she almost felt good, felt relieved, when he was putting her down. It felt familiar, it felt like love. It felt like what she deserved. That thought scared her. Would she ever be able to feel loved by someone who was nice to her? She wasn't sure but she knew she had to start by treating herself lovingly, treating her own body well rather than continue her self-abuse and self-criticisms. She had to do her share of the work before she could expect anyone else to be good to her. She determined to become more aware of when she was pushing him into his attacks on her and when she was putting herself down.

As she gradually started to feel better about herself he found new names to call her, new ways of trying to belittle her and to ridicule her, criticizing the meals she served him, trying everything he could to make her feel bad about herself so she would be there for him.

Sometimes he would take another tack and subtly sabotage her efforts to lose weight by bringing home her favourite baked goods, little "treats" as tokens of his "love" for her. "You deserve a treat now and then," or "You're doing so well, a little something won't hurt," he'd say as he served her a large slice of pie.

At first she would eat them, fearing that he would feel rejected or get angry if she didn't. But she would always regret it the next day and she started throwing the rest of the pie in the garbage and pretending to him she had eaten it all up. This was a giant step for her, throwing away perfectly good food, as she had been brought up with a "waste not, want not" philosophy—even if the extra calories were completely wasted on her body, far more wasted than if she threw them in the trash.

Then one day when he brought home a rich chocolate cake that in the past would have tempted her beyond her feeble resistance, she said "No. I appreciate you thinking of me, but I have decided I don't want to eat that kind of food anymore."

As she had expected, he did get angry. "You ungrateful witch. Who do you think you are? You think you are too good to eat the gifts I bring you. Well, you aren't. You're still just a fat cow."

She started to feel angry herself. Why should she be grateful for something she hadn't wanted in the first place. As a child she had hated when her parents told her she should always be appreciative for any gift she received from them even if it was something completely inappropriate for her. She felt so unseen for who she was and yet she was supposed to be grateful.

She had always thought that the fat she carried was a layer that protected her from the world, kept her safe from the criticisms and rejections. If that was its supposed function, she realized it wasn't working very well. One day she realized that rather than a protective shield of fat around her, what she had been doing was taking in and storing in her body, in each cell, all the slurs, criticism, put-downs, rejections, and negative comments. She had been carrying them all around with her all these years. So, as he insulted her she started to examine each insult, piece by piece, to see if it really fit for her rather than just accepting it as the truth. "Ungrateful witch"—well, yes, she was ungrateful, why wouldn't she be. But a witch—no. At least not in the negative sense of that. Or come to that even in the positive sense. She never really had claimed her feminine power, her feminine wisdom, her capacity to cast a spell. Maybe she would like to become more of a witch. "Ugly, stupid cow"—well she knew she wasn't a cow in any literal sense. She had never given milk or provided meat—actually cows were rather wonderful animals, at least in human terms although the cow might not appreciate these sacrifices. Maybe she did tend to sacrifice herself rather, perhaps in a docile cow-like way. Something to think about. Stupid? Perhaps in some ways—being in a relationship with a man who treated her with such disrespect might be a fairly sure indication of stupidity. But there were other ways in which she didn't think it fit. She'd never taken an IQ test, but she had done quite well academically at school. She could do the crosswords quicker than him, although she never let him know that. Ugly? Yes, she was overweight but as she stood in front of the mirror and examined herself she didn't think she was ugly. She had rather nice eyes, and good lips. Maybe her nose was rather large for her other features, but no-one gagged as she walked down the street. All-in-all the overall picture wasn't too bad. Maybe she could do more to make herself attractive but "ugly" didn't really fit. "Ignorant bitch" he'd called her. Ignorant—well yes, there were things that she was ignorant about, things he knew a lot about—football, guns, racing scores, politicians. He seemed to know an awful lot about everything that was wrong with politicians. But there were other things she wasn't ignorant about. How to make a soufflé without it collapsing as soon as she took it out of the oven, for example, how to help people balance their books, do their year-end statements and fill out their income tax. She was quite good at that. "Bitch" certainly didn't fit for her. Perhaps she should learn to be a bit more of a bitch seeing as he saw her that way anyway. She'd see then how he liked that.

The day she went to the store on her lunch hour and bought herself a size 16 dress she decided to leave him.

When Bill realized she really was leaving, his initial reaction of anger was followed by panic. He saw the years of loneliness stretching ahead of him. He even briefly considered the possibility that some of his behaviours might have contributed to her going. He promised to change, told her he would do anything she wanted if she would just stay. At first her heart softened. She felt empathy and sadness for him. She felt the pull to give in so as not to hurt him. She felt guilty that she was betraying and abandoning him. And then she felt something new. She felt a barrier go up between her and him, a protective shield. She felt her heart hardening a little. She didn't have to sacrifice herself to protect him from his feelings. With trepidation she refused his request. She had changed too much to turn back now.

She moved into a small apartment by herself. She took the wedding dress with her as a reminder of how she had hidden her worth from herself and others not only under layers of fat but more importantly of disrespect for herself. It represented for her the way she used to be that she was afraid she might slip back into if she wasn't careful.

After the initial excitement of the first couple of weeks she found it really hard living alone, going home each night to the empty apartment. She started to wonder if she had done the right thing. She told herself no-one else would ever love her. She was so tempted to call him, to go back to her old home, to tell him she was sorry and ask if he would take her back. On a few nights she bought herself "treats" to try to help herself feel better. But within minutes the "treat" was finished and she felt worse about herself. She gained a couple of pounds. She realized she needed to get back on track.

"I can either treat myself or treat myself well," she said to herself, "and I would rather treat myself well." She repeated that to herself: "I can either treat myself or treat myself well." She liked the sound of it. "I can use that", she thought, "when I feel like buying myself a treat that I know isn't good for me or doesn't fit with how I want to be as a woman who can make good choices for herself, be in charge of her destiny rather than a victim to others' meanness."

One evening when she was feeling particularly lonely, she went into her closet and took out the wedding dress and thought about how she had had the opportunity to be married, maybe even to be happy, and had thrown it away. She tried on the dress and stood in front of the mirror looking at herself. It hung loose on her. As she stood there, she remembered what it had felt like living in that old body, in that old life, how lonely and sad and unhappy she had felt even though she was with him, how much lonelier she had felt living with him than she ever felt alone. Wearing the dress brought it all back vividly. She realized her old dreams of getting married and living happily ever after, of having a "normal" life, didn't fit her any more either. In losing the weight she realized she had expanded in other ways. She was now in charge of her own happiness and needed to figure out what it was that would make her happy that wasn't dependent on a man loving her, especially a man who wasn't capable of love. She realized that what she had longed for, what she had worked so hard for was self-respect. If she felt good about herself, about the kind of person she was, no matter what she weighed, it would matter a lot less if other people didn't like her. She realized that losing the weight had only been a part of the journey to gaining her self-respect.

"No," she said, looking at the dress hanging loosely on her body, "I am never again going back to that. I would rather be alone and have my self-respect than be with someone who can't love and respect me." She took the dress off and hung it in the closet, right in the middle where she would see it and remember, rather than in the back, where she might forget. That week she looked into evening courses and she signed up for one. She joined a gym. She started to meet people and make some friends.

She continued to lose weight. Generally, she ate healthily: cereal and fruit for breakfast, some fish or chicken and a salad or vegetables for dinner. Lunch was often a soup or a sandwich. She was careful not to keep food in the house that would tempt her to binge. She returned repeatedly to her mantra, "A woman of normal weight." Each month she set herself a new intention. One month it was taking a brisk walk each day before eating dinner. Another it was making sure she completely chewed and swallowed her food before taking another mouthful, which she found quite a challenge as she became aware of how quickly she tended to stuff her food in her mouth and swallow before she had even chewed or tasted it. Another month she tried eating off small blue plates instead of her usual red set because she read somewhere that blue cut the appetite whereas red increased it and smaller plates helped you take smaller portions. She didn't notice any difference due to the colour. When she tried drinking at least 4 glasses of water a day she only lasted a week. She hated having to go to the washroom every few minutes and found it especially inconvenient when she was out walking. She found that getting 7 ½ to 8 hours sleep a night really helped. It cut down on her cravings for snack foods when she was well rested, and the weight seemed to drop off faster. Whatever worked she continued and whatever didn't she dropped.

She had her ups and downs. As a bookkeeper for an accounting firm she was very busy during tax season. She put on 4 pounds in a month. She didn't have time to cook properly for herself, was eating high carbohydrate foods when she was exhausted to give her some quick energy which didn't last long. She often didn't get home until after 8 to eat her dinner. One time in November she slipped and twisted her ankle on the wet leaves. It was very painful, so she had to stop walking for a while. The days were getting shorter and were cold and wet. She felt shut in and lonely. She wondered if she would always be alone and if so, what was the point of all this. She put on three pounds that month. Each time she got herself back on track without beating herself up too much for the slips and most months she lost at least her 1 pound but often she lost 2 or 3 pounds.

She went through a particularly hard time when she was promoted to a new position at work with more responsibility. Her new boss could be quite critical at times and Dawn at first felt devastated by her harsh remarks. She went right back to the old feelings of being worthless. She wanted so much to get it all right so she would be appreciated and valued. Another of the women she worked with noticed how upset she was and followed her to the washroom, where she had gone to hide her tears. She was so kind, Dawn couldn't believe it. She told Dawn not to let it get to her, that it wasn't about her. The boss was going through a hard time and tended to take it out on her employees sometimes. She did it with all of them. Each of them had been upset by it at first but they had learned to let it roll off their backs. Dawn was so grateful to the woman and realized that she wasn't alone in her feelings. Over time, rather than wanting to leave her new job, she began to see it as an opportunity for her to learn how to deal with criticism in a new way so that she would be less destroyed by it. She still felt hurt by it but realized there was sometimes some truth in the criticism, that there was something she could improve on, but it didn't have to mean she was no good at all.

Three years after she moved out from living with Bill, she met a guy that she really liked at the gym where she worked out. She had dated a little but no-one she felt she wanted to go on more than a couple of dates with. Harry was kind and caring and treated her well. They became friends, got to know each other slowly and gradually their love deepened. After 2 years of dating he proposed to her and she accepted. The day she bought her wedding dress she decided the time had come to let go of the last vestiges of the past. She put an ad for the old wedding dress in the *Free Trader* flyer: "For sale: Wedding Dress. Size 20. Never worn."

Both of them wanted children, but when it came to her getting pregnant she kept putting it off time and time again. Finally, they sat down and talked about it.

"I'm scared you'll stop loving me if I put on weight during my pregnancy," she admitted. "I used to be fat and hated myself. I'm scared that as I get bigger and bigger I'll disgust you and you'll see me differently." Harry held her as she cried and cried, releasing all the uncried tears from her childhood and her relationship with Bill. As she became aware of her fear and Harry responded with love and reassurance rather than making her feel stupid for doubting him, she felt able to take the risk of becoming pregnant.

During her pregnancy she continued to work hard at keeping herself fit and healthy, not just for her own sake but for the growing life inside her. One day she said to Harry, "A miracle is happening inside me. A new life is growing in my body. It is totally changing the way I experience my body. Rather than seeing it as a traitor that is lurking to overtake my life again, I now see my body as a sacred temple, the vessel of the miracle of life."

Harry looked at her with love and awe. "In my eyes, you are a goddess, a divine creator of new life" he said. She saw herself mirrored in his loving eyes. Never again would she feel the same way about herself or her body. Not only was she a woman of normal weight, but she felt like a normal woman who was loved and loveable with all her strengths and insecurities, a woman who could love in return—a woman with self-respect and respect for the man she loved.

The Invitation

What did you think about the connection between Dawn's weight and her self-hatred and self-esteem? Were you offended?

Surprised? Or did it seem obvious to you? How might you write this sort of story? Have you ever had issues with your body image? Have you ever felt too fat, too thin, too tall, too short, too ugly, too pretty (Yes, even that? "People only relate to me because of the way I look"), too big busted, too flat chested, etc.? Has this affected the way you feel about yourself? Are there ways in which you feel you have to be "normal", fit a certain mold, to feel love-able? What is the story that is pushing to be birthed from you about self-rejection, self-acceptance, body image, the impact of how we experience love in our childhood on our way of being as adults? How might your characters feel about themselves? How might they express this? What are they really longing for under the immediate surface wishes like weight loss? How might they move beyond this, or not? Do you have empathy and under-standing for your characters, even the mean or abusive ones? How might this come across in your writing?

Blown Away*

(To be read with a strong southern drawl)

"Frankly, my dear, I don't give a damn," said Bertt. "You could get married in your petticoats for all I care. I'm sure you'll look lovely for our wedding, no matter what you wear."

Ruby was shocked at hearing him refer to her undergarments, but the thought of standing at the altar clad all in the white frills and lace of her petticoats was just too amusing a picture.

"I'd do anything to save Lara," she said. "I have to raise some money somehow to make the loan payment on the plantation. If we can just make this payment, we can keep it going until the cotton is picked and sold to the British merchants. I am sure my wedding dress would raise the few dollars that we still need to make the payment and save Lara from being repossessed by the bank."

So, the next day she rode into Atlanta and placed a small advertisement in the *Atlanta Free Trader* "For Sale: Wedding dress. Size 20. Never worn". She was very sad to part with the beautiful gown she had had imported at huge expense back before the civil war, but everything had changed over the years of that dreadful conflict and "Beggars can't be choosers," she told herself. "If we are to rebuild Lara to her former grandeur, or even keep her, we must all just keep on making whatever sacrifices are necessary." The gown was a beautiful rich, scarlet-coloured silk affair with rows of frills around the bottom, worn over a white petticoat.

"Maybe Bertt is right," she thought. "Maybe there is something I can do to make the petticoat do instead." She had heard that since Queen Victoria wore a white wedding dress, they were becoming all the fashion in England.

She sold the dress to the wife of a carpetbagger from the North. They were the only ones with any money these days and they seemed to have plenty. She was able to make the payment on the loan and breathed more easily.

The day after it was sold, she had one of the former house slaves help her transform some old net curtains into an overskirt for her petticoats and fashion a bodice out of an old shawl that had belonged to her mother. By the time they were finished only she and the slave woman knew that she was standing up to be married in her undergarments with barely anything beyond a bit of netting covering her frilly, lacy, white petticoats. She didn't even pause to wonder if her former house slave took some satisfaction in seeing her "mistress" so reduced that she had to be married in her underwear.

The wedding was certainly not the grand affair it would have been in the pre-war era, but the guests were blown away by the magnificence of the bride all in white.

*With apologies to Margaret Mitchell author of *Gone with the Wind,* an epic novel about the American South in the Civil War era, and also to all those offended by the stereo-typed racial portrayals of such antebellum stories.

The Invitation

Take a classic novel, perhaps one you read as a teenager when you were supposed to be sleeping, under the covers at night with a flashlight (as I did *Gone with the Wind*), and then pun around with it. Pick just one or two characters and write a short vignette.

No Going Back

He had meant to go back to her, but he never did.

They had waited until they were engaged, until all the wedding plans were in place—the church, the reception, the dress, the invitations sent out—before having sex. Both of them were that rare breed—virgins—in a world that seemed full of people having it off with anyone, anywhere, anytime. They wanted to be sure before they actually did it.

Tony didn't enjoy it as much as he had thought he would. He had waited so long for this moment and then it was over, and he felt disappointed, let down. He didn't like the faces she made when he entered her, when he was thrusting in and out or when she came. He didn't like the sounds she made—the grunts and moans, the heavy breathing and sighing, and the final crescendo of shouting. He found it distracting. He didn't like the ripe, fishy smell of her or the taste. He came too quickly and then it was over and she quickly wiped away the mess he had made in her.

He didn't know if it was her, or him, or just that it was the first time and they'd do better next time. He didn't like the thought of a next time. He dreaded a life of making love to her, of pretending he was enjoying it. Was it like this for everyone? He didn't think so.

He heard his friends talk about sex. They made it sound like the greatest thing ever—to fondle a girl's breasts, get into a girl's panties, and then inside her, have it off with her. It was like they couldn't get enough and just thought about doing it over and over again. They talked about it like it was a taste of heaven, a life purpose. It didn't seem to matter to them who it was with, even someone they didn't know or care about. But Tony had grown up being the cautious type. His mother was always giving him warnings about the dangers of this or that, so he was scared he'd catch a disease somewhere, or get Lucy pregnant if they had sex. Even when he masturbated, he was scared his mother would know and admonish him.

He brooded over the matter for days. He developed a plan. Before he got married he would taste other fruit in the garden—that way he would know if it was him, if it was her, or if it was inexperience that had been the problem.

He realized he didn't really know much about how to go about getting laid. He had been slow to develop as a teenager and had always been rather shy around girls. He and his fiancée had been together since their teens. He decided to ask his friends for help. He didn't tell them about his experience with his fiancée or that he hadn't enjoyed it much. He just said he wanted to get some sexual experience before he settled down, so he could know what it was like with other women and be a better husband. His friends certainly didn't need long explanations of why a guy wanted to get laid and they took him on as a bit of a project.

That Thursday night they took him to a bar where they said the beer was cheap, the music was good and the women were easy. There certainly were plenty of women there, of all ages, who didn't seem to be accompanied by a man. They danced with each other or sat around in groups, chatting and drinking. One of his friends grabbed him by the arm and took him over to ask a couple of young women to dance with them.

He said to the one he pushed Tony towards, "He's getting married soon. He wants to get laid so he knows what he's missing. Take care of him, will you?"and laughed as he went off to dance with the other girl. Tony thought this would put an end to all his chances of even dancing with the girl, but she didn't seem to mind at all and led him out onto the dance floor.

"So, you're getting married are you?" she said as they started to dance. "When's the big day?"

"In two months' time," he responded.

"Well, you'd better get on it then," was her comeback.

She let him buy her a couple of drinks and they danced together a lot. Between times they sat down and chatted a bit. She worked in a shoe store in the town and lived in an apartment close by with her girlfriend who had been dancing with Tony's friend.

Finally, she said, "So, do you want to go back to my place for a drink?"

"That would be nice," he said, not quite sure what this meant but game to find out, although a little anxious. He couldn't believe it could be that easy to go to a bar, meet a girl and get laid. He could hear his mother's voice in his head saying "You don't know her. Be careful," but he chose to ignore her.

When they got back to her place she cracked open a couple of beers, then left him for a few minutes while she went to the bathroom. He could hear her brushing her teeth. When she came back she led him into her bedroom. She seemed just a little drunk, but not much.

"Do you have a condom?" she asked, rather brazenly he thought, but it excited him.

"Er, no," he stammered, "This is all very new to me. I could find an all-night pharmacy, perhaps."

"Don't worry, love" she said. "I've got plenty. I don't take any chances. Come on over here then and sit beside me on the bed." He went and sat, and she started kissing him. He could taste the toothpaste and the beer. It tasted strange, unfamiliar. He could feel his cock starting to harden. She pushed her tongue in and out of his mouth getting him more and more aroused.

She paused and said, "So you want something to look back on to remember what you're missing, do you? Well, we'd better make this good then, hadn't we? What do you like?"

"I don't know," he confessed. "How about you show me and I'll tell you if I like it?"

"Alright, you've got a deal."

She took another sip on her beer then turned to face him and took off her top and then her bra. Her tits were much,

much smaller than his fiancée's but they were perky and looked straight at him—large, erect nipples with dark brown circles around them.

She took his hands and put them on her small, firm breasts. She showed him how to roll her nipples around between his thumb and forefinger.

"Yes, that's nice," she said, "Just like that." He was getting very excited and didn't know if he should take his clothes off or whether he should wait until she told him to, so he waited and concentrated on her breasts.

"Would you like to suck my nipples?" she asked.

"I think so," he replied. "Yes, I think I would very much." He couldn't quite bring himself to add "I would very much like to suck your nipples" but he thought it and the word 'nipples' in his head turned him on too.

She stood in front of him between his legs and put her left breast in his mouth.

"OK, suck my tit," she said. "Lick it and suck it. Mmm. Yes, suck it harder now. Like you really mean it."

He did as he was told. He was getting so aroused he thought he would come before he ever got inside her. He didn't want to do that. He'd feel like a real fool if that happened.

He pulled away and said, "I need to go to the bathroom. Don't go away."

He stood with his back against the bathroom door and breathed heavily, calming himself. He thought perhaps he should urinate but knew he couldn't with the boner he had. He continued to breathe. Again, he could hear his mother's voice warning him, "Be careful, you'll catch something nasty from her, she's not a nice sort of girl." He pushed that voice away but at least it impacted his erection enough that he could pee.

"This is more like it," he thought, "And we've barely begun." He went back into the bedroom. She was lying on the bed naked playing with herself. He'd never seen a woman do that before, didn't even know they did. He thought it was just guys who wanked off in the dark and then wiped it away quickly with a tissue so as not to get it on the sheets.

"Are you alright? I was starting to wonder whether you were coming back. You'd better get undressed and come and join me," she said.

Seeing her lying there naked with her perky little tits pointing up to the ceiling and her fingers playing in and out of her vagina made him erect again. He pulled off his clothes quickly and threw them on a chair, without even folding them. She reached for the condom on the bedside table and as he stood in front of her she slowly rolled it on him. He watched her do it. Everything she did turned him on more and more. She didn't seem at all embarrassed or shy about what she was doing, she just went ahead and did it. He liked that a lot.

"So do you want front door, back door or sideways, or some of each?" she asked him.

"Whatever you like best," he said, not sure what she meant and not wanting to seem too ignorant.

"I like it best on top," she said. "Lie down on the bed and I'll get on you."

So he lay down and she climbed on top of him, straddling his body and then gently slid onto his sheathed penis. She moved up and down him a couple of times and then sat still. She took his hands and put them on her breasts again and showed him how to play with her nipples to maximum effect. He liked the little moans she made. He liked her smell. Then she started to move her pelvis, slowly at first and then with hard thrusting movements, grunting softly as she did so. It didn't take much before they both came in a glorious moment of release.

"Now this is something I could get used to," he thought to *himself. "I could get to like this."* He smiled.

"So did you enjoy it?" she asked, getting off him and lying down beside him. "Will you think of me when you're married and banging your wife? It was a bit quick, but I didn't think you could make it last much longer. Maybe another time, if you like, we can take a bit more time. But don't come and see me when you're quite so hungry, next time. OK, you'd better leave. I have to work tomorrow. Let yourself out, will you?"

He put his clothes on and left. He thought he could hear his friend and the other girl having it off in the other bedroom as he quietly closed the door to her apartment behind him. He walked home, replaying each moment in his mind. Well, clearly the problem wasn't him. He wasn't gay, or lacking something essential that other men had, some capacity to enjoy sex, as he had feared. He wondered why it had been so different with this stranger than it was with his fiancée.

He decided he needed to do some more research and see if he could have a similar experience with other women or was it specific to this one girl who had been so open and brazen. He texted his fiancée the next day and told her that he wasn't feeling well and didn't want to give her his flu, so he wouldn't be able to see her over the weekend and then he called his buddy. "So did you get laid last night?" he asked.

"Yes," said Tony.

"She's not bad, is she?" said his friend. "I wouldn't say no to her. In fact, I've had her a few times myself. Tits are a bit too small for my liking but otherwise she's quite serviceable. Her friend was pretty good too. You should try her some time."

"Are you going out again tonight?" asked Tony. "I'd like to come along."

So began Tony's new life. Once he'd started, he couldn't stop. He didn't want to stop. He felt a freedom he'd never felt before. He went out with his buddies on the Friday night and the Saturday night as well and the following weekend. Each time they went to different bars or clubs and picked up different girls. At first he used his original line to chat the girls up—that he was getting married and wanted to know what he was missing. Many of the women seemed to hear it as a challenge that goaded them to do their best for him. It seemed like they wanted to be unforgettable, to find a little bit of eternity by continuing to hold some place inside him across his years of married life.

After two weeks he called his fiancée and told her he wasn't coming back. He didn't try to explain. He just said he'd changed his mind and couldn't go through with the wedding. He was very sorry to hurt her but it was better this way in the long run. He dropped using that pick-up line after that. It didn't seem right.

Each week he'd go out on Thursday, Friday and Saturday, sometimes on Tuesdays too. Sometimes he went with friends and sometimes alone. Sometimes he'd have sex with the same woman a few times but mostly he tried to find someone new each time. Each one felt a bit different, introduced him to different ways of having sex, varied the pace. He loved the variety, the novelty, the unexpected, the feel of different flesh, different sounds, different smells of different perfumes or body odors. He wondered occasionally why he hadn't been aroused with his fiancé—had he known her too long? Was she too familiar? Did she remind him too much of his mother? He didn't like to think about it. He did notice that the nightmares he'd had since childhood of being smothered by a large pink blob went away.

He had sex with white women, black women, Asians, even a few Arabic women, big women, small women and whatever he could get in between, ugly women and pretty women, women with enormous breasts and women with hardly any breasts at all, women with large loose vaginas and others whose vaginas were small and tight around his cock. Some seemed to like it a bit rough and others smooth and slow or more romantic. Some liked lots of foreplay and some seemed to just want to plunge straight into the main event. Each woman was unique to him, and he felt grateful to each one. Some were more memorable than others. He had particularly fond memories of the night he frolicked with a pair of identical twins, who were full of surprises. He'd had an interesting experience with a woman with a pet boa constrictor although he wasn't sure he got off on the snake quite as much as she did. The trampoline artist was certainly a lively act.

He also developed a softness for an older woman at work, probably older than his mother, whom he helped out a few times after she'd had a hysterectomy and wanted to make sure all her equipment was working well, and she could still enjoy sex. She had lots of experience and a maturity to her that more than made up for anything she was lacking in youth. She usually cooked him a decent meal to go along with it, which he appreciated.

If any of the women looked like they wanted more than sex and were interested in getting into a relationship with him, he beat a hasty retreat. There was no way he wanted to be pinned down ever again. The thought made him feel suffocated, like he couldn't breathe. He never wanted to give up this new freedom he had found. He didn't brag or talk to his friends about his experiences, as they did with each other, but he privately savored each one, like he was cherishing each beautiful fruit in the garden. He learned to read each woman's desires, to become a flexible and responsive sex partner.

He had never felt so free in all his life. As a child he had been kept close to his mother, who was an anxious woman. He could remember her constantly warning him of the dangers of the world. "Don't touch that, it's got germs," "Don't do that, you'll get hurt," "Don't play outside, you'll get dirty," "Stay here with me, you'll be safe," "Don't have anything to do with those children, they aren't nice," "Don't watch those filthy TV shows,"

"Be careful," "Be careful," "Be careful" and so on and so on and so on. She was a big woman and when she hugged him tight he felt he would suffocate in her enormous bosom, drown in her flesh. He didn't like the cloying smell of her perfume. Whilst the other children were out playing and having fun, he would stay at home and read, do puzzles or watch the few shows on the television that his mother thought were suitable. His dad was around in the evenings and on weekends, but he was never really there. He was never engaged with him and his mother, off somewhere in his own world, or down at the bottom of the garden in his shed. While he sensed that his mum thought about him and what he was doing all the time, had little else to think about except all the things that could harm him, he felt that his dad never really thought about him at all—out of sight out of mind, and even when he was in his father's sight he didn't feel like his dad really noticed him. So he and his mum formed a close little unit with his dad off in space somewhere.

He had rather fallen into relationship with Lucy, his fiancée, rather than fallen in love. They had known each other since elementary school and their mothers were friends. They started dating during high school, as others in their group paired up—he wasn't sure it wasn't all engineered by their mothers. When they had finished their studies and both got jobs and steady incomes, marriage just seemed like the next step. They started talking about where they would buy a house and how many children they wanted in an abstract sort of way at first but then it seemed they were setting a date. He wasn't quite sure how it had all come about but it seemed inevitable, like it was the only possibility. He never even considered any others.

Lucy didn't like going out much. She was self-conscious and anxious in public. Mostly they stayed home and watched the television, usually shows she liked, or they rented movies—her choice. Occasionally they went to see a film at the cinema, if there was something special on she wanted to see. Once in a while they would go to a party but never stay very late. She liked to cook and was endlessly looking for new recipes in cooking magazines and trying them out on him. It had seemed like a good life, even if somewhat predictable and boring. Although he still woke up sometimes from nightmares of being smothered or suffocated he didn't really pay much attention to them. He'd had them since childhood in one form or another. Often they were of some great amorphous pink blob that grew and grew until it covered his face and he couldn't breathe. He'd wake up gasping for air. Mostly, though, he just got on with his daily life in his usual safe, predictable way. Until he didn't anymore.

About a year after he had told Lucy the marriage was off, he was flipping through the *Free Trader* looking for a new car, something a little sportier. He saw her ad. "For Sale: Wedding Dress. Size 20. Never Worn." He knew it was her because he recognized her phone number. He told himself she must have finally given up on any hope of him coming back and he sat back and breathed deeply and freely.

The Invitation

I invite you to think about a part of yourself that you don't get to live out because of the childhood messages you got from your parents or your culture. Is it, like Tony, your daring, exploratory part? Is it your willingness to speak up and express your opinions? Did you give up feeling your emotions in the face of messages to not exaggerate, not show anger, not be emotional? Did you surrender your sexuality to the messages that "Nice girls/good boys don't." You might find some clues in what other people say to you, such as "You should be more…" or in the aspects you criticize in others where you hear yourself say "I would never…" Now write a story about a character who expresses that to an extreme degree, lives out that part of you fully. What happens to this character when they do express that? Let your fears and longings about expressing that part of you surface and write them into your story. How does your character react?

BBW

I proposed six weeks after we met through a BBW dating site. After exchanging emails and photos for a couple of weeks and feeling we had a connection, we decided to meet for coffee. When I arrived at the café and looked around, I knew immediately which one was her. She was sitting across the room with her back to me. I went towards her and introduced myself. When she stood up to shake my hand and say hello, she was magnificent.

I am a small man—5 foot 2 and slight of build. I'm what is known in some circles as an FA—a fat admirer. I have always been attracted to Big Beautiful Women—BBWs. I love their mountainous breasts, their rounded bellies, their wide hips and large buttocks. And she was gorgeous—tall, about 5 feet 10 and ample in every way, probably about 250 lbs. Wow! I couldn't believe my luck.

I went and bought us both a coffee and a piece of double layer chocolate cake with icing for her. As we sat talking, I couldn't take my eyes off her as she ate each mouthful of the sweet, rich cake. Her unembarrassed pleasure in each bite told me this was a woman with a lust for life, with a capacity to savour all life's possibilities. I found myself aroused as she took each piece into her mouth, her lips, her teeth, her tongue covered in chocolate. I wanted to kiss her right there but held myself back with great difficulty. My cock was getting hard as I imagined her naked, eating the cake. That wasn't all that was hard—the harder my cock got, the harder it was to concentrate on what she was saying but I really wanted to listen fully. When she finished and wiped off her mouth, I wanted to offer her another piece but was sure my boner would be obvious if I stood. I have a larger penis than many would expect on a man my size. We drank our coffee and found we had so many things in common, similar tastes in film and music, politics and literature. We both love to go for long walks.

I don't know what took me so long to propose. I knew right away she was the one for me. Perhaps I was worried she'd find me too small, not enough for her. She told me later she worried I'd find her too much. When I proposed she agreed to be my bride and I felt like the luckiest man alive. She was my zucker baby, my sugar dumpling, my pride and joy. Walking down the street with her I felt like I was 10 feet tall, although I knew some sniggered at our difference in size. I didn't care.

We hoped to get married over the Christmas holidays, which was just three months away and we started to make preparations. She had her dress made—she told me later it was a magnificent creation of lace and frills with pearls sewn all over the bodice. We decided we would marry in Vegas with a small group of family and friends from the BBW and FA communities joining us. We all loved Vegas—we didn't feel like freaks there. Anything goes in Vegas. We booked a chapel, rooms in the hotel and our flights. We spent a lot of time discussing and deciding on the menu.

Then my mother got sick and had to be hospitalized and we decided to postpone the wedding. It was important to me that my mother be there with us for the ceremony. I really wanted her to share in this joyous day. Although we wanted to be legally joined together as soon as possible, we didn't mind waiting. We were blissfully happy. One of my greatest joys was feeding her little tidbits, sweet stuffs, dates, pastries. She let me pop little bits into her mouth and watch her as she slowly ate each mouthful. I found it so exciting. It turned me on sexually and seemed to excite her too. She was my queen bee and I her little drone. The more she ate, the more excited we would get and then I would disappear between her mountainous breasts, sinking into the soft, warm flesh, holding, squeezing, kneading, sucking, slapping her great mounds as I dived in and wallowed in her magnificence. I sank between her legs into the enormous wetness of her lips, feeling I was smothering and disappearing right back inside her great feminine body. Sometimes she would sit on top of me until she almost suffocated me. My cock would get so large and rigid until I would scream out for air and then ejaculate in great spurts all over her. She seemed to enjoy our lovemaking with the same delight she took in the food I fed her. She was my goddess, the epitome of womanhood and I adored each inch, each curve, each pound. The more there was of her, the more there was to love.

The following summer, when my mother was again well enough for us to go ahead with the wedding, she took out the wedding dress she had had made and tried it on. It no longer fit. She had gained at least 10 pounds since Christmas. She put an ad in the *Free Trader* "For sale: Wedding Dress: Size 20. Never Worn", and quickly had another one made in a size 22, this one in shiny satin to show off her wondrous curves to fullest advantage.

The wedding was a marvellous affair. I was too excited to eat much of the food we had chosen so carefully, but I watched her eat with awe and delight. I arranged to have a tray of little cream-filled pastries delivered to our room to be awaiting us there when we retired for our wedding night. Some I fed to her by mouth, getting so aroused with each bite she took, and some I smeared on her buttocks, her breasts, her enormous vagina. We wallowed in delight all night in the pleasures of the flesh—oh, so much flesh!

The Invitation

Pick a fetish, any fetish that you want to write a story about and go for it. What is it about the fetish that turns your characters on? Do both partners engage willingly with the fetish activity or is there an element of coercion? Do you want to include any background of how the fetish developed? Enjoy yourself.

Second Time Around

"I bought my wedding dress today," she said over dinner that evening. "I saw an ad in the *Free Trader,* "For Sale: Wedding Dress, Size 20, Never Worn" and got in touch with the woman who was selling it—a nice girl called Bettina. It was really inexpensive. She said she wanted to sell it so that she could start a baking business, specializing in wedding cakes. I don't know what happened that she didn't get to wear the dress herself. I didn't want to ask. It seemed a bit like a can of worms I didn't want to open. I hope the dress isn't imbued with any negative energy. Maybe I'll get my friends together and we'll smudge it with a cleansing stick of sage and have a ritual to fill it with the energy of light and love before I wear it."

It was a second marriage for both and they had decided to have a simple wedding and cut down on the costs. Both agreed that it was more important to spend money on their marriage when the need arose, rather than on their wedding and they didn't have much to spare. They had three children already from their first marriages, who were approaching adolescence and a child of theirs on the way. They wanted to make the day special in ways that were more meaningful to them—involving the children in the ceremony, writing their own vows. They were going to host it in their home and prepare much of the food themselves. Their friends had offered to help and to bring their favorite dishes. She hadn't been going to buy a fancy wedding dress because of the cost but she realized she really wanted one and when she saw the ad in the *Free Trader*, she made the call.

It was a wonderful wedding, simple yet profound. Several friends told them afterwards that it was the best wedding they had ever attended and it had moved them to tears. They both felt they had done it the way that was right for them, and she felt very special and radiant in her dress that her friends had helped her cleanse with sage. The look of love, gratitude, awe in his eyes when he saw her in it gave her a sense of joy and aliveness she felt she would hold within her always.

When the wedding was over, she wrapped the dress up carefully in tissue and put it in a beautiful box. She put an ad in the *Free Trader:* "For sale: Wedding dress. Size 20. Worn once with great love and joy". She sold it for a lot more than she had paid for it and put the money away to use should their relationship ever reach a point where they needed some help. She knew from her first marriage that what feels initially like great, everlasting love can turn sour and transform into conflict and acrimony. She was scared that they would "lose that loving feeling", that they wouldn't "bring each other flowers any more", as the songs suggested. She had seen it in her friends' marriages also. So she tucked the money away in an account that earned interest against that rainy day, and mostly forgot about it.

One day, some years later, she was watching the Oprah Winfrey show. She didn't usually watch daytime television, rather looked down on people who did, but she was home and doing some ironing, a job she found excruciatingly dull, so flicked on the television. Oprah had a guest on, a psychologist whom Oprah described as "the best couples' therapist I know."* He had written a book and developed a new approach to working with couples. What he was saying made a lot of sense to her and really rang true. She watched in fascination as he worked with the couple to help them understand each other better, have empathy for each other's experience and connect deeply. He mentioned the weekend workshops he offered for couples.

As she watched she realized that she and her husband had reached that point where their relationship needed help. She knew they were both unhappy and dissatisfied but it had crept up so slowly she hadn't stopped and said, "We have to do something about this or we'll end up in the same place we ended up the first time around".

She realized they had let their busy lives take over—house, kids, jobs. They barely spent any quality time together anymore and seemed to be constantly arguing. "Don't talk to the kids like that. You can't just lay down the law and expect them to do whatever you want," she would say to him, her voice full of criticism covering the anxiety of feeling she wasn't adequately protecting her children from his anger.

"Why not? They never listen unless I yell. All you ever do is explain and explain to them endlessly which doesn't change anything. You don't set any boundaries for them," he argued back. This usually triggered her into sanctimoniously preaching at him about child rearing and respect for 45 minutes without pausing for breath, only to repeat herself the next time he yelled out of his own frustration.

Family life was in chaos and they were taking it out on each other, blaming each other—or rather she was blaming it all on him and he was taking it all on as his fault. "Why do you have to be so angry and unpleasant all the time," she'd accuse. "We could all be happy if you would just be in a better mood," she pleaded longing for peace and harmony with no awareness of how she was contributing to them not having that. "You'd all be better off without me", he said, wanting to be persuaded otherwise. He needed to feel important and loved. They were limping along with the spectre of another divorce, another split up for the kids, never far away.

And their sex life was on the trash heap. Just that morning they had had the same old repetitive row. He'd started coming on to her just as she was getting up to get the kids up and ready for school and she'd rejected him with annoyance at his timing. He always seemed to try to initiate sex at inconvenient moments but she wasn't sure if any moment would be convenient. She just didn't feel any desire for him when they were in a constant state of conflict. "You never seem to want me anymore," he'd complained, yet again. "You're always too busy with everything else to be interested in me. My needs didn't count for anything. I'm just here to do stuff around the house and bring home a pay cheque but no-one cares about me," he'd tell her over and over again.

"If you were nicer I might feel more inclined to have sex with you. You only ever seem interested in me for my body. All you ever want to do is have sex. It's all you ever talk about and who the hell would want to have sex with someone as angry and dissatisfied as you are anyway. It's not exactly a turn-on," she had responded.

It was an impasse. "I used to feel so loved and now I just feel inadequate all the time," she said. He'd come back with "You feel inadequate! How do you think I feel? Why does everything have to be my fault all the time? You knew how I was when you married me. You didn't seem to mind it when we were dating." Sometimes she would just give in and have sex with him to try to reduce the tension and stop him complaining and he would go along with it because he figured it was the best he was going to get, even though it didn't really count for him because she wasn't into it. Often neither of them really enjoyed it, even if they both reached an orgasm—it seemed functional rather than the emotional and spiritual connection they used to feel. Both of them came away feeling they had violated something that had been so precious and wonderful at the beginning of their relationship.

"Why can't it be the way it was in the past" he'd complain, grieving the loss, and she would come back with "Grow up and be realistic. Things don't stay the same. Relationships change. Get used to it," wanting him to change so they could move forward to something new and better.

After seeing how the therapist helped couples empathically understand each other and connect through a process called the Couples Dialogue, she bought the book and it blew her away. It sounded as though it was speaking right to her and the issues they were struggling with. The reasons couples fought made sense and there were specific tools that could help couples make real changes. She made enquiries and found there was a workshop in New York City on the weekend of her husband's upcoming birthday. She remembered the money she had put away from the wedding dress, a symbol of their commitment to each other, to use when their marriage needed it. She took it out of the bank and reserved a place for them on the workshop. Fearing he wouldn't agree to go if she just asked, she gave it to him as a birthday present. She made arrangements for the children and booked a room at the hotel. Although she thought it would be good for their relationship, she really gave it to him because she thought he needed it. Fundamentally she thought that he was the problem and that if he would just change then everything would be fine. She hoped the workshop would set him right, get him to see the light so that he would make the changes necessary so they could recapture the love they had felt for each other at the beginning.

When she told him about the workshop he was anything but thrilled. He thought New York was dirty and dangerous as well as overpriced. Spending a weekend in a hotel facing their relationship problems was a version of torture he would like to avoid at all costs. He anticipated that she would spend the weekend complaining to him about all the things that were wrong with him and he wouldn't be able to escape. His way of coping with their marital problems was often to just not think about them, whereas hers seemed to be to dwell on them and talk about them endlessly. He'd rather put his nuts in a vice-grip than endure that. However, he figured, "If I just put my head down, go along with it, I'll 'keep the wife happy' and then I'll be safe and she won't be able to complain—and then maybe the sex will improve. Yes, that would be good, if the sex improved." He believed that if they could make love again they'd feel that loving connection again. Maybe a weekend away from the kids wouldn't be such a bad idea. He'd put up with the workshop but at night in their hotel room perhaps they'd get something on that resembled what they used to have. That would make it worth it.

Well, the workshop turned out to be nothing like either of them had expected. They found themselves in the huge ball-room of a hotel with about a hundred other couples, and yet once they got into doing the exercises, talking to each other about their feelings, their fears, their childhoods, their desires using the Dialogue process, it was like none of the other couples existed and there was just this precious, intimate connection between the two of them. It felt that each couple was encapsulated in its own little bubble of intimacy doing the work they needed to do. The psychologist she had seen on the Oprah show was a wonderful speaker and shared his ideas about why couples are attracted to each other and why they almost inevitably then end up in conflict. He explained in a simple, easy-to-understand way that made so much sense to both of them. But he didn't stop there, he gave them some concrete tools to help them work through these inevitable conflicts, to understand what was beneath them with empathy and compassion for each other. He also gave them specific ways to focus more of their energy on what they loved and appreciated about each other and to express this with passion and aliveness.

A turning point came for them in one of the exercises quite early on in the workshop. They were directed to talk about their experiences as a young child to the partner, who took the role of one of their parents. At first they thought it was a little hokey, but went along with it like all the other couples seemed to be doing. The simple structure of the exercise allowed them to go very deeply, very quickly, into what had been good and what had been painful for them as children. It brought up a lot of emotion in both of them to reconnect with their own painful and joyful experiences from the past and to see the hurts in their partner that were behind their reactions and needs in their relationship with each other today. They realized how they were both behaving in ways that triggered old pain in each other.

As the eldest of four boys with a father who was away much of the time he had felt he had to put his own needs aside to be there for his frustrated, dissatisfied mother. Going back to being a 10-year-old boy and talking to his wife in the role of his mother he said "I wish I could just make you happy so I could feel safe and maybe you'd be able to pay attention to me, meet some of my needs. I never seem to be able to make you happy. I feel small and inadequate but I'm expected to be big, the man of the house because Dad is away so much on business. Sometimes I feel angry I have to be there to help you take care of my brothers rather than just be a kid and play with my friends. I feel as though my needs don't matter. Then I yell and lose my temper, which just gets me into trouble and sent to my room or spanked. But afterwards you give me a hug and some attention and I like that a lot. Sometimes it seems like the only way of getting hugs and attention is to misbehave. What I long for most, have always longed for, is to feel that I'm important for who I am not just as your helper, and that my needs count."

She felt her heart soften as she saw in her mind that little boy who had so needed the hug, the touch, the attention of his mother, and got for the first time how she might be triggering similar feelings in him when she was too busy with the kids or whatever projects she was giving importance to rather than him. Instead of blaming him for only thinking about sex she started to realize that that was how he felt connected and loved, wanted and important, as though his needs counted. She too wanted those feelings, she just went about it in different ways—probably no more effective than his.

When they switched and it was her turn to talk with a parent, he took the role of her mother and she explored how she had felt as a 12-year-old. There were many good things about her childhood but there was also some pain she had never really acknowledged. "I feel there's no room for me to be me. It's like you want to control everything about the way

I am—how I wear my hair, how I talk, who my friends are. Who I am as a person doesn't seem to count against how you think I should be. What I want or need doesn't matter. You just want to feel good about yourself as a mother so I have to behave the way you think I should all the time so everyone sees what a good mother you are. But I don't want to be the way you want me to be. I want to be me—to figure out who I am. I get so frustrated and angry I rebel and do everything the opposite of what you want, but that's not me either. I still feel I'm being controlled by what you want. Or I become sneaky so I can do what I want but then I'm scared of being caught and getting into trouble." Like him, she felt that what she wanted for herself wasn't important, someone else's needs took priority. Her father also was absent a lot, working hard to get ahead to provide for the family, which contributed to her mother's lack of fulfilment. "I just want to feel that what I want is important, that I can make my own choices."

They started to see the similarities between them, the similarity of their childhood hurts, rather than the differences in circumstances and details. They started to feel empathy, and a longing to be a healing person for each other. They also realized that their parents had been doing their best with the knowledge and resources available and had not caused them pain intentionally.

"What do you think we are doing to our kids?" he said as they sat having dinner in the hotel restaurant that evening. "I'm too exhausted to think about that now," she said, "but I think it's a really important question. Let's talk about it some more. I don't want to blindly repeat our unconscious patterns from the past."

The second day of the workshop they learnt a way of working through their frustrations that took them beneath the negative energy to what was really bothering them and helped them ask each other for what they wanted in ways where they could hear and be empathic to the wish rather than defended against it. They discovered some ways to bring the romance and pleasure back into their relationship and created a shared vision of the relationship they wanted that they could work towards.

By the end of the workshop, although they felt so much more connected, they were also exhausted, far too tired to make the eight-hour drive back home. They stopped and took a motel room for the night. After a bite to eat they went to bed and fell asleep in minutes. In the morning they made love for the first time in several years—really made love, not just had sex. She had to reconnect with her own sexual desire for him, which she had shut down a long time before, in order to reach out and initiate their lovemaking. He had to slow down, let her find herself sexually, rather than just go for it all out and get it over with out of fear he was bothering her.

Thus started the long and, at first, often very rocky journey into a deeper, more passionate and loving relationship. It took a lot of work, often very challenging work. It required that each of them give up being right and be open to hearing the other's perspective and seeing it as equally valid as their own. They had to replace their judgments and criticisms with curiosity about each other and to eliminate all the put downs, no matter how subtle. They realized that every time they put each other down, criticized, shamed or made the other wrong, it elicited defensiveness and that took them out of the connection they yearned to experience with each other. They realized how addicted they were to these silly yet hurtful little criticisms. They learned to put the effort and energy into making their relationship fun, doing new things to spark up the excitement and sense of novelty. The work of building the relationship of their vision was rarely easy, but at least it was doable, given the tools they had acquired at the workshop. Even though it was often so much easier to go back to old patterns, somehow they got themselves back onto the new path, sometimes her, sometimes him getting them there. They saw that when they did things the old way it always ended up with the same old, unsatisfying outcome but when they used their new skills, it got them back into connection and into a deeper understanding of each other, even if it took a while.

Gradually over the years they saw their marriage transform from being like a box or prison that shut them in and limited them, to being a crucible for personal transformation, to being like a beautiful flowerpot that allowed each of them to grow into all of their fullest potential yet stay grounded and connected with each other, with roots that were deeply intertwined.

Years later as they sat together looking back over their journey, sharing their experiences and joys, they realized how grateful they were for the money that had come from the sale of the wedding dress which had allowed them to attend the workshop all those years ago. It was the symbol of their commitment. They just needed to know how to live that commitment in ways that were effective.

On their twentieth wedding anniversary she wrote him this poem:

> *A thousand connecting strands*
> *Defy the space between,*
> *A cord of woven moments,*
> *Each silken thread unseen.*
> *A kiss, a touch, a smile,*
> *A glance across a crowd,*
> *Memories of times and places,*
> *Of thoughts we've spoken—shared.*
> *Slowly, tenderly woven*
> *Through a history of years,*
> *With loving hands we wove it*
> *From laughter and shared tears.*
> *When we're apart it stretches,*
> *Mere distance cannot strain.*
> *When anger comes between us*
> *It draws us close again.*
> *And now the bond is hardy,*
> *It stretches across the void,*
> *Death has no power to break it*
> *Forever, through love, we are joined.*

*This story is written with gratitude to Harville Hendrix and Helen LaKelly Hunt, creators of Imago Relationship

Therapy and authors of "Getting the Love You Want" and the workshop based on it.

The Invitation

Today I invite you to write a love poem to someone who is or has been important to you.

The Wedding War/or Out of the Frying Pan into the Fire

"Samuel and I are getting married," I announced to my mother and father.

Dad responded warmly.

"That's wonderful, Sandra! I hope you'll be very happy," he said and gave me a hug. He shook Samuel's hand vigorously.

Mother responded rather more coolly with a simple, "That's nice, dear."

A while later, whilst we were having dinner, she said to us both, "Now, don't you worry about a thing. Your dad and I will organize everything for the wedding."

Dread spread through my body. *"Oh no"*, I thought. *"I can just see it now. I'll be caught between Samuel and my mother. If I side with my mother, Samuel will quite rightly feel I've betrayed him, and if I side with Samuel my mother is going to get all hurt, make me feel terrible and probably won't talk to me or will punish* me some other way until I give in. *This wedding could end up being a nightmare rather than a joyous celebration.*"

I know my mother is rather domineering. She always wants things her way. My dad and I have learnt to give in. We know ahead of time we're never going to be able to win, so we don't bother fighting, we just go along with whatever she wants. We've done this pretty much as long as I can remember. It's so much easier than the fights and arguments or the terrible silences on the rare occasions when one of us has tried to stand up to her, like I did a few times in my teens. Sometimes we roll our eyes at each other behind her back, but we rarely even put up any protest. There just isn't any point.

I am aware that Samuel can be a little like that too. I love his clarity and determination. He's a lawyer and can argue circles around me and just about anyone else. His father was rather a force to be reckoned with, a former lawyer who is now a judge. He lays down the law at home with a gavel-like decisiveness. His mom has always wrapped her life around his wishes and needs, anticipating what he might want before he even asks and apologizing profusely if she ever gets it wrong. I gather she had been very bright as a young woman, one of very few women of her era studying law. She seemed headed for a career as a university law professor, but she gave it all up when she married his father and never mentioned it again.

Samuel, on the other hand, learned to cope by being even more determined than his father was to get his way and to never give up until he did. Apparently, there were some monumental battles of will, especially when Samuel was a teenager.

Consequently, he's really good at standing up to people and getting what he wants. He never takes "No" for an answer. If we go to a restaurant and they don't have a table, he will persevere until they find one for him. I really admire these qualities in him a great deal. However, I have a sense that in a head-on battle between Samuel and my mother a lot of blood could be spilt before either of them will give in.

"That's very kind of you to offer, Mrs. Jones. Thank you very much but Sandra and I want to organize our own wedding. It is our special day and we want to make it perfect for us." I loved the way Samuel responded so graciously and felt a flicker of hope that this once Mom would back down. But I could see my mother bristle. The dread that I would be caught in the middle of a no-win situation ratcheted up a notch.

"Coming from your background, you probably aren't aware that it is the parents of the bride who put on the wedding. And pay for it," Mom added pointedly. "That is the way things are always done in this culture."

Mom's voice was dripping with condescension. Samuel is Jewish and my family is totally WASP. His family isn't religious so I won't have to convert to marry him, although I would if he wanted me to.

I could almost hear Samuel's hackles go up.

"Please, Mom," I begged. "Can we talk about this another time." Samuel must have seen the tears in my eyes because he took a deep breath, relaxed his shoulders and said, "That sounds like a good idea. Right now let's just celebrate—here's to a wonderful wedding and a very successful marriage that lasts as long as yours and my parents' marriages have."

Mom took the tiniest sip of her wine to honour the toast and went out to the kitchen where she clattered around with the dishes. I felt torn between following her out there to try to soothe her ruffled feathers and staying with Dad and Samuel, pretending like nothing had happened.

That was the start of the "Wedding War" which consisted of many bloody battles—battles about the church or registry office, battles about the location for the reception, battles about the colour scheme, the flowers, the bridesmaids' dresses, the guest list, the invitations—the look and the wording—battles about the food, the band, even where we should go on our honeymoon! Samuel seemed to take on each issue as if it really mattered to him. I sometimes wondered if he wasn't more interested in getting his own way and winning the battle with my mother more than the actual details of the wedding. Finally, after weeks of acrimonious encounters where neither of them would back down, we managed to divide up some areas of responsibility. Mom got to make all the decisions about the church, the invitations, the flowers and the food, while Samuel and I decided on the reception, the music, the colour scheme and the honeymoon. I say "we", but it was mostly Samuel because I felt too worn down to engage in any more battles with him. I was only too happy to go along with whatever he wanted. I sometimes thought he actually enjoyed the struggle of wills with my mother, saw it almost as a game that he was determined to win. Living at home was pretty miserable though, as my mom took it all out on me and Dad whenever she felt she wasn't getting her way.

One day Samuel asked me, "Sandra, have you got your wedding dress yet?"

"No. Mom's been talking about it, but I've been putting it off. I'm rather dreading it," I said. "She has very definite views about what she thinks I look nice in."

"You have to go on your own and choose your own dress," he said firmly. "You cannot let your mother choose your wedding dress for you."

"How could I possibly do that? She'd never let me."

"You just do it and tell her afterwards," he said. "Take a day off work and go shopping. Tell her you got some time off and decided to go and look at dresses and saw one you liked and bought it on the spur of the moment. She can't argue once you've already bought it."

"I'm not so sure about that," I countered.

"You have to stand up to her on this one, Sandra. Really you do. I'll be very disappointed if you let your mother choose your wedding dress. We've talked about this before and I've told you many times that you have to learn to stand up to her."

I could see Samuel's point, but still, I knew my mother would be upset if I didn't go shopping with her and I knew that if I did I would probably come away with a dress that she wanted rather than one I chose freely. I decided I would go along with Samuel's idea. I asked my boss for an afternoon off work to look for a wedding dress and he agreed.

One day the following week I left the office at lunch time and went down-town to where all the big stores with wedding dress departments are. I'm quite a big woman and there weren't all that many to choose from in my size. At the first store they only had three. I tried each one on but as I looked in the mirror, trying to decide whether I liked it or not, I couldn't help wondering which one my mother would want me to buy and which one Samuel would like best. It was hard to know what I liked myself with all that going on in my head. It was pretty much the same in the next shop and the next. At the end of the day I was no further ahead than I had been at the start, but I had to buy a dress if I was to follow through on what Samuel wanted.

With much trepidation I went back to the first shop and bought the first dress I had tried on. It was very simple and plain and I thought it couldn't offend anyone. It was on sale and they had to make a few minor alterations so I wouldn't be able to return it. That was perfect, I thought. My mother wouldn't be able to make me take it back. They would deliver it in a few days.

When I got home, I plucked up my courage and told my mother I had been shopping and had seen a dress that I really liked so I had bought it. I told her that as it was the only one in my size and on sale. I was worried it would be sold if I waited.

"Oh," she said in her hurt voice. "I thought that we were going to do that together—mother and daughter. But if you don't want me involved in such an important decision I'm not one to impose myself." She left the room. Even though I had expected this, my heart sunk.

The wedding dress was delivered three days later. My mother had already opened the box before I got home from work. Her face looked like thunder when I walked through the door.

"You can't possibly wear that dress for your wedding," she said before I even had my coat off. "It's totally unsuitable. It's so plain you'll look like a church mouse. This is the biggest day of your life, except for when you give birth, so you have to wear something special that makes you look and feel like a princess, not something plain and drab like that. I won't allow it. No daughter of mine is walking down the aisle in that."

"But Mom," I said, "I've paid for it and I can't send it back. They made some alterations. I'll have to wear it."

"No, you'll just have to sell it and start again. I'll put an ad in the *Free Trader*. I'm sure we'll be able to off-load it to someone and we'll start again from scratch. We'll go out together and choose something much more suitable. We'll make a day of it. Go for lunch in the restaurant at the department store like we used to when you were little."

She put an ad in the *Free Trader* "For Sale: Wedding dress. Size 20. Never worn." Someone bought it and came and took my wedding dress away.

I must admit I didn't put up much of a fight and I didn't tell Samuel either. I figured he wouldn't know the difference whether I had chosen it or my mother had. So, she traipsed me around the shops again. We took a whole day looking at every wedding dress in town in my size. We had lunch together in the same restaurant where we had had lunch each time we had been shopping when I was a child. I realized she had always chosen my clothes even back then—the grey skirts, white blouses and red cardigans she dressed me in on Saturdays, the itchy woollen dresses she sent me off to Sunday school in. I had had no more say in the matter than I had today. She even ordered my lunch for me—the same fish and chips I had always eaten in the past. Talk about déjà vu!

The dress we bought had lots of lace and frills. I thought it made me look even bigger than I was, like some enormous fairy, some grotesque white confection—all I needed was the wings and wand. I think Mum would have liked a much smaller, daintier daughter than she got, and she was going to dress me up as if I were that on this day of days for all the world to see.

On the day of my wedding I walked down the aisle feeling awkward and embarrassed. I was scared that when Samuel turned around and saw me his face would drop, he'd look aghast and he would run out of the church as fast as he could. He didn't and I loved him for that. He gave me a beautiful smile and reached out for my hand.

We were wed. As soon as I could I left the reception and put on my going away outfit, which I had chosen myself. However, the whole evening I was scared Samuel would overhear my mother bragging to everyone that she had chosen my dress. I had to make sure to keep him away from her, which was not actually that difficult to do as he was only too happy not to spend time in her company.

When we came back from our honeymoon, that he had chosen, I put an ad in the *Free Trader:* "For Sale: Wedding dress. Size 20. Worn briefly." I couldn't wait to get rid of the thing.

It was about a year later that I really began to wonder if I hadn't jumped out of the frying pan into the fire.

The Invitation

What do you think Samuel and Sandra's marriage would have been like? Can you imagine them two years after their wedding? What might a conversation or argument sound like? Can you write one scene in their marriage—or any other couple's marriage, if you prefer? You might want to write out one of those repetitive scenes from a relationship you have been in. Most of us have them, I think. It's like we know our lines by heart and churn them out when we get triggered. They may include lines like "You never listen to me," or "Why don't I ever get to choose?" You could even write it as the script for a scene for a play or movie.

The Couple on the Train*

Michael

I'm not sure how or when it started really, how we first struck up a conversation. I just remember that at a certain point I would look for her on the platform in the mornings and in the evenings. In the mornings she almost always took the same train as me, the 8.02 from St. Albans to Farringdon and quite often she'd take the 5.13 home that I usually tried to catch in the evenings. I think I'd noticed her in a guy kind of way, sizing her up, seeing she was attractive, for some time before we ever talked. No harm in looking, I always say. I think it was probably her height that caught my attention at first. I'm a big man, have always been tall for my age, so I tend to notice a woman's size. I've always dated big women, never any of these skinny little broads with no meat on their bones. I feel as though I might crack them in two if I hug them too tightly. No, I like a woman who is strong and can stand on her own two feet, won't need

189

too much from me, although I admit that's not always how my relationships have turned out in the long run.

I think initially we just made occasional comments about the weather, or something connected with the newspaper headlines—the elections or another terrorist attack somewhere in the world—banal comments. Getting on at St. Albans I could usually get a seat. I noticed she started to sit beside me. I like to read my paper on the train in the morning and she didn't seem to mind that or expect us to chat or anything. She usually read a book on her iPad or pulled some papers out of her briefcase to work on. Occasionally I would share a tidbit of news with her and she would look up and smile. She had a warm smile. She always looked really interested so I'd start looking for little items to share with her—bizarre or funny things to make her laugh. No harm in that.

Sometimes I would share my opinions on what was reported about some of the politicians or financial policies they were proposing. I work in banking, on the investment side, so I know what I am talking about and can make well-informed criticisms. It drives me crazy when a lot of stupid promises are made by politicians in order to get elected. I found out she worked in human resources for a world-wide photocopier machine company. Her name is Rachel—pretty name. It suits her.

I suppose that gradually our conversations started to get a little bit more personal. If we met on the train coming home, I'd ask if she'd had a good day and she would start to tell me about something that had happened at work, or a new pension plan she was implementing. I started to tell her about my colleagues and some of the crazy things that would happen during the day. It really was a cast of rather bizarre characters that I worked with and some of the petty things they got up to made for a good story. I can be quite funny in a dry sort of way and she would laugh out loud at the shenanigans that went on. She has a nice laugh.

I started to talk to her about some issues I was having with a new female boss who took over our department who I felt was always on my case wanting something or other from me. Whatever I did, it never seemed to be enough. It drove me crazy. Just to be able to talk to Rachel about it on the way home I found really helped me to let go of the frustration I would leave the office with. I missed her if she wasn't on the platform for that 5.13. She often had to work late when her company was going through a merger or implementing a new pension plan. They always seemed to be taking over or merging with some other photocopier company. It opened a whole new world to me. Working in HR, she sometimes had some really helpful suggestions about how I could handle the situation with my boss more effectively. No harm in that.

The truth is I didn't like talking to my fiancée, Hazel, about these issues I was having with my boss because she would immediately start telling me what I should do, and then she'd go on and on about it. For days she'd check up on me to make sure I had done what she told me to do and nag me half to death about it. Rachel wasn't like that.

Maybe at some point I did start to talk to Rachel about some of the problems I was having with Hazel. I didn't see any harm in it. After all she didn't know Hazel.

Hazel and I had met three years previously and started dating. She was very outgoing and we had a lot of laughs together. She had a good group of friends. When I had to give up my flat, she suggested I move in with her. It seemed like a good idea at the time—I often stayed over at her place, so wasn't using my flat much anyway. It'd be cheaper and there'd be fringe benefits, if you know what I mean. The following summer a couple of her friends got engaged and she decided it would be a good thing if we did too, so one Saturday we went shopping for a ring and the next thing you know we're engaged. Well, after that we were setting dates for the wedding and she was choosing her dress and flowers. I just sort of went along with it, I suppose. Somehow there never seemed a good time to talk about whether this was really what we both wanted. I didn't think about it too much.

The problem was Hazel never seemed satisfied. She always seemed to want more from me, but I never had any idea what more she wanted. She criticized me for not spending more time with her but she knew I was busy at work and had a stressful job. She knew I needed to go to the gym to work out in the evenings before coming home, and that sometimes I had to bring work home with me or liked to just chill out in front of the TV. Besides I'm not really much of a talker usually so the idea of sitting around so she can bang on endlessly about all the wedding details and her friends and who said what to whom at work wasn't very appealing. When I did try to spend some time with her, that didn't seem to be enough either. She said I wasn't really listening and I didn't share enough with her, but whenever I tried she'd interrupt. I just felt puzzled and confused. Maybe I made it sound a little worse than it was when I talked to Rachel about it, but she listened so sympathetically I felt I could tell her anything, even though I don't usually talk about my feelings to anyone much. I liked the way her eyes softened as she looked at me when I told her about my troubles at home and at work. Sometimes she squeezed my hand and her skin felt warm and soft.

Rachel told me she was also engaged. I was rather surprised actually. She started to tell me stuff about her fiancé, Alex. I don't know the bloke, so I don't see any harm. It just helped us both to get stuff off our chests with a stranger, I suppose.

One night it was pelting down with rain when we got off the train. I happened to have my car parked at the station that day. I often rode my bike to the station in the mornings but that day the forecast was bad so I took my car. Most nights I go straight to the sports center for an hour or so for my workout when I get off the train. I saw Rachel pull her umbrella out as she stepped down onto the platform. The way it was teeming down I figured she'd get drenched even with her umbrella, so I offered to give her a lift. No harm in that—the only decent thing to do. She seemed very grateful. She asked me to drop her off at the end of her street. It was still pouring when we got there so I suggested she wait a few minutes and see if the rain slowed down a bit. We sat and talked in the car for about 15 minutes or so before the rain let up at all. I was really surprised when she reached across and kissed my cheek before she got out of the car. Guess it was just her way of saying thanks for the lift.

After that I drove her home whenever I had my car, which was most days now that winter was drawing in, and she managed to catch the 5.13. We often sat and talked for 10 or 15 minutes before she walked up the street to her flat and I drove off to the gym. The physical contact never went any further than a touch of our hands, a kiss on the cheek—no harm in that. I wouldn't do that, go any further, given that both of us are engaged to be married—although I was probably tempted sometimes. I did look forward to our daily 23 minutes together each morning and again in the evening. The rhythm of the train was very soothing and I don't think I have ever confided in anyone like that before. But it was never a sexual thing between us—how could it be on a train?

Then one day it all came to an end. My fiancée accused me of having an affair. It's ridiculous and I told her so, but she won't listen to reason. She said the wedding was off!!! I couldn't believe it. She was screaming and yelling and made me move out that night. I had to go and stay with my brother on the other side of London. I'm devastated. It's so unfair. How could she even think that of me?

I take a different train now—that goes to Victoria Station. I don't see Rachel anymore. I kind of miss our daily chats but it's probably just as well this way, given she's getting married in a month or so. I haven't tried to contact her. It wouldn't be fair.

Rachel

I had often noticed him on the platform in the mornings before we ever spoke. A nice-looking man. He was tall. He looked like a businessman, was well-dressed and carried a briefcase, but athletic looking at the same time, like he kept himself fit. I like athletic, fit-looking men. Alex, my fiancé, is like that. He has a wonderful firm, muscular body. He plays a lot of sports—football in the winter and tennis in the summer. I've always had a bit of a problem keeping my weight down although I do my best. I'm a big woman and have a sedentary job. I also love to cook, and Alex seems to enjoy the meals I prepare. Perhaps I shouldn't be sizing up other men like that but I think it's only natural. No harm in looking....

We first spoke on the 24th of January last year. It was a bitterly cold day and the train was late. I was stamping my feet and clapping my hands trying to stay warm. He turned to me and said,

"Cold morning, isn't it."

I answered, "Yes, I hear it's supposed to stay like this for several days."

Perhaps not very deep as conversations go but it broke the ice, so to speak. I got on the train right ahead of him and he sat down beside me. We didn't say much more that day, but when we both got off the train at Farringdon I turned to him and said,

"Have a good day," and he replied, "You too."

I know all this because I wrote it in my diary. I have a lot of time to myself in the evenings so I write in my diary about my day—silly little details really about people I meet, conversations. Alex, my fiancé, is actually quite sports mad. When he isn't playing some sport himself he's either watching sports on his big screen TV or checking sports scores on his computer. He says I should be happy that he's not off in bars every night like some of his chums or running around with other women. I suppose I am happy about that, but I don't feel very happy. Mostly I feel lonely. Sometimes I cry and tell him he doesn't care about me, that I need him to be around more, to show me more affection, but then we end up in a big row and I feel even more unhappy. I don't know why I stay, but I do. I suppose it's because I love him. I can't imagine living without him. I think I'd feel even more lonely coming home to an empty flat every night.

Anyway, Michael and I (Michael is the name of the guy on the train—we eventually introduced ourselves and shook hands rather formally), we started exchanging greetings with each other every day and would often end up sitting together. He reads *The Times* on the train and sometimes he would comment to me on an item of news. I liked his voice and the intelligent way he would comment on government financial policies. He works in finance and seems to be very well informed. He has nice eyes, although he often has a serious expression.

On April 6th he talked to me about his job for the first time. He has a lot of stories to tell about the people he works with. He tells the funniest stories with such a straight face, he makes me laugh out loud. I told him a little about what I do. I work in Human Resources for an international photocopying machine company. Not very glamorous but I am good at my job and we often have challenging issues to deal with—relationships between department heads and staff, or between members of a team who can't get along with each other. I'm really good at helping them work things through so they can work together more effectively.

At the end of May, Michael got a new boss—a woman. He didn't like her from the start. She sounded like a real bossy bitch who was never satisfied. Anyway, he would talk to me about his problems with her and I would listen. I liked to listen to him telling me stuff. I felt important and he seemed to appreciate it when I made suggestions. I've dealt with a lot of managers like that—women and men who like to throw their weight around, who think they will get the best from their team by criticizing their work and always demanding more. I'm usually very good in situations like this at work, at helping people to listen to each other. I wish I could do that as effectively with Alex, but he just never seems to want to listen no matter how hard I try to tell him nicely what I need from him.

Michael listens. I sometimes tell him about my day, some of the stresses of instituting new pension plans or the challenges when we do a takeover or merger. It always involves a lot of added work for me so I often miss the 5.13 train but I look forward to seeing him the next morning on the 8.02. I must admit that I started to have fantasies about being in a relationship with him. In my fantasies we would meet up on the train after work, talk about our day with each other—I would make helpful suggestions that he would appreciate and implement and he would listen to my tales of woe and admire me for how I was handling them. In the evening I would cook him a wonderful meal and we would talk some more during dinner—about world affairs, theatre and art. Then we would watch a little television—a BBC drama or current affairs show, and then go to bed and cuddle close. I didn't let myself stray into too many of the details after that. I knew I shouldn't be thinking about him that way but if Alex took more notice of me I am sure I wouldn't.

June 27th : "Dear Diary—I found out today that Michael is in a relationship—he's actually engaged to be married. I am pretty devastated to hear that. I don't know why because I'm engaged too. I know I shouldn't be upset but I guess it kind of puts a dent in my fantasies! His fiancée's name is Hazel. He got on the train in a real state this morning. I think they'd had a row—something about her having planned some event with friends and him not being available for it because he'd made plans to work out with someone—he's training for some triathlon event. I can actually sort of see her point of view and once he had finished telling me how upset he was I think I was able to help him to see what it might be like for her a little bit. Although he didn't say so, I don't think she appreciates him enough."

After that, he would talk to me sometimes about his relationship with Hazel. It sounds as though she is always going on at him to be there more. I get the sense she's very demanding and doesn't understand him, poor guy. I feel sad for him. I don't think she knows how lucky she is to have a guy who is willing to talk about his day and listen to her problems, like he does with me. I sure wish Alex would. I try to listen really attentively even when I don't understand everything Michael's saying about financial policies or new government regulations.

In August he didn't show up for two weeks and I was in a panic that I would never see him again. I wrote in my diary: "I feel like I did when I was in the 2nd form and my best friend moved away. I never saw her again. I really miss him. The train seems so empty without him. I think I have a bit of a crush on him."

I was so relieved when he was there again on the Monday morning the first week in September. I must have greeted him with the biggest smile. Of course, I didn't tell him how worried I had been. He seemed to be quite relieved to be going back to work. He told me that he and Hazel had gone to stay with her parents in Devon. He didn't say much about it but I think it was quite stressful.

November 10th: "Dear Diary. Today Michael gave me a lift home from the station. It was raining heavily when we got off the train, a horrid slanting, sleety kind of rain, full of that dreadful November chill. I was so grateful when he offered me a lift home. He had his car parked at the station. He usually rides his bike in, so I was really pleased when he said he had his car. I asked him to drop me off at the end of the street. I don't want Alex seeing me drive up in a car with another man. For someone who barely seems to notice me much of the time he can be very jealous if I pay too much attention to someone else, or even talk about some of the men at the office. It was still pouring when we got to my street. Michael suggested that I wait a few minutes to see if the rain let up any, and I was happy to do so. It felt so cozy in his car with the heater on, the windows fogged up and covered with rain drops. It is the first time we have ever been alone together. Mostly we just listened to the sound of the rain. I told him how much I loved that sound as it brought back memories of childhood when I would lie in bed at night all cozy and warm and listen to the rain on the windows. I think he felt very peaceful too. When I got out of the car I kissed him, just to say thank you for the ride. His cheek felt rather scratchy from his 5 o'clock shadow. I know I shouldn't have done it, but it just felt right to do."

After that he often gave me a lift to the end of my street when I was able to catch the 5.13 from Farringdon. We would usually sit and talk for a while before I jumped out and walked up the street. Sometimes I would kiss his cheek or touch his hand as I got out of the car, but he never came on to me. I don't know why not. I know it was wrong of me but sometimes I wished he would, although I don't know what I would have done if he had. What we had seemed so precious and special.

24th January—the anniversary of our first conversation. I wondered if Michael would mention it, but he didn't so I didn't say anything directly, although I did mention that it wasn't as cold as it had been this time last year.

All through the winter Michael and I continued like that—traveling up to town together in the mornings, sometimes coming home on the same train in the evenings and him often giving me a lift to the end of my street. As we rattled along in the train each day we watched the seasons change, from winter to spring. We saw the fields being ploughed and planted. We saw the trees burst into flower and then turn green as spring painted the landscape with her fresh palate. In the spring he started riding his bike to the station again most days so we would see each other on the train, but only occasionally got the chance of private time together in his car. I knew I shouldn't miss it, but I did.

The last time I saw him was on 23rd May. The weather had turned nasty after a warm spell—torrential rain from morning till night and Michael had driven his car to the station. He offered me a lift home and I accepted gladly. We stopped as usual at the end of the street and sat in the car for some time chatting on and off and listening to the rain. When I got out of the car, I leaned back in and gave him a kiss and thanked him for the ride. He made a joke about people getting the wrong idea and I laughed as he pulled away and I walked off up the street.

He wasn't on the train the next morning. I thought he must be sick although he had seemed perfectly healthy the night before, but somehow in my bones I knew something was wrong. I panicked when I realized then he had no way of contacting me. We had never exchanged any more than first names. He knew the street I lived on but not the building or the apartment. He had no phone number or email address and I had even less information about him.

I don't know how I knew but I did. It was just like when my 2nd grade friend had moved away. I knew somehow I would never see him again. I cried and cried at night as I poured my heart out to my diary. I didn't want Alex to see that I was upset but I couldn't hide it completely. My eyes were red from the crying and I was probably a little sullen and uncommunicative.

June 17th: "Dear Diary: Alex has left me. I came home this evening feeling really bereft. It has been three weeks since I last saw Michael. I miss him so much on the train. Every morning I look for him on the platform, and every evening I stand around at Farringdon station looking for him. I keep thinking I see him, but then it turns out to be someone else. When I got home I walked into the flat and went into the kitchen. There, on the table, was an envelope. I opened it with a sinking feeling. It was a note from Alex—short and to the point. 'It's over between us forever. I don't need this shit in my life. How could you? Alex.' I can't stop crying. I keep wandering around the empty flat. He had taken almost all his stuff. My wedding dress, which had been hanging in a corner of the closet in a bag, was on the bed where I couldn't miss it. He had drawn a big cross in black marker across the bag. I have no idea why he's gone. What have I done wrong?"

June 20th: "Dear Diary: I can't bear seeing my wedding dress in the closet with that big black cross on the bag. I feel like I have that black cross right across my heart. I haven't heard from Alex or Michael. I don't know how I can go on. Thank goodness I have my work, although I am having trouble concentrating and keep having to go to the bathroom where I break down in tears. I think my boss knows there is something wrong. I called the *St. Alban's Free Trader* newspaper today and placed an ad 'For Sale: Wedding Dress. Size 20. Never Worn,' and added my phone number." I guess it really is over. Alex isn't coming back. He won't even return my calls.

January 24th: "Dear Diary: It was two years ago today that Michael and I first talked to each other and seven months since I have spoken to either him or Alex. I concentrate on my work and get through each day. I got a promotion last week but I wasn't really that excited. Everything still feels rather flat. I keep looking for Michael on the platform, I feel like I always will, but he's never there. I had to cancel all the wedding plans. It was awful. I didn't know what to tell anyone except that Alex had left. He picked up the rest of his stuff one day when I wasn't home. He never did talk much but I think he could have at least said something.

Alex

I know I shouldn't have read her diary but what the hell, I did. And a damn good thing I did if you ask me. She'd been moping around looking miserable for a couple of weeks, looking like she'd been crying. I figured it was pre-wedding nerves—we were supposed to be getting married in a couple of months. I know a lot of girls get them, so I didn't ask. I figured it would blow over. Best not to stir things up. But I was looking in her desk for some papers I needed to pay a bill and it was sitting right there so I opened it. I couldn't believe my eyes. She's made a right fool of me, I can tell you. She says in her diary that she kissed him and that she has fantasies about him! You can be sure it's gone further than that even if she doesn't say so specifically. I didn't read it all anyway. I didn't want to know all the details. I was so disgusted. How could she do this to me, the bitch? I wonder if any of my mates know. They'd think I was a real chump, especially if I'd gone ahead and got married to her when she was fooling around on me. It's a good thing I found out in time. I wonder if my pals did know why didn't they tell me? Would I tell one of my mates if I knew his girl was fooling around on him? Yes, you bet I would. I would never let him make a fool of himself like that. Well, if they don't know, they aren't going to hear it from me, I can tell you that. I'll just tell them I changed my mind, that I found out she's not the girl I thought she was and so decided not to go through with the wedding. They'll understand.

I can tell you I was pretty angry. That was it, it was over for me right there. I didn't even want to see her face again. I didn't know what I might do. So I called one of my mates and asked if I could hang out at his place for a few days until I could find a new flat. I packed up most of my gear in a couple of my big sports bags. I'll come back for the rest in a few days when I've calmed down a bit. I wrote her a note and left it on the table. Perhaps I shouldn't have broken off with her in a note like that, but what the hell—I did.

Hazel

I still can't believe it. I feel sick when I think about it all. My friend Stephanie phoned me and said she needed to talk to me. She asked if Michael was home. It seemed a bit strange but I told her to come over. Michael was out at the gym and would probably be there for some time yet. At least that's where I thought he was. Now I don't know anything anymore.

Stephanie told me she'd seen Michael on the train with a woman—every day. And that he talks to her like she's never seen him talk to me—all gooey-eyed. She says it's been going on for a long time, that they meet on the train every morning and most evenings. She said they also get into his car together when they get off the train. I didn't know what to make of it. Perhaps she goes to the same gym as him and he's just giving her a lift when he has his car. I started making up all sorts of excuses for him, but Stephanie seemed pretty certain there was something more going on.

I decided to follow him. It was May 27th. He took his car that morning because it was raining. I made sure he didn't see me when I followed him onto the platform. I saw the way they smiled at each other and their eyes lit up when they saw each other. I saw the way they huddled together under his umbrella. I bought a ticket and got on the train. I hid behind some people so I could see them but they couldn't see me. I don't think they would have noticed me even if I'd been standing right in front of them with flashing lights all over me, the way they were engrossed in each other. I saw the way they talked with each other! Talked! Michael never talks to me. Hell, he never talks to anyone! But they were deep in conversation. I saw the way they laughed and the way her hand brushed his. I saw how comfortable they looked together. When they got off the train I heard him ask 'See you later?' with hope in his voice. I heard the way she said 'I'll do my best' as she headed off in a different direction. I took the next train back home.

It was a miserable, rainy day and I sat and brooded all day. I work from home but I got very little work done that day. My stomach was churning and I felt sick when I thought of them together. I decided I would go down and see what happened when they came home that evening. I knew he usually took the 5.13 that arrives in St. Albans at 5.36 so I was waiting, concealed, when they got off the train that evening and headed to the car park together as though they did this every day. I followed them through the rainy streets wondering where they would go. It certainly wasn't in the right direction for the sports club. They parked at the end of a street, in a secluded area away from the blocks of flats. I parked nearby. I couldn't see into the car because it was raining so hard, but they were there for about 20 minutes—long enough to get up to whatever it was they got up to. Doing it in a car! Really—how adolescent! Then the rain let up a little and the woman got out of the car, but before she left she leaned in again and kissed him.

I went home and packed up as much of his stuff as I could. When he came home from the gym a couple of hours later I told him to leave. I told him I knew about his affair. I called him a "cheating bastard" and another few choice names. He played all innocent but I'd seen them with my own eyes. He took his bags and went to stay with his brother.

It took me nearly four weeks to pluck up the courage to call the *St. Albans Free Trader* to place an ad to sell my wedding dress. It was the strangest thing. When I told her to put, "For

Sale: Wedding Dress. Size 20. Never Worn" she kept insisting someone had already called a few minutes earlier to place the ad. It was really weird. It was only when I gave her my phone number and my credit card number that she would accept it. I was so surprised when I got a copy of the paper the following week. Right next to mine was an identical ad, "For Sale: Wedding dress. Size 20. Never worn."—identical except for the contact information. What a coincidence!

*With gratitude to Paula Hawkins, whose book 'The Girl on the Train" gave me the idea of locating the story on a commuter train, and to my father who traveled the commuter train each day for many years back in the days of steam trains and individual carriages that seated about 6 or 8 people—mostly men in bowler hats. I had the joy of traveling with him for a couple of years when at college and in my first job.

The Invitation

Have you ever had an interaction with a stranger on a train, or boat or plane? There is often a "time outside time" quality to these interactions, like they are bracketed off from the rest of life. Do you ever fantasize about meeting someone on some form of public transport? I invite you to write a story about such a chance meeting of strangers—real or imagined. Who are your characters? What might they be looking for? How does it play out? You could try writing it from the two different points of view.

The Journey

It was minus 24 degrees Fahrenheit when Mary and Mitch left Malone for the drive to Dorval Airport in Montreal—exceptionally cold even for February. They had never flown before and didn't know what to expect on the long journey to New Zealand. It would be summer there when they arrived. Weird!

They were going to New Zealand for a month. It was a pre-wedding honeymoon. They both held junior positions at the prison where they worked, Mary in the kitchens and Mitch as a guard, so they couldn't get extended vacation in the summer when they were getting married. Also, Mitch was needed then on the farm his family owned, so they decided to go before the wedding.

The trip was Mary's dream really. Ever since she had seen the Hobbit movies she had wanted to take a trip to New Zealand even though she had never been anywhere far from home before.

Everything went smoothly at Dorval airport. Their first flight took them to Los Angeles. Mary was amazed by the whole experience: the de-icing process, the views from the window as they flew across America, the wide choice of movies to watch on the tiny little TV screens, the meals served in little containers on plastic trays.

During the eight-hour layover in Los Angeles as she looked around at the other passengers the thing she noticed most was how many appeared to be obese and how much unhealthy, high calorie food was being consumed. She considered herself about 60 lbs overweight but there were many people much larger than she. She had always thought that America was the greatest country in the world, the country everyone looked up to and would want to live in if they had the opportunity, the country of freedom and possibility, but as she saw all those overweight people around her she wondered what was going on that so many of her countrymen seemed to be eating themselves to death. She was shocked and decided that during the vacation she would try to be more careful what she ate.

The thirteen-hour overnight flight to Auckland was uneventful. The flight staff looked very smart in their colourful, purple and black, bold-print dresses. She loved the video they played before departure that was a take-off on *"The Hobbit"* to tell them about fastening their seat belts and what to do in an emergency. She decided to watch *"The Lord of the Rings"* on the little TV during the flight. She even slept for several hours—she figured she was pretty beat from all the excitement and anxiety as well as traveling all day and the time differences.

When they landed in Auckland it felt amazing to get off the plane into the heat of summer. They found their way to the car rental place and after a bit of a fuss and an hour's delay because they didn't have international drivers' licences (they had assumed their American licences would be good anywhere in the world) they got on the road, remembering to drive on the left.

They got lost getting out of Auckland but eventually found their way north. They thought that the New Zealanders weren't very keen on having clear road signs to the major highways, and Mary found following the map they had more of a challenge than she had expected, used as she was to the long straight roads of North America.

They drove up on what seemed to be the only highway that went to the north of the North Island. It was two lanes, one in each direction and went right through the centre of the towns. Mary was amazed that it was such a small highway. Progress was slow because there were many large trucks. Periodically there were areas where slower traffic could pull over to let faster cars pass. She was impressed that the trucks and some cars seemed to observe these well. It seemed a very polite sort of thing to do. There was also a lot of construction going on to widen the road in some places, which made the trip even slower. Mary realized that with a population of only 4.2 million there probably were a lot of things that she took for granted in the States that a smaller population just couldn't afford—like good highways. She hadn't really thought about the effect that population size had on highways and other infrastructure before and how many of the things that she took for granted or even complained about at times just weren't available in other places.

They decided to stop for lunch and turned off the highway at a town called Warkworth. They found a little restaurant and sat outside eating their rather expensive chicken and avocado wraps. They were horrified that the coffee cost over $4 Australian a cup, although with the exchange rate it was a bit less in American dollars, but still. It was wonderful to be outside. They chatted with the waitress and she told them that, whilst they were in town, they should visit the Kauri Park and the nearby Tawharanui Regional Park. They decided they wanted to be spontaneous and flexible and figured that even with the slow going on the highway the distance they had to travel that day wasn't so much that they couldn't take a couple of detours.

They went for a walk along the river that ran through Warkworth and saw some birds with long spoonbills perched on a dead tree. At Kauri Park they walked through a rain forest. One of the Kauri trees was over eight hundred years old and was huge around the trunk, like the redwoods in America that she had read about. They went for a beautiful walk through the forest and saw all kinds of trees and plants she had never seen before. It even rained gently for a few minutes which seemed like just the right thing for it to be doing in a rain forest.

At the Tawharanui Reserve they had to go through a fence. Mary was amazed to learn that there were only two land mammals that were native to New Zealand and those were two species of bats. No other land mammals had evolved here. She couldn't believe it. She had assumed there were mammals everywhere. She had watched a TV show on Australia not long ago. She had sort of assumed that being so close New Zealand would be something like that—with koalas, maybe kangaroos, and lots of poisonous stuff. The show on Australia had kept emphasizing how they had the world's most poisonous this, and the most dangerous that—snakes, spiders, jelly fish, plants, etc. etc. It seemed New Zealand wasn't like that at all. It was like a tiny version of Canada, or at least many of her friends' perceptions of Canada—a safe place where people were polite and nothing much happened, nestling beside the more violent and dangerous country of the United States.

Mary had grown up a Baptist and had been told that evolution was a fiction for which there was no evidence. She had been taught to take the Bible literally, that the world was created by God in seven days. Because God was perfect, all he created was perfect. Therefore, there could be no such thing as species becoming extinct. As she got older she had grown away from the church seeing the hypocrisy of people saying one thing and behaving differently. Her mother told her that her father had had affairs and left her for another woman despite the commandment to not commit adultery. There had certainly been plenty of taking the Lord's name in vain around her house as she was growing up and her mother had encouraged her to steal little things they couldn't afford from the big stores, saying it didn't hurt anybody. Mary didn't think she was a true creationist anymore but hadn't really thought about evolution very deeply. It really impacted her to hear that there were no real land mammals, and that as a result of there being no predators several species of birds had evolved into being flightless, such as the kiwis, which only came out at night, and the pukekos, a blue and black bird with a bright red beak and feet, which they saw running around everywhere. She learned that Europeans had introduced rabbits so they could have some meat to eat, but with no natural predators these had proliferated to an unmanageable degree. In their wisdom, the Europeans had then introduced ferrets, stoats and weasels to keep the rabbit population in check. As these animals didn't have any natural predators there either, they too had proliferated and proceeded to kill off not only the rabbits but the native birds who, being flightless, couldn't get away. Hence the fence! It was an attempt to provide a safe sanctuary for the native birds and wildlife before they got completely eradicated by the introduced species and became extinct as other species had already done. Ferrets, stoats, weasels and possums (another introduced species) seemed to be public enemies number one in New Zealand. Mitch and Mary were to see many traps for them in their travels.

All this put evolution in a completely new light for Mary. It became a real thing with consequences, not a religious argument that set her apart from her schoolmates. She also saw how things that might seem like a good idea at the time, without sufficient study and thought, can turn out disastrously.

Back on the highway they drove through much beautiful countryside that turned from the green hills and forests to golds and browns as they went further north. They arrived in Paihia in the late afternoon. It was a small town with the beach on one side of the road and restaurants, bars, shops and a few hotels on the other. The bed and breakfast they were booked into, that they had found online, turned out to be about 3-miles out of town, up a very steep driveway.

They were greeted warmly by the hosts, Chris and John—two men who referred to each other as "my husband". Mary was surprised and shocked to hear them be so open about their gay relationship. She didn't know any gay people back home, at least no-one who openly admitted they were. She knew that there were places like San Francisco where they had gay pride parades and where people lived openly as gay partners. There was even legislation now in some states legalizing gay marriage, but she had never actually met anyone who was gay, at least not as far as she was aware. One or two people she knew were suspected of being gay but they were mercilessly made fun of and called names and they denied it emphatically. It certainly wouldn't have gone down well in high school or for any of the guards at the prison. Mary wasn't sure how she felt about her hosts being gay but figured it was only for a couple of nights. Mitch was even more uncomfortable, but the room was nice and the secluded setting was lovely. Besides, they had already paid for the room when they had booked on-line, never doubting that Chris was a woman, so they unpacked their bags and settled in. They were pretty beat.

They went back into town and found a restaurant where they could sit outside on the terrace to eat supper. There were lots of dishes with strange names and lots of weird combinations of ingredients on the menu so they both settled for a hamburger, which at $19 was about the cheapest meal available. Again they were shocked at how expensive the food and drinks were and decided they would have to be very careful about what they ordered or their money wouldn't last the month. When the plates of food came there was so much they thought they could have shared a meal. They decided they would do that sometimes and would go without the beer and wine, which added a lot to the cost. They were very surprised to find that, in addition to the usual meat patty, cheese and bacon, there was also a fried egg inside the bun of their burgers! Mary had never seen a burger with a fried egg in it before. It seemed a little excessive but it tasted really good.

After they had eaten they wandered along the sandy beach to the end of town and then back again past the shops. When they got back to their room they went straight to bed, without even watching any television, and fell asleep immediately. Mary had been worried she wouldn't sleep with the 13-hour time difference, but she was so tired she slept right through until morning.

Their hosts put on a wonderful breakfast and they made light conversation with the three other guests who were staying there. John suggested they visit the newly opened Waitangi Treaty Centre whilst they were in town and also that they take a day boat-trip round the Bay of Islands. Mary didn't like just lying on the beach in the sun—she felt too fat in her bathing suit and tended to go red rather than get a tan so having some other ideas of things to do suited her fine and Mitch was happy to go along.

After a leisurely breakfast and sitting outside for a bit listening to the strange forest sounds, they drove to the Treaty Centre. They joined a group led by a Maori guide. He was very entertaining and told them lots of stories about the original people from Polynesia who came to New Zealand around 1,400 AD. Unlike Australia where the aboriginal people dated back thousands of years, there had been no people at all, along with no other mammals, until about 600 years ago. When the British and Europeans started showing up in the early 1,700s and at times unwittingly violated the Maori's traditions and taboos, they got into conflicts with them and there were some violent skirmishes. The guide seemed to take great delight in letting them know that the Maori would eat their foes after they had killed them—that they had been cannibals! He proudly showed them the signature of his ancestor who had been one of the Maori chiefs to sign the treaty with the British at Waitangi in 1840. He said that what was unique about the treaty in the history of British colonialism was that the British and the Maori pledged to treat each other as equals. It didn't work out that way but the pledge was there and it was a lot better than many places the British and other Europeans had taken over. In recent years the Maori and others were increasingly demanding that the agreement of equality be honoured.

Mary thought about how the Native Americans had been treated—put on reservations, their land taken away and killed by guns and disease. It was not a history she felt proud of. She realized that, even though there was a reservation just north of Malone and she had driven through it several times, she really didn't know much about how the native people lived there today, what kind of lives they had, beyond selling cheap cigarettes and gas and running gambling casinos because they didn't come under some of the same taxation laws as other Americans. She'd also heard Mitch talk about the Native American prisoners at the jail in derogatory ways. The guards seemed to have a lot of negative attitudes towards them as a bunch of drunks. She decided she would try to find out more about them, their history and how they lived today when she got back home.

When they came to the part of the tour where they entered the Maori meeting house to watch a show of aboriginal dance, they had to go through a greeting ritual where the Maori decided if the visitors were friends or enemies. Fortunately, they were considered friends so they were invited into the highly carved and decorated interior, rather than killed and eaten, as they might have been in the past.

Once inside Mary noticed that many of the fantastic carvings had bulgy white eyes made of abalone and their large tongues stuck out. These facial expressions were repeated by the hake dancers. Four Maori men and four women performed the war dance and other ritual dances, swinging balls, throwing sticks and making loud grunts, wearing costumes in red, black and white woven cloth. Mary thought they were very good and really enjoyed the show. Mitch said that on TV he'd seen the All-Blacks rugby team do a dance like that before a match and figured it was a way to intimidate their opponents. He thought it was probably quite effective. Afterwards they had a chance to meet the performers and Mary was surprised when one of the men, who must have weighed 300 lbs. and had looked very fierce during the dancing, told her in perfect English he liked her sunglasses. She didn't know what she had been expecting but not that. She realized that many of her assumptions were being challenged.

After the show they walked around the grounds some more and spent some time in the museum getting a little more of a sense of New Zealand's history. They were glad that they had decided to do that at the beginning of their trip to give them a context for their travels.

When they felt saturated with dates and information they went into town and walked around. There was a food-market on the pier with stalls where vendors were selling all kinds of delicious smelling foods, so they bought a couple of dishes which they shared and sat on a couch and listened to the singer—a young woman with a lovely voice who also played guitar. It was a beautiful setting and they felt very happy as they sat there holding hands.

The next day at breakfast they chatted with Chris and John and Mary was surprised to find that she really liked them. Again she didn't know what she had expected but felt her assumptions were being challenged. They again did as their hosts had suggested and took the boat trip around the Bay of Islands. Mary couldn't believe the beautiful green colour of the water and all the wonderful islands dotted around—about 144 according to Captain James Cook, who was the first westerner to visit them. The commentary that was provided gave lots of neat little stories about various of the islands and things that had happened—like when the French had violated the taboo of not fishing in a bay where a Maori chief's son had been buried. They got killed and eaten for their troubles. Mary felt she was starting to get a sense of the history of the area and realized she had never even been curious about how Malone was settled or why, although daily she saw the beautiful old Victorian mansions on Elm Street. Why had those people lived there, how did they make their money, what had happened to turn it into the financially depressed area it was today? What had life been like before the Europeans arrived?

The highlight of the boat trip for Mary, though, was when they sailed through an enormous school of blue fish—there must have been thousands, maybe hundreds of thousands of them all round the boat. She had been fishing in the local lakes and rivers of her part of New York state and, if she was lucky, in an hour or two she would catch two or three trout. But here in the ocean there were fish beyond numbers and so beautiful. Mitch's favourite part was when the captain steered the boat through a narrow archway made of rock, where the water was crashing and swirling on all sides. That took real skill!

The next day they drove the same road again going south, through Auckland and out the other side, without getting lost. The roads were better there, more like what would be considered highways back home. It was a long day of driving, much longer than they had expected, based on mileage and the expected travel time from the web site they had checked out. Mary found the scenery to be incredibly beautiful, especially the large plants along the side of the road—the golden toitoi and the black spires of the flax made a very dramatic combination.

They got to Hamilton in the late afternoon and found their hotel easily. The parking garage was very small and the cars were stacked using some kind of mechanized lift contraption that Mitch couldn't figure out so he parked in the handicapped space that was such a tight squeeze he didn't think anyone with a disability would be able to maneuver it. He had to back out and let Mary out and then drive in again after she'd been unable to squeeze her body out of the car.

"I must do something about this weight of mine," she thought, not for the first time on this trip. *"At least I'm eating less and walking a lot more than I usually do. I spend far too much of my spare time sitting in front of the TV watching rubbish and eating rubbish. That's got to change. There's so much more to life than that and I'm starting to see that clearly."*

They didn't like Hamilton much. It was an ugly town, except for the Riverwalk, not unlike many similar industrial towns in North America. It's only claim to fame seemed to be that the guy who wrote *"The Rocky Horror Picture Show"* had written it when he lived there and worked in a dentist's office. There was a memorial to him on the main street. They had started watching it late one night on the movie channel back home but couldn't figure out what was going on and thought it was stupid. They gave up and switched the channel after half an hour, unable to figure out what all the cult hoopla had been about.

Mary awoke very excited the next day. They were booked for an 11 a.m. tour of Hobbiton, the movie set where they had filmed the parts of *"The Hobbit"* movies that took place in The Shire. They followed what looked like the shortest route on the map but ended up on some seemingly endless road that appeared to lead nowhere. They came to a T-junction neither of which direction meant anything to them. Mary was getting more and more anxious that they would miss their tour. They were sitting at the intersection trying to figure out where they were and which way to go when all of a sudden, out of nowhere, a woman appeared and asked if they needed help. She then drew them a map of how to get to Hobbiton and disappeared again. Mary was convinced she was an angel.

They arrived just in time for the start of their tour. They had to get on a special green coach to go to the site from the parking area and reception centre. The driver told them stories about how the film crew had found the location for the site—that the farmer had been watching an All-Blacks rugby game when the location scout showed up at the door to make him a substantial offer to lease the land. The farmer told him to sit down and wait until the game was over and then he'd talk to him. The scout did and when the game was over they engaged in a conversation that must have led to a very lucrative deal for the farmer.

When they got off the bus they were greeted by a young woman who would be their guide. They had to stay in a group around the site and she would give them a commentary about the making of the movies as they went.

Mary thought Hobbiton was perfect! She thought it was the most wonderful place she had ever been! It was exactly as it had looked in the movies and as she had imagined it when she had read the books. Her mother had had a job at the town library when Mary was 12 and she had to go there after school every day and wait for her to finish her shift. She thought the librarian had taken pity on her as she often recommended books that she thought Mary might enjoy and during that year Mary had developed a love of reading and found a way to escape from the loneliness and pain of her own life. One of those books was *"The Hobbit"*. She got a bit bogged down when she tried to read *"The Lord of the Rings"* series but she loved *"The Hobbit"*—the tale of Bilbo Baggins, a home-loving Hobbit heading off on a journey of adventure with Gandalf, the Wizard, and a cast of other unlikely characters. Simple, stick-in-the-mud Bilbo had discovered himself on that journey, found his strength and his courage and ended up the hero of the tale.

Yes, Hobbiton was perfect in every detail, from the round doorways of the hobbit holes to the flowers and vegetables in the gardens, the fish hanging up to dry, the little clothes on the clothes lines, the water mill beside the pond and the Green Dragon pub where they ended up their tour with a glass of the most delicious ginger beer. Peter Jackson, the director of the *"Lord of the Rings"* movies, had attended to every detail down to having the tree on the hill over Bilbo Baggin's home custom-made and then having each leaf repainted by hand a week before shooting because he thought the colour was wrong. If Mary hadn't been told which tree was fake she would never have guessed. She felt she could have moved into Hobbiton very happily and lived there the rest of her life. It felt like home, so friendly and welcoming, even though the doors were just fronts with nothing behind them.

Talking to Amy, the guide, Mary found out that she was from Scotland and was working in New Zealand for a year on a permit. She said that immigration to New Zealand was very restricted but that it was easy to get a one-year permit because they needed the manpower to do the jobs like serving the tourists and picking fruit, given that their own population was so small. Amy had filled out an application for the Hobbiton job and got it. She loved working there. Other staff were from many different countries and they had a lot of fun together. She had also traveled around New Zealand getting jobs as she went wherever she felt like stopping or when the money ran low. She adored New Zealand and would love to come back and live there at some point. Mary wondered if she would ever be able to do something like that—get a job for a year working at Hobbiton. It seemed like a delicious dream. She had never even thought of doing something like that before. She had gone straight from high school to her job at the K-Mart and then the prison. She had started dating Mitch the last year of high school and then they just continued. She had never questioned what else she could be doing, how else she could live her life. The trip to New Zealand had been her one big, out-of-the-ordinary dream.

As they drove away from Hobbiton, Mary said wistfully to Mitch, "I don't want to go back home. I want to stay here and live in a Hobbit hole in Hobbiton for the rest of my life, taking care of the gardens and growing vegetables."

After talking with Amy, Mary made sure she chatted to everyone they met in restaurants and bars, shops and hotels. She was fascinated by their stories. Most of them were from somewhere else, visiting for the year on a work permit. They all seemed to love New Zealand, found the people friendly and although it was expensive living there and they weren't able to save any money, they were able to make ends meet as they traveled around and worked. Wages, even in restaurants, were decent because there was no tipping expected. Occasionally people would add a tip, for example in a fancy restaurant if the service had been exceptional but it was never expected. Mary found that strange. In restaurants around where she lived wages of waitstaff were appallingly low because 20% tips were the expected norm. If you didn't give at least 15% they sometimes got nasty, which was understandable given how poorly they were paid.

From Hobbiton they continued south. Mary loved the beautiful rolling hills, like folds in a fabric, carved out by she knew not what forces of nature but nothing like anything she had ever seen back home. Their next stop was a farm just past Owhango that Mitch had found on-line. He thought it would be interesting to stay on a farm and talk to the owners about farming in New Zealand, see how things were done down here, and whether he could get any ideas for his farm back home that he would one day inherit from his parents.

After they had arrived and settled in, Phil and Merle, the owners, who looked like they were in their 50s, served up a wonderful meal of lamb chops, roast potatoes and kumara, a starchy thing like a potato, and lots of vegetables. Merle did the cooking and Phil served them at table. Mary had never eaten lamb before, although it was available in the supermarket. Mostly she ate hamburgers, pork and chicken or pre-cooked pasta dishes she bought in the frozen foods section. She really liked the lamb and was reassured to learn it wasn't one of the ones they had raised themselves on the farm, although most of the vegetables were from their garden. Mary had already met a couple of the pet lambs when she had been out for a walk before dinner.

After dinner the couple sat with them and talked about farming. Even in this mild New Zealand climate it wasn't an easy life. It was a mixed farm—sheep which they raised for wool and meat, and beef cattle, but with changing world conditions, including the increased use of synthetic fabrics rather than wool, it wasn't always easy to pay all the bills. They took in guests and were constantly looking for other ways to supplement their income. They sold the sperm of their prize ram and did a trade of cattle for 500 jars of Manuka honey from a bee farmer who lived further north. Phil had tales of driving the cattle there himself with the help of one of his sons. They had two sons and were sad that neither of them wanted to go into farming, especially given that Phil's father and grandfather had owned the farm before him. One son worked in Japan as an English teacher and the other was an IT guy. Phil said that Mitch's parents were lucky to have a son who wanted to take over. It seemed strange to Mitch that Phil was up early, working outside all day and then serving guests at table in his own home in the evening. He certainly couldn't see his dad doing that and wasn't sure he liked the idea himself. It showed him that he might have to think creatively to keep the farm going back home in a situation where so many family farms had already been taken over by big corporations.

Over the huge, delicious breakfast Mary told Merle that they were planning on going to Tongariro National Park. Mary commented on how many of the places seemed to have Maori names, except for the cities like Auckland, Hamilton and Wellington, and that all the signs were bilingual. Merle gave Mary some tips on how to pronounce some of the Maori words, like Owhango—where the wh was pronounced like an "f" or "ph", and the "au" in names like Tauranga were pronounced like an "o" as in toe. Mary was really surprised to find out that New Zealand has three official languages—English, Maori and sign. The children all learn some Maori in school and are taught about the culture and customs. That seemed very different from back home and much more respectful, especially given that the Maoris were themselves immigrants who had only arrived about 300 years before the white people. Unlike Australia, where many of the early settlers were convicts sent there to serve time in a harsh penal colony, early New Zealanders went there by choice to build a new and better life.

Their day in Tongariro National Park started out beautifully sunny but then the dark storm clouds moved in giving the place an eerie, doom-like feel. It was the first time that Mary had seen a volcano and a recently active one at that. The most recent eruption was in 2012, when Mt. Tongariro had blown its top and scattered rock and ash all around the surrounding countryside. The landscape was incredibly barren for miles. As they went up Mt. Rapahui in the chair lift and looked around, nothing seemed to be growing anywhere and yet it was majestic and beautiful in its own way, especially when beams of sunlight shone through gaps in the dark clouds. She recognized Mt. Ngauruhoe as Mount Doom in the *"Lord of the Rings"* movie she had watched and understood why they had chosen it to represent that dark and evil place. It was such a stark contrast to the gentle, green, sun-filled countryside of The Shire.

They stayed three days at the farm. Mitch helped Phil out and learned a lot more about farming in New Zealand, while Mary went for long walks and sat and read on the beautiful porch surrounded by flowers. Merle was the gardener and had done a wonderful job making the farmhouse and garden look really attractive. Mary thought about Mitch's farm and wondered if she would ever be able to do something similar. It seemed a monumental task and she wasn't sure she had the heart for it. She wondered if it would ever feel like her home, that she belonged there, even after they were married or after Mitch had inherited it. She wasn't sure it would ever feel like anything other than Mitch's parents' house, even long after they were dead.

Merle seemed sad when they left. She had told Mary that while it was a good life and a busy one, at times she felt lonely, with Phil out working from early morning till late, and no women to sit around and have a coffee and a chat with, the nearest town being about thirty miles away. She'd grown up in a town and been trained as a teacher before she married Phil. She really missed all the bustle and comradeship of people.

The next stop was Waikawa Beach on the west coast north of Wellington. They were renting a "bach" there for 5 days. A "bach" was the New Zealand term for a cottage or beach house. Mary had also learned that flip flops were called "jandals" derived from "Japanese sandals." She realized that although New Zealand seemed like a Western country, it was actually closer to Asia, hence all the Asian tourists they had seen in some places, and the banners in so many places celebrating the Chinese New Year.

They found the key where they had been told it would be and let themselves in. It was a simple, single-story building with one bedroom, a bathroom and a large room in the front that served as living-room, dining-room and kitchen. It had large windows that looked out over the mountains in the distance, sand dunes and a garden of grasses that danced in the breeze. It had sun decks on two sides. They unpacked the groceries they had bought at the store in the town they had passed through on the way and then went for a walk down to the beach. They couldn't believe it—there was endless sandy beach in both directions, miles and miles of it as far as the eye could see, and not a single soul in sight. And the shells! Mary immediately started picking up some of the numerous, beautiful shells that lay scattered everywhere.

Their days at the bach were idyllic. They ate simply and went for long walks. One time they saw a man riding a horse along the beach and another day they met a woman with a dog but apart from that they had the beach to themselves. They made love in a slow, leisurely way, like never before. They read books and felt more relaxed than they probably ever had. Mary was sleeping well and starting to feel healthy in her body as well as peaceful in her mind. There was no TV so they had no idea what was going on in the world outside. Mitch said he missed watching the sports but Mary enjoyed being insulated from the killing and nastiness that was constantly portrayed, not only in the news but in most of the shows they usually watched. She felt as though all that stuff had been polluting her mind and her spirit in ways she hadn't realized until it wasn't there.

In their long walks on the beach Mary gathered shells but had to put most of them back because she didn't have room in her suitcase. The ones she kept she spent time soaking and cleaning to make sure there was nothing smelly still living in them. She took a lot of photos of the beach and the ocean and the driftwood that was scattered about. Sometimes they swam a little and jumped in the waves.

"I don't want to leave," said Mary as they left the bach at the end of their stay there.

The next day they caught the ferry across to the South Island. The only boat ride that Mary had been on before was when one of her mother's boyfriends had taken them on a day trip to Burlington, Vermont, and then they had taken the ferry back across to Essex. She had loved it—the feel of the wind in her hair, the ploughing of the boat through the waves, the sense of freedom as if she could take off and fly like the gulls swooping and dipping. Her mother had promised they would do that again someday but they never had.

The trip across the Marlborough Sound was beautiful and exhilarating for Mary. The way the land rose up from the water, all the little inlets and coves, the clouds and the sun streaming through—Mary felt an excitement and joy that filled her with a sense of aliveness. She even saw a porpoise swimming beside the boat.

They picked up another rental car after they docked and drove across to the west coast, through miles and miles of vineyards and then over mountain passes. The roads were better here, and she couldn't believe how few cars there were. When they reached the ocean at Westport, they turned south down the coastal road, stopping periodically to gawk open-mouthed at the views—the amazing rock formations, the crashing waves, the blue sea that spread out to the horizon. It was only later they realized how many sand flies had dined on their juicy American flesh, and how long these bites would drive them crazy with itchiness. Whereas the scenery in the North Island had been beautiful, the South Island was stunning—mountains on one side, ocean on the other. She imagined this was what the California coast might be like, except here there were a lot fewer people. They stayed overnight in a chalet-style cabin near Franz Joseph and in the morning went for a walk to see the glacier, which was very beautiful, but sadly receding rapidly due to global warming. They didn't linger long however. Mary told Mitch that she hadn't come all this way from home in the wintertime to see more snow and ice!

Back on the road they wound through mountain passes over very narrow, windy roads, barely wide enough for two cars, never mind the campervans that they occasionally passed. Mitch was tense as he drove slowly up and down the steep, curvy highway with sheer rock on one side and sheer precipice on the other. As they rounded a bend Mitch didn't have time to swerve to avoid the sharp shards in the road from a rock-fall and the result was they got a flat tire. He had to keep going for quite a way because there was just nowhere to pull over. Finally, he found a lay-by and pulled off the road and started to try to figure out how to work the jack and change the tire. Whilst they were there almost all the cars that passed pulled over and offered help and one guy, who must have been in his seventies, got out to give Mitch a hand, even though it had started to rain heavily by then.

Mary wondered if people back home would be so friendly and helpful. She hoped they would. She knew there were many kind, friendly, helpful Americans, but it seemed there were also a lot of people who were so suspicious and paranoid, probably due to all the horror stories reported in the media of people trying to help others and ending up murdered. Perhaps working in a prison and hearing Mitch's stories about some of the inmates didn't help her own levels of trust either. That kind of fear of strangers just didn't seem to be present in New Zealand from what she could tell. She wondered what the crime rate was like compared to the US. She imagined it was a lot lower, although she had heard that there was a lot of drunk driving among the young people and deaths that resulted from that. She had seen quite a few roadside memorials. She wasn't surprised if they tried to drive these mountain roads after a few beers.

They spent several days in Queenstown—an attractive town on the north end of Lake Wakatipu. It had a very holiday feel about it. They did a couple of excursions, including an overnight boat trip on Milford Sound. It was a long coach ride up and down over craggy, mountainous roads to get there, but the views were amazing and the driver made it interesting with his commentaries. It seemed that New Zealanders had a bit of a thing for jumping off high places. He claimed that bungee jumping had started there. Mary wasn't sure if he was just pulling their legs when he told them about how deer had been rounded up. Initially they were imported and released into the wild to provide Europeans with good hunting. This experiment in importing animals had apparently gone no better than the other such experiments and someone had had the bright idea of rounding them up and transferring them to farms. Mary had seen several deer farms alongside the road. According to their driver the way to catch them was to ride around chasing the deer in a helicopter and when they got near one, some young daredevil would jump out of the helicopter onto the back of the deer and wrestle him or her to the ground. This sounded decidedly far-fetched to Mary but made for a good story.

Milford Sound was breathtakingly beautiful with the sheer cliffs rising out of the pristine waters and mountains surrounding on all sides. They were served a bowl of soup and then taken on a nature walk along the last part of the Milford

Track—a 4-day hike through the wilderness. She told Mitch she would love to come back and do the whole trek one day and maybe some of the other famous hikes in New Zealand, carrying her supplies on her back and sleeping in lean-tos provided along the way. In the dinghy on the way back to their boat they saw seals lying on the rocks and swimming around in the water, paying no mind to the human intruders.

At 10 p.m. when the engines were turned off, the absolute stillness and silence of the night, the brightness of the moon and the stars inspired a sense of awe in Mary and she and Mitch sat quietly on deck for some time before turning in for the night. They had a cozy little cabin and the gentle rocking of the boat lulled them into a deep sleep.

After an early breakfast the boat got moving again and took them out to the ocean before turning around and retracing their route up the Sound. The captain took them right up to the base of great waterfalls that came crashing down the sheer cliff faces. They saw more seals lying on the rocks. The beauty of the place inspired Mary to want to paint, to capture the essence of the place in a way that she felt a photograph couldn't, although she took plenty of those. She didn't have any paints but she did make a pencil drawing in her notebook and was quite pleased with the effect.

Mary realized how much beauty she was surrounded by back home living just north of the Adirondack Park—the largest State Park on the US mainland and a place of incredible, unspoiled, natural beauty, with miles and miles of mountains, rivers and lakes. She thought about how much she took it all for granted and didn't even go there, although tourists came from around the world to camp, canoe and hike there. It took her going all the way across the globe to start to appreciate the splendour of nature that she had at home. She determined she would be more aware in the future, live with her eyes wide-open instead of glazed over as she felt she had been living. She would look up and see the stars and the moon. She would gaze with awe on the colours of the sky at sunset. She would open her ears to the sounds and the silence of the night. She would let herself feel the air on her skin, feel the breeze in her hair. She wrote about it in her notebook beside the drawing she had made of Milford Sound to remind herself when she got home.

On the way back they stopped for lunch in the town of Te Anau. They bought a steak and kidney pie at The Pie Shoppe, which they ate at a table outside in the open air. They got chatting with a group of men at the next table. They had just finished hiking the entire Milford Track and said they were celebrating World Pie Day. They were surprised when Mary and Mitch said they'd never heard of it and wondered how they had been taught about the mathematical number pi. At their school they had always celebrated March 14th by eating meat pies. Mary didn't get it at first until she realized that it was the 14th of March and 3.14 was the value of pi. She couldn't remember what pi was all about but knew it was an important number in math. The pie was memorably delicious, and she decided she would in future honour every 14th March with a meat pie!

Queenstown was their furthest point south. After that they headed north again, taking a couple of days to cross the strange and changing landscapes on their way to Christchurch. Arriving in the city they were stunned by the devastation caused by the earthquakes of 2011 and 2012. The whole downtown core had been razed and consisted mainly of rubble-covered ground, although a few brave souls had set up a sort of shopping mall consisting of shipping containers. A temporary cardboard cathedral had been built to replace the one that stood in ruins. Everywhere they went the earthquake of February 6th, 2012, came into the conversation, people harking back to it and recounting their memories. There had been another big tremor as recently as Valentine's Day, just a month previously and everyone seemed pretty shaken up even though it hadn't caused much damage. Mitch figured the whole city was suffering from a case of PTSD. They went to visit the exhibition, *"Quake City"* which gave them a sense of the devastation and they listened to people telling their stories of grief and loss or of miraculous survival and rescue. It touched them both deeply.

They only stayed a couple of days in Christchurch but there were at least two small tremors whilst they were there and they couldn't wait to leave. Mary couldn't imagine living with that kind of threat day in and day out. Then she thought about how she herself as a child had lived with uncertainty, never knowing when her mother would get drunk and shake the very bedrock of her existence. A different kind of threat maybe, but constant anxiety nonetheless. She was surprised that people were staying and rebuilding there, although she figured it was probably pretty hard right then to sell their homes to make a new start elsewhere. She understood, perhaps for the first time, why her sister had left home as soon as she could and wondered why she herself had stayed living at home with her mother for so long. She wondered whether it is possible to rebuild a life in the same place it has been shattered.

They both breathed a deep sigh of relief as they drove north up the coast road towards Kaikoura. The road passed inland through rolling hills, again very beautiful but different from any part of the country they had seen so far. So much beauty everywhere. *Do the New Zealanders take it for granted as she did the beauty that surrounded her back home?* Mary wondered.

They found a b&b where they had the whole top floor to themselves with views overlooking the ocean. Mary woke quite early next morning and sat for a long time quietly by herself gazing out at the blue sea and sky and thinking about her life. She was poignantly aware that their vacation was coming to an end and that in another week she would be heading back home. After all she had seen and experienced she wondered if she would ever be able to settle down again to the dull routines she was used to. She didn't know if she could. It would be like trying to make herself go unconscious again after finally waking up from a coma.

After getting a muffin and coffee at a little bakery in the town they made their way to the south end of the town where they were told they could see fur seals. It was a large area of flat rock that spread from the bottom of the cliffs out to sea. They spotted three huge fur seals lying in the sun seemingly asleep.

Mary was delighted, but even more so by all the different types of seaweeds in the rock pools that abounded—green, brown, yellow, white and crimson. She was amazed at how beautiful some of them were especially the delicate, lacy crimson and pink ones that lay flat against the grey rock. She took masses of photos. She even saw the fossil of a scallop shell in the rock and took photos of that.

Leaving Kaikoura, they continued north and took a detour to visit a lavender farm. Mary had wanted to see one since she had seen photos of fields of lavender in a magazine, but it turned out to be too late in the season and the lavender had been harvested already.

"Oh well, that stays on my bucket list," she thought, but she did stop in the gift shop and bought some lavender oil for people back home.

They had been told that they might see another colony of seals further up the coast road at Ohau Point where there was another fur seal sanctuary, so when she saw the sign Mary asked Mitch to pull off the road. What she saw was more than she could ever imagine. There were hundreds of seals including lots of baby ones frolicking and playing in the swirling waters between the rocks very close to the shore. She was able to get up close and see the babies with their sleek black coats and big, round, bulging, black eyes. One in particular seemed to be playing peek-a-boo with her. She stayed there for ages in absolute awe. She even got to see four little ones clambering awkwardly over the rocks to get to their mother to nurse, sucking hungrily and squirming around as she lay peacefully in the sun. Then off they went again to play in the water.

After Mary and Mitch had sat there for a long time they decided to go up the trail to the waterfall that they had been told about. The trail ran beside a river with several pools at various points along the way as it cascaded down over rocks. In each one there were seals, swimming and playing. At the top of the trail they came to a much larger pool with a beautiful waterfall flowing into it. Beneath the waterfall were many more seals—adults and young swirling around, swimming hither and thither and seemingly having a wonderful time. The beauty of the spot, with the bright green mosses and ferns, was stunning, and the magic of the playful seals almost broke Mary's heart. She lingered and lingered, trying to fill her heart with the joy and awe she felt. It was as if, if she got enough of it, it would last her the rest of her life.

She wondered if Mitch's friends, who loved to hunt and fish, would be able to appreciate the beauty of these seals, or just see them as something else they could shoot. The seals had been hunted almost to extinction until a ban had been put on it in 1894.

Eventually they tore themselves away and continued up to the harbour town of Waikawa on the north coast of the South Island—a different Waikawa than the Waikawa Beach on the North Island where they had stayed in the bach. Here they were booked to stay in a bed and breakfast for a couple of nights before taking the ferry back to the North Island from nearby Picton. It turned out to be owned by a woman called

Lynette who worked as a chef twice a week on tourist boats for groups of high-end tourists. She cooked them gourmet meals of local delicacies, like green-lipped mussels. Mary thought that sounded really funny as she could imagine the mussels looking up at her with large, pouty green lips. She also cooked two meals a day for three hundred migrant workers who were picking grapes in the local vineyards. Mary asked her a lot of questions about the kinds of meals she made and how she managed with just two helpers. Mary was one of a team of five who worked her shift at the prison cooking meals for the prisoners. It sounded as though the grape-pickers were fed much more interesting and healthy meals. She wondered if she could suggest some improvements when she got back, although the thought of being back in that environment made her stomach turn. She imagined herself working alongside Lynette on the boats and in the vineyards.

They spent a day exploring Waikawa and Picton. They walked around the town and along the shore. Mary spotted at least three different kinds of starfish on the beach, clusters of beautiful orangey-pink scallop shells as well as great clumps of mussels clinging to the jetty. The next day they drove along Queen Charlotte's Drive. They stopped in many of the beautiful coves and inlets of Queen Charlotte Sound. In Havelock they had lunch in a restaurant and Mary bravely ordered a bowl of the famous, green-lipped mussels cooked in a white wine and cream sauce. They were indeed well-named. They were each about 3 inches long, sandy brown in colour with bright green edges around the top. And they were delicious! Mitch decided to play it safe and stuck with a chicken and avocado wrap. Like many New Zealanders it seemed, Lynette didn't own a television and that evening Mary really enjoyed playing a game of Scrabble with her. The score was really close although Lynette won in the end.

Next morning they caught the ferry from Picton to Wellington and bid a sad farewell to the South Island. The sun was shining and the journey back across the Marlborough Straits was perhaps even more beautiful than it had been on the way down, although for Mary it was tinged with sadness as she got closer and closer to the end of their trip.

They only stayed one day in Wellington. Mary was very aware, after their experience in Christchurch, that it was situated right on a fault line and she looked with amazement at the houses built seemingly precariously up the sides of the many hills. Like San Francisco it seemed to be a matter of when rather than if the big quake would hit and she couldn't begin to imagine the damage it would wreak. They went to the Te Papa Museum and discovered that the whole of New Zealand's geography was the result of violent happenings of nature—volcanic eruptions and earthquakes. They also walked around town and visited Zealandia where they saw strange birds, bugs and reptiles.

Early next morning they caught the train from Wellington to Auckland—an eleven-hour trip across the heart of the North Island. The scenery was exquisitely beautiful—farmland, forests, rivers, ravines and glacier-capped mountains. Mary was very quiet on the journey—in fact she spent much of it in the last carriage, which had no seats and was open, with no windows. When she did sit beside Mitch in the coach seats, she said little and he, as usual, didn't say much. Mary didn't know if he was sad to be going home or if he was looking forward to it and when she asked him he just said he didn't know, both perhaps. Growing up in a large family as Mitch had you either learned to shout louder and talk more than everyone else or shut up and say nothing because you weren't going to be heard anyway. Mitch had chosen the latter option and kept his own counsel, especially if something was going on inside him.

It was after they got to their hotel that Mary told Mitch she needed to talk to him.

"I can't go back," she said.

Mitch looked at her.

"I figured as much. I've seen you change during this trip. But what do you mean exactly—you can't go back? We're booked on the flight tomorrow."

I don't know exactly," said Mary. "I just know I can't go back to the old life I was living or rather that I was slowly dying in. I can't go back to being the person I was, and I can't marry you. It's different for you. You have the farm and your family. Even if they are a bunch of idiots who drink too much and act stupid, they are your family. But I don't have any of that. I like you a lot. We get on so well. You've always been such a safe person for me, which I needed after my crazy childhood. But I realize now, it's not enough. You're too safe, too comfortable. I want more. My eyes have been opened. Maybe I love you but not the way I want to love the man I marry and I don't think I'm anywhere near ready for marriage yet. I am so sorry to do this to you, but I can't do it. I don't know what I am going to do, maybe apply for a job cooking for tourists at one of those great camps in the Adirondacks, maybe I'll apply to come back to New Zealand for a year, or go back to school, maybe something completely different. I just don't know yet. What I do know is that I can't go back to my old life and I can't marry you."

Mary held Mitch in her arms for a long time before they fell asleep.

It was a long journey home. Mitch didn't say much, although Mary thought he seemed sad. He wouldn't tell her what he was thinking even when she asked him.

His brother was there to meet their flight and drive them back down to Malone and they told him some highlights of their trip, but after they told him the wedding was off, conversation lagged rather.

Mary spent the next few days letting everyone know that the wedding wouldn't be happening and cancelling the plans they had made. She put an ad in the *Malone Free Trader:* "For Sale: Wedding Dress. Size 20. Never worn," and then she felt ready to step forward into her new life, although she had no idea what that would be.

The Invitation

Have you ever taken a journey that has changed you in some ways—opened your eyes to new possibilities, helped you to question some of your assumptions? If so, I invite you to write your story. What impacted you most strongly? What changes happened inside you? What beliefs did you question in new ways?

The Wedding Dress

I am very beautiful but for many years I thought I was cursed.

Perhaps I should start at the beginning. I am a wedding dress and I have a rather long and curious tale to tell, so why don't you make yourself a nice cup of tea and settle down comfortably. Yes, there you are. Would you like to put your feet up? Another cushion for your back? Good. Comfortable? So I'll begin.

I came into being quite a number of years ago now in the studio of a dressmaker, or "haute couturier" as she preferred to be called, who was quite well-known at the time in the city where I was conceived and "born," so to speak.

There is something I think would be helpful for you to know. When babies are born, humans generally see them as coming into the world devoid of knowledge and consciousness. This may or may not be true. Wedding gowns, however, come into being with the collective consciousness of all the wedding gowns that have gone before. While this knowledge is strongest from those that have been closest geographically and in time, somewhere in our fabric is woven the awareness and understanding of all wedding "dress-ness".

The dressmaker's studio was a happy place full of beautiful evening gowns, bridesmaids dresses and, of course, wedding dresses of different shapes and styles. None of us stayed there long for we left as soon as we were completed, but we were all full of excitement about the lives we were setting out to lead. The evening dresses would chatter away about the glamorous balls they would attend. The bridesmaids' dresses twittered away like a flock of excited birds, but always demurred to those of us who would take centre stage on the big day. I'm sorry to say some of us could be a little condescending in return.

We wedding dresses would dream endlessly of our big day when we would be the centre of attention, when all eyes would be on us as we glided down the aisle, the day on which the life of our bride would change irrevocably, when she would be transformed into a fairy princess, a queen, an empress, a goddess! Just for this one day she would be the most beautiful woman in the eyes of the world to make the biggest transition of her life—from maiden to wife. We knew we would only be worn that one day but what a day that would be! We all picked up snippets of information about our up-coming great day as our brides chatted with the dressmaker about the groom, about their plans for the flower arrangements and the bouquet, for the food to be served at the reception, the music to be played, the dancing. Some even shared thoughts and fears about their wedding nights and we were all very curious about what would happen once we had been removed.

Let me describe myself a little so you have a picture of me. I was made to perfectly fit the body of a magnificent, voluptuous woman with flaming red hair and a fiery personality. When she arrived for her fittings I could hear her sweeping up the stairs and into the studio in a great whoosh of air. I was a little afraid of her, if truth be told, scared that she would find fault with me, that I wouldn't please her, but there was nothing the dressmaker couldn't adjust to suit her exacting standards. Mostly, however, I would really enjoy the fittings. I felt so elegant and beautiful as I was draped around her body and fitted snugly to contain and support her ample breasts and flow over her rounded hips. I am made of yards and yards of satin tightly fitted in a strapless, sleeveless bodice with a low plunging neckline to show off her endowments to fullest magnificence. This is all discretely covered over with a long sleeved lace over-bodice which ends just below the waist. I have little pearl buttons all the way up the back. My skirt is lightly pleated at the waist and then it cascades into a wonderful train that swirls behind when she moves. There is a delicate lace trim all the way around the hem. Can you picture me?

My bride filled the space when she entered the studio. She had the grace and magnificence of a ship under full sail as she moved around the room wearing me and I imagined us sweeping up the aisle to meet the man she was to marry, whilst the congregation gasped in awe at my beauty and her groom's eyes teared up with love and gratitude.

It was a charming dream and I cherish it still, but life doesn't always turn out the way one expects, as I have come to realize. That certainly wasn't the reality of what transpired. But I'll come back to that shortly.

We wedding gowns were as proud of our brides as they were of us. We bragged about their beauty, their charms, their figures, their wealth or social standing if they had any—anything we could find to one-up the brides of the other gowns—a harmless and friendly rivalry that helped to pass the time and make us feel even better about ourselves, or so we hoped when we scored a point. So while some of the other dresses, especially the smaller sizes, who barely took up any space at all, scoffed and snickered at times at the size of my bride, I took tremendous pride in her magnificence, her girth and splendour. She was a woman of substance and I felt blessed to be her gown.

The day after I was completed she came to get me. She took me home and hung me in the closet. I couldn't see anything of course, because it was dark and I was very carefully wrapped in a special bag to keep me safe and hidden from his gaze until our big day. As a result, I didn't see what happened but I certainly overheard the scene as it unfolded and let me tell you, I was very shocked and totally devastated. All my hopes and dreams came crashing down around my hem that day.

It was a weekday so neither of them should have been at home. They both left as usual in the morning, but around mid-morning I could hear some strange noises in the bedroom. It was his voice I could hear but it definitely wasn't hers. First of all I could hear them taking their clothes off, zippers coming down and clothes being thrown willy nilly in great haste. Then I heard noises as though they were thrashing around on the bed in a most vigorous manner. They were breathing heavily, grunting and squealing. I couldn't tell what was going on, but suddenly I heard the bedroom door fly open. It was then that I heard my bride's voice. She was yelling and calling them terrible names. I can tell you I was in a state of complete shock to hear my bride using that kind of language. I would never have believed her capable of it. I could tell she was terribly upset. Suddenly I heard her curse me! I didn't hear the whole sentence but I did hear something about "the f@#king wedding dress!" and just after she said it I could feel the curse land on me, even protected as I was in the closet. It was like something dark and dank creeping into my soul. And then it sounded like she threw up all over the bed—it smelt really awful! Well, there followed a lot more cursing and then a lot of weeping. I was so angry and hurt, so let down by my bride that she was not the beautiful, elegant, exquisite, refined creature I had made her out to be, the one with the dignity to show me off in the way I deserved, I was caught up in my own misery. I felt so betrayed by her and so angry at him. How could he do this to my bride?

It soon became very obvious to me there was not going to be any wedding now and my big day was completely ruined. What would become of me? A wedding dress without a wedding, without a bride. A wedding dress with a curse hanging over me. I had lost my sense of purpose, my raison d'être. It was all too much for me. She seemed so angry and hurt herself I was afraid she would come in the closet and tear me to shreds.

Instead, she just cursed me every time she saw me hanging here. At other times I could hear her sobbing uncontrollably into her pillow.

The next day I heard her on the phone. She was telling someone she wanted to place an ad in the paper, "For sale: Wedding dress. Size 20. Never worn". Well, she added some extra words in there but I will not repeat those to you. Suffice to say, she clearly wasn't the bride I had been so proud of. I had no idea what would happen to me after that. All I could do was hang around and wait to see what fate had in store for me. I am embarrassed to say that I think I went into a bit of a depression hanging around alone in that dark closet with no sense of purpose and all my hopes crushed.

It was probably about a week later when she came to get me—a terrible, endless week of grief and uncertainty. I was very surprised to see, when she took me out of the bag, that it was a man standing in front of me, looking me up and down—a somewhat strange looking man, but a man nonetheless. I had never heard of a man buying a wedding dress except perhaps a few gay or trans men but my understanding was that even they did not generally get married in gowns like me. As yet the general information on gay marriage was not very extensive among wedding dresses as it was not permitted everywhere and was only recently even a possibility. I had never actually met or even heard of a gown that had been worn by a man.

He asked to try me on and I can tell you I was shocked and disgusted at the idea. I don't have any objections to men getting married, I had just never expected personally to be placed on the body of a man. But I was really too depressed to care what happened to me at that point and my bride still seemed too angry to care either. In fact she almost seemed amused that I was not going to be worn by another beautiful woman who would be walking down the aisle to meet the man of her dreams at the altar.

The man's name was Suzanna and he stood in front of the mirror gazing at me from every angle. He seemed totally delighted with the way he looked in me so he paid what my should-have-been bride was asking without quibbling and took me away with him.

The next thing I knew I found myself hanging on a rack with a lot of other gowns in the dressing room of a theatre. I can't begin to tell you the state I was in. I hung there limply, taking no interest in my new surroundings, not even bothering to get to know the other gowns hanging on the rack. I felt hopeless and purposeless. I think I would have set fire to myself or thrown myself off a tall building if there was any possibility of that. I had lost everything and now I was to be worn by some ghastly male! What would the other dresses back at the studio have thought of that. Oh, how they would have made fun of me! The shame was all too much. My self-esteem was at rock bottom.

The next night I was the last gown to be taken down from the rack. Each of the others had taken their turn. They had been placed one by one on this strange male body. He also had a variety of wigs and make up, including false eyelashes. Other parts of his anatomy were also false to make him look very like a large voluptuous woman, although I don't think he really fooled anybody—it was all so over the top!

I was surprised when he finally took me off the shelf, changed his wig to a long blond affair with mounds of cascading curls, touched up his make-up and dashed back out onto the stage of the theatre. I could feel him take a big, deep breath and then release it. I could see that there were hundreds of eyes from the people in the audience on me and I didn't care. I wanted to fall through the floor. I wanted to run away and hide in a dark closet and never come out again. I wanted to turn towards the audience and scream, "This is not who I really am. This is not what I was made for." I didn't do any of these things. I just hung there limply and waited for the end to come.

Suzanna stood there striking poses and trying to look coy and virginal whilst a person whom I thought had to be a woman dressed as the groom (I later found out she was a well-known drag king named Vesta Shields), sang the Joe Cocker song "You Are So Beautiful." This was supposed to be their new grand finale. They had worked on it for some time and rehearsed diligently. Suzanna had bought me specifically for this number. I was supposed to bring the house down. However, after Vesta finished the last note and it hung in the air, there was barely any response at all from the audience—a little bit of lame clapping and people started leaving immediately. The curtain came down and Suzanna and Vesta left the stage in tears. I was removed in the dressing room and hung back on the rack with the other gowns. I couldn't believe my own misery. Was this to be my life? Was this my destiny? The ignominy of it was too much to bear.

This appalling scenario was repeated for several nights in a row. Vesta was obviously trying harder and harder, without success, to wring the emotional response she wanted from the audience. Suzanna was trying harder and harder, without success, to appear as the most beautiful bride who ever was told she was beautiful. Night after night I hung there limply trying to survive the shame and disappointment of all I had lost and what my cursed life had become. Night after night the act fell flat and Suzanna and Vesta returned to the dressing room in tears. Finally one night I heard them talking about cutting this final number and developing a new finale to their act. They threw around some ideas, none of which involved me.

At first I was terribly relieved. I wouldn't have to go through this ordeal any more. Then I started to wonder what would happen to me next. Would I be thrown in a dumpster, left in some dark corner of some theatre dressing-room as they moved on to new places, sold to god-knows-who for who-knows-what purpose, cut up to make cushions or dust rags? Was this what I wanted? No! I was better than that! I was a made-to-measure gown! I was designed to adjust to the curves and circumstances of the one who was to wear me. I was not some ready-to-wear dress who has to hang around waiting for the right fit to come along. I was flexible and adaptable and I had better remember that before it was too late. It was time I pulled myself together and realized that the life I had was the life I had, even if it wasn't the life I had expected. Besides which, I realized, this way I would be in the spotlight night after night with all eyes on me, rather than just the one time as I would have been had my bride worn me down the aisle.

The next night, when Suzanna put me on for the final number, there was obviously something different about me. He could feel it through his skin, he could sense it in his being. I no longer hung limply on his body but shaped myself to his contours, glowed with a new radiance and showed him off to full advantage. Vesta picked up on it immediately and there was a new authenticity in her voice when she looked at Suzanna and sang, "You Are So Beautiful To Me," down to the last high, quavering note. The audience erupted into applause. They leaped out of their seats, clapped and cheered and Suzanna and Vesta took bow after bow, encore after encore, until finally the curtain came down and they hugged each other in disbelief.

After that life really became very exciting. We travelled a lot from town to town putting on shows, meeting new people. We became rather famous on the cabaret circuit. It was a busy life, constantly packing up and moving, unpacking in new places, some seedy but many quite posh. We worked hard and had a lot of fun and night after night I finished the show with my big number—the grand finale, the piece de resistance. I was the star of the show. It may not have been my original purpose in life but who is to say how fate guides us towards our true vocation. I have to admit I did love the spotlight and all the admiration. I liked being looked up to by the other gowns who were all very beautiful in their own way. I made some good friends—you have to learn to get along with others when you are traveling around like that. Suzanna took exquisite care of me. I felt precious and cherished by him. Three wonderful years we had together. Then one night it all came crashing down—literally.

I had been getting a little concerned about Suzanna's drinking for some time. Initially it was a glass of champagne here or there or a drink or two to celebrate our success. Then the pressure started to build. How to stay on top, how to keep going on night after night and feel fresh? What if some new act came along and took over the place we had carved out for ourselves? There were always young upstarts hungry for success, hungry to take away what was ours. I could feel the tension in his body each night when he put me on, but then he would look in the mirror, see his own magnificence, see his beauty reflected in Vesta's eyes as she put all she had into this wonderfully evocative, emotional love song, and I could feel the tension drain away for those few minutes. I felt proud of the power I had to relax him and bring him back to his sense of confidence. Unfortunately, it didn't last once he took me off and hung me back up on the rack, took off the wig, the make-up, the eye lashes, took off the falsies and got back into his street clothes. Without me he looked more like any old stage hand as he left the theatre than the top-billed performer of the show.

It happened one evening during one of the early numbers. Suzanna was wearing a very short, red, sequinned dress with matching boots. They were the most amazing boots you have ever seen. Suzanna had ordered them from a very well-known company in Northumberland, England, that specialized in making custom-designed boots for drag queens. He had only had them a couple of weeks. They had 1 ½ inch platform soles and 10 inch heels. They were shiny and red and stretched right up his long legs almost to the crotch. He had had to practice walking gracefully and even dancing along the catwalk in them, as he sang a song from a new musical which had just opened on Broadway. It was not easy from what I had seen when he staggered back into the dressing room on previous evenings. I don't think the alcohol helped any.

Well, that fateful evening, there was suddenly a great buzz in the theatre. It took a while for the news to get back to us but when it did we were all in a state of shock. Suzanna had fallen off the catwalk in the middle of his song and dance number, right into the lap of a woman in the audience, hitting his head on the arm of her chair. He had passed out. An ambulance had been called and immediately whisked him off to hospital.

As you can imagine, we were all extremely worried about Suzanna, and also about what would happen to us. We received little news and it was a very uncertain time for us. A few days later we were all folded up and put in a hamper in a corner of a storage cupboard where it was hard to even get a sense of the gossip going around the theatre. We were literally left in the dark.

We languished there in a state of uncertainty for some weeks. It was a dreadful time but at least we had each other for comfort and reassurance and we spent a lot of time reminiscing about past glories, places we'd been, funny moments and this cheered us up a little.

Then one day, unexpectedly, we were pulled out of the storage closet and hung up on a rack in one of the dressing rooms. And then there was Suzanna. I barely recognized him—he had changed so much! He had lost a lot of weight and can you believe it—he had grown a beard. A beard of all things! Unthinkable. It seemed that we were there to be auctioned off to raise some money for him to go back to live on his family's farm in Arkansas!!! Poor Suzanna—how ghastly for him. No more bright lights, no more adoration from his fans. Just corn and cows! My heart almost broke. We had been so close night after night for three years and I had become so fond of him. I had found a new purpose and a new life with him. He had made me a star when I had thought that my life was over. I would be forever grateful.

One by one the other costumes were all auctioned off, including the kinky red boots Suzanna had been wearing the day of his accident. I was the last item left and most of the people had left. I was starting to feel a little desperate when Suzanna asked who wanted me. I am of a scale where I require a body of a certain size and shape to display me to my fullest advantage and not everyone has the stature to carry me off well. I had noticed two particular men eyeing me furtively through-out the proceedings, trying not to show the degree of their desire for me, I thought. Suzanna seemed quite tired by this time and I think he just wanted the whole thing to be over, so rather than auctioning me to the highest bidder he set a price and asked if anyone was willing to pay that. The two queens who had been eyeing me, whom I knew by their stage names of Roberta and Cassandra, stepped forward. They immediately started squabbling over me like a couple of cats. I was scared they would each grab me and tear me in two and perhaps Suzanna had the same fear because he held up his hand to stop them. They tried to figure out a way they were going to decide who would be the one to get me, but every time it deteriorated into an argument that was going nowhere. Seeing how they were behaving I knew I didn't want to be owned by either of them, but I didn't have much say in the matter.

Finally Suzanna suggested that they play a hand of cards and the winner would get to take me. Can you imagine! Me, who had been destined to be worn by a magnificent bride, had her sad fate not befallen her, me, who had been the star of the show, who had been applauded by audiences around the country, having my fate decided on a hand of cards! I must say I was rather angry at Suzanna for doing this to me after all we had been through, after all the times I had been there for him. It was the final ignominy. The curse was still with me.

I watched with lack-lustre interest as Suzanna pulled a deck of cards from a dressing-table drawer and dealt out three cards each. Cassandra had a gleam in his eye and a slight smirk on his face as he put one card face down on the table and asked Suzanna for one more card. Roberta was inscrutable as he put down two and asked for two more.

"I'll see you," said Cassandra.

"A pair of queens, ace high," responded Roberta. "You?"

Cassandra threw his cards on the table. I could see he had tears in his eyes.

"That beats my pair of Jacks," he said. "You win. The dress is yours," and he stormed out of the room looking like he would gladly have scratched Roberta's eyes out.

"A pair of Queens. How ironic." said Roberta, as he carefully packed me up, gave Suzanna a big hug, wished him all the best and left. So started my new life.

Roberta had neither the class nor the talent that Suzanna had had and I never really got into the spirit of show business again. Roberta was full of big dreams but didn't really have the follow-through to make them happen. He complained a lot about what other people weren't doing for him, how they weren't giving him the breaks he deserved, that he wasn't getting the lead billing, that the dressing rooms were not properly cleaned or were too draughty, that people were cheating him out of his take and an endless list of other things. As a result, over the next two years we played a bunch of third-rate clubs to audiences who had been drinking too much and weren't really there to see our act. They just wanted the dancing girls to come out and take their clothes off so they could ogle some ass and tits. Occasionally we were actively booed off the stage but mostly we were just ignored. I hated it all and gave as little to the performance as I got. I missed Suzanna horribly and his beautiful gowns that I had become friendly with. I didn't bother to make friends with the shabby new companions I found myself in the company of.

The gigs got fewer and fewer and eventually I spent most of my time hanging around in closets of seedy hotel rooms. I was sure I was going to attract moths or other bugs. Roberta didn't give me the care and attention Suzanna had, so I felt sorely neglected. I slid back into a state of depression. It sounds like an oxymoron—a depressed wedding gown, but there you are. It was the truth.

One day I heard a woman's voice in the room.

"I read your ad in the *Free Trader*," she said. For sale: Wedding dress. Size 20. never worn. Let me see it." I was brought out of the closet and the small, grey-haired woman looked me up and down.

"If this has never been worn, I'm a monkey's uncle," she said, "but it'll do I suppose. I'm going to have to pay a fortune for cleaning, so I'll give you $25 as is."

"Twenty-five dollars!" Roberta sounded outraged. "It's an insult." I had to agree with him about that. "I won't take a penny less than $200." I was still feeling stung by the insult of this. A mere $200! I considered myself worth much more than that.

"Twenty-five and not a penny more," said the woman as she turned to leave.

"Oh, very well then," capitulated Roberta, to my utter shock and horror. The woman slapped down twenty-five dollars, grabbed me off the hanger, rolled me up in a ball, shoved me in a plastic bag she had brought with her and was out the door with me faster than you can imagine.

After a short car ride she took me out and I found myself in a dry cleaner's shop. I must say the process of being cleaned was not very pleasant but I felt a lot better at the end of it. I felt quite restored to myself, almost virginal again. I was starting to feel curious to see what my new life would be. Who was this middle-aged woman? Why had she bought me? It was clearly not for herself as she was a woman of small stature and I would never fit her. For a beloved daughter perhaps but why was the daughter not with her to choose me herself? Unanswerable questions. I would just have to wait and see but I was so grateful to be out of that musty closet and to be all clean and fresh again I felt ready to face anything.

When I was unwrapped from the dry cleaner's bag I found myself in a small windowless room in a large old mansion-style house. I was surrounded by other dresses including many wedding gowns of various styles and sizes, but also bridesmaid dresses, tuxedos, top hats and tails and other wedding outfits—mother of the bride, and so on. Many of the women's outfits were quite décolleté and on the risqué side of good taste, but far be it from me to criticize. Feeling more myself and very curious to know what was in store for me, I quickly struck up conversations with the gowns around me.

Well, I thought I had hit rock bottom with Roberta but this was a whole new level of degradation! I would never have even guessed such a place could exist. Apparently, my new home was a whore-house that specialized in wedding scenarios. Have you ever heard of such a thing? Apparently there are men and women out there who have sexual fantasies and fetishes that involve wedding scenarios or gear—men who get off on ravishing "virginal" brides, mothers-of-the bride who want to get laid by all the ushers and the best man, best men who can't wait to get into the knickers of the bride, the ushers, the bridesmaids or even the bride's mother, and bridesmaids who can't wait to ravish each other. There are even people with sexual fetishes involving wedding cakes. Hearing all the other gowns talk as well as the crosstalk with the tails and tuxedos, I can tell you it was an eye-opener. As you can imagine, wedding dresses are quite sexually naive because we are usually kept closeted until the big day and then hung up carefully in another closet before any of the work of sexual consummation begins. Of course, we know that it happens but the details are pretty hazy for most of us and I had very little sexual education beyond that, despite the unusual and exciting life I had led. Not much happens of a sexual nature in the dressing rooms of drag queens, at least not Suzanna and Roberta's.

Once I got over my initial shock I actually got to quite like the other gowns and outfits hanging in that room. They were rather a bawdy lot but generally good sports and we all had a lot of laughs about the shenanigans that the humans got up to. None of them took any of it very seriously. I must admit that almost all the others were of the ready-to-wear variety, so not up to my standard in many ways, but they seemed to have accepted their fates. All of them had actually had their day in the limelight and had been sold by their brides after the great event. They lived with no regrets and were happy to have found a home with amusing company to hang out with, rather than being packed up in a damp attic until they turned mouldy or were eaten by moths. I didn't share much about my own early history—I certainly didn't want to be pitied by a bunch of ready-mades for never having walked down the aisle, but I did tell them about my experiences as a cabaret star and some of them seemed impressed and wanted to know more.

After only a couple of days in the wardrobe-room the madam, the short lady with grey hair who had bought me, came to get me. She introduced me to a rather large, plump young woman, with doughy hands. She helped the girl to put me on and had to do up all the little pearl buttons up my back herself. She kept telling the girl, whose name was Bettina, to be nice to the man, to make him feel good, to do whatever he wanted. I guessed she was fairly new at this game. I am ashamed to admit I was a little curious as to what would happen when the "bride" and "groom" got together.

The madam met the "groom" at the door and introduced him to Bettina. He was an older man with grey hair and a large paunch of a belly—not exactly a stud of a man, although he looked nice dressed up in his tuxedo. She then took them upstairs to one of the rooms. There was a bottle of champagne and two glasses on a dresser. When they were left alone, Bettina and the groom seemed rather awkward and uncomfortable with each other. I got the sense that neither of them really had a lot of experience or knew what to do. The groom poured some champagne for both of them and they sat on the bed to drink it. After a couple of sips the groom took her glass away and very gently asked her to stand up and turn around. He then undid all my buttons, fumbling rather as he did so. Then he slid me off her shoulders and let me fall to the floor. She stood there plumply naked. He picked me up and laid me gently on the chair from whence I had an excellent view of the proceedings, whilst still being able to pick up the vibes of my "bride."

The groom did his best. I felt sorry for him because he tried really hard to very tenderly arouse Bettina in a variety of ways, telling her she was beautiful and gently stroking her breasts and other parts of her body, but none of it seemed to be doing it for either of them. Bettina really wasn't into it and he didn't seem to be getting aroused either, no matter what she did. She just wasn't a very enthusiastic participant and I imagine that he sensed it.

The problem was the cake. Bettina had baked a cake just before the man's arrival. I could smell the aroma of it on her body when she put me on. I could feel her longing for it. I could hear her stomach rumbling. The smell of it had filled the house and it had smelt so divine. While he wanted to take his time and get her aroused, she seemed to just want him to get it over with as soon as possible so she could get back to the kitchen. She was getting more and more discouraged and frustrated. Eventually the poor man suggested that they give up on it. She just shrugged when he apologized repeatedly for his inability to be a better lover. Then he left.

Bettina poured herself another glass of champagne. She figured the cake would have all been eaten by now and didn't want to waste a perfectly good glass of bubbly. She was sitting, naked, on the bed drinking it when the madam walked in.

"Bettina," she said, "I just talked with your client as he was leaving. It seems as though the sexual experience was less than satisfactory to him, although he did say that he got something very important out of it. Something about realizing it wasn't all his fault. The point is, Bettina, that I don't think this is the right line of work for you. You don't seem to have any enthusiasm or artistry for the craft and the clients pick up on it. It just won't do. I won't be able to keep you on."

I could feel both relief and anxiety rising in Bettina as she listened. Where would she go? What would she do?

The madam continued.

"I know you love to bake and that you are very good at it. That cake you baked earlier was wonderful. All the girls enjoyed it and I even had some myself." Bettina thought she could see the crumbs still around the madame's mouth and down her blouse and felt an overwhelming sadness that there would be no cake left for her.

"What I will do for you is give you that dress you were wearing. I can't imagine I'll have any more use for it. It is not a size that clients usually request. Perhaps you can sell it and set yourself up in business as a baker. If you specialize in wedding cakes I'll hand out your business card for you and when I have clients who want a cake as part of the scenario, I'll be sure to order from you. You're a good girl and I'm fond of you. But I just can't keep you on." With that she left the room.

That simple act of kindness on the part of the madam, that act of giving me to Bettina to start up a new life, a life she was more suited to, had a huge impact on me. It was as if the curse that I had been carrying since that fateful day in my bride's bedroom was lifted. I felt light, airy, hopeful.

Bettina sat and looked at me for a while, then slipped me back on and we went downstairs. She didn't even bother to do up my buttons but I didn't mind. (The cake had indeed all been eaten.)

The next day she packed me up and we left the brothel together. We moved to a very small apartment in a run down area of town, but it had a large stove. Bettina placed an ad in the *Free Trader* "For sale: Wedding Dress. Size 20. Never worn." She struggled over the last two words because technically she had worn me to go upstairs and then down again but I hadn't been worn for a wedding and she knew nothing of my history, assuming I had been new when I was brought to the brothel.

During the short time I was with her, Bettina talked to me constantly about her plans. She would buy some cake pans, icing materials and ingredients with the money she got for me. She would also have some business cards made and some flyers. She already had a commission from the madam for a cake for an upcoming wedding scenario where the client wanted to include the cutting and eating of the cake. She talked to me about the life she imagined living and I felt happy and hopeful for her and for myself. I shall always be grateful to Bettina for being such a lousy whore and to the madam for her act of generosity.

The woman who came to find me in response to the ad had a lovely energy. She had curly brown hair and an ample figure. I sensed that she was already pregnant but I had seen too much to become judgmental. I liked her immediately.

She took me home and a few days later she had a group of her friends over. It was a sort of hen-party but not like the young girls have where they get drunk and wild and do things they later feel ashamed of. No this was an evening with some very dear close friends who clearly loved my bride a lot. At one point in the evening they got me out of the closet and with a sage stick they smudged me. It was an amazing experience. It was like the very last of the negative energy in me, the curse and all the bad experiences I had had, were drawn out of me, transformed and dispersed back into the universe. Then they sang and celebrated and blessed me and my bride with wishes of happiness and health. I felt radiant and beautiful all over again, filled with light and love.

A month later I finally had my big day, or perhaps I should say that my bride had her big day. It wasn't really all about me at all. It was about my bride and her groom, the love they had for each other and the loving family they wanted to create for their children including the new baby. It wasn't in a church as I had always imagined. It was in their home, which was warm and welcoming. Their friends all brought food to share that they had made themselves with love. They had written the service themselves to make it personal and meaningful to them. Their children each had a role in the weaving together of this new family. Their vows moved me in every fibre of my fabric. I shall carry that always within me. I think I look more beautiful than I ever did before because I am imbued with their love.

She has put an ad in the *Free Trader* for me: "For Sale: Wedding Dress. Size 20. Worn once with great love and joy." I don't know what fate has in store for me next but I welcome it with open arms.

I hope that you have enjoyed my tale and that it will give you some hope in the darkest moments of your own life, when you are feeling depressed, disappointed and cursed, that sometimes things can change for the better through simple acts of kindness.

The Invitation

How have you been doing with your own writing? Have you been having fun? For this invitation I thought I would ask you to write a story from the perspective of an article—a dish rag, a camper van, a piece of clothing—a sweater, pair of pant-ies—or a creature—a dog, a turtle, whatever. What kind of personality emerges when you put yourself into the "shoes," so to speak, of something else? Have fun. I hope you have enjoyed journeying with me and the size 20 wedding dresses and that it has inspired you to do some of your own writing. Now there is just one more story to read and my final invitation to you.

The Start of It All—Part 2

While Sophie was meeting with her women's group and trying to get them to write some stories, David had been spending time with his buddies. He had vaguely raised the idea of them coming up with some scenarios but with no more success than Sophie. In fact, David himself wasn't that interested in making up stories about the ad. He wanted to know the truth. He wanted to know what had really happened to lead the person who had placed the ad in the paper to put it there. Why hadn't the dress ever been worn? What had gone wrong? He was a practical, down-to-earth sort of person and knew he would never be satisfied with his own, or anybody else's, made up stories. His need to know stayed with him. He couldn't seem to let it go. He was sure there was some sad tale behind the ad. The picture of this somewhat overweight woman coming so close to being married and then having it all fall through touched him deeply. He imagined how sad and perhaps angry she might have felt when she placed that ad. David had a big heart and was very attuned in some ways to others' feelings. As the eldest son with a frequently distraught mother, he had taken on a lot of her feelings as a child. He was her confidant and also the recipient of the brunt of her anger. Although he didn't think about it in these terms himself, perhaps unconsciously he felt that if he could just find out what had gone wrong he would be able to fix it, as he tried to do unsuccessfully so many times as a child. He couldn't bear it when women were sad and he protected himself mostly by taking on responsibility for their feelings, although sometimes with Sophie he would withdraw and shut down rather than get enmeshed in her frustration.

On the long drive home from his get-together with his buddies he thought about finding out the real story and imagined himself as a great detective tracking down the relevant parties, following the leads, eventually finding the person who had placed the ad and getting the "true" story.

He had recently retired from work but Sophie still had her job and traveled frequently on business, so he had a lot of time with nothing much to do but read the newspaper, watch all the documentaries he liked on television, take the grandchildren out sometimes and take care of things at home. He started to wonder how difficult it would be to track down the person who had placed the ad and how he might go about it. He wondered if the paper kept a record of the ads they ran and who had placed them. He figured that might be a place to start.

The next morning after breakfast he called the newspaper.

"Oh no, we couldn't possibly give that kind of information over the phone," said the woman who answered. "You'd have to fill out a form and pay a fee because we would have to do a search. You'll have to come down to the office."

David nearly dropped the whole matter there, but something drove him on. It was a beautiful day and he'd enjoy the drive to the town a couple of hours away where the newspaper office was located, near to their little summer cabin. It was fall and the leaves were changing colour. The woods around the cabin would be brilliant with crimsons, reds, oranges and yellows. It was his favorite time of year to be there.

"This is crazy," he said to himself as he headed off, but he felt excited and a bit daring. It was a little like playing at being a detective. He loved the cop shows on TV and always tried to figure out the plots ahead of time and identify who had committed the crime. He often figured he could write some of the scripts himself.

When he arrived at the newspaper offices and found his way to the right department the woman behind the counter looked a little puzzled by his request, but he had white hair and a pleasant face and didn't look like a stalker or axe murderer. He sweet-talked her a bit and used his winning, boyish smile on her and she soon came around and said she would do her best. He didn't have much information, which would make it difficult to find, but she would see what she could do. He paid his fee and she told him to come back in three hours' time.

He walked around the town and found a place to sit outside to have some lunch. He wasn't used to being there by himself because Sophie was generally with him when they went to their cabin, but he found he was rather enjoying his solitary adventure and he'd tell her all about it when they spoke next. He could imagine the surprise and delight in her voice when he told her. He went for a walk in the nearby park and watched the clamour of the migrating geese massing on the lake. It was one of those spectacular fall days when the air is warm and yet crisp and clear and holds a poignancy from the knowledge of rapidly approaching winter.

Three hours later he was back at the newspaper office.

"All I have for you is a phone number of the person who placed the ad. The responses were to go to a post box number. Somehow the name doesn't seem to be there. Sorry I can't do more, but I did my best," said the woman behind the counter.

"Thank you very much for trying," he said as he left. Okay, so now he had a phone number. It wasn't much to go on, but at least it was something. He called the number, not quite sure what he'd say if someone answered, but it was out of service. He didn't know if he was relieved or disappointed. Alright, so what was his next step? Perhaps he could contact the phone company and find out who had held that number and see if he could find a name, an address and new phone number for them. He went back inside the newspaper office and asked the woman how he could contact the phone company. She looked it up on her computer and gave it to him. He thanked her again and left.

He called the phone company on his cell phone. When he told the person on the other end of the line what he wanted again the response was, "Oh, we couldn't possibly give that kind of information over the phone. You'll have to come into the office and fill out a form. There will be a fee for that kind of a search. However, everyone from that department will have left for the day now. You'll have to come in tomorrow."

Once again he thought to himself, "This is crazy. What am I doing this for?" He went back to his car and headed off in the direction of home.

"It was a nice outing," he thought to himself as he headed out of town. But then, as he passed the road that led to their cabin he changed his mind and turned the car around. "Why not follow this through?" he thought. "I have nothing particular I have to do tomorrow and this is rather fun."

When he arrived at the cabin he went for a lovely walk through the woods revelling in the beauty of the colours and the early evening light shining through the trees. He felt very alive and proud of himself that he was following through on this, even if it didn't lead anywhere. Back at the cabin he made himself some soup which was all he could find to eat. They had taken most of their stuff back to town in preparation for closing up for the winter. He watched a couple of cop shows on TV and went to bed. He felt a bit strange being there by himself and missed Sophie being there.

Next morning he drove back into the town, found a small restaurant and ordered bacon, eggs and sausage—his favorite. Then he headed over to the offices of the phone company. The young man who worked in the records department didn't seem to be at all interested in helping him but when David insisted a little, he said he'd go and find Mrs. Peters who had been around a long time and maybe she would be able to help him.

He waited around and about 15 minutes later Mrs. Peters came in. Again his pleasant face, warm smile and charming, rather old-world manner seemed to have the desired effect and she helped him fill out the requisition form and pay his fee for the search. She told him to come back again in two hours and she would see what she had for him. He went and had a coffee and walked around the town some more. It had clouded over and was a lot colder than the day before. There was a definite wintry bite in the air. Again David asked himself why he was going through all this, but he didn't seriously consider packing it in having come this far. It was the most excitement he'd felt in some time—probably since he'd retired. He felt a sense of purpose and accomplishment again.

When the two hours were up he went back and Mrs. Peters gave him a name and an address to which the phone number had belonged up until 3 years ago when the line was discontinued. Mrs. Elizabeth Hutchinson, Hill Rise Farm, RR #2. Well, this was progress. Mrs. Peters had no idea where the farm was so he went to the town offices to inquire there. He found someone to show him on an ordnance survey map where the property was located. It wasn't far out of town, so he got in his car and headed out there, his excitement mounting.

When he arrived at the farm it was starting to rain, a cold diagonal rain. He had headed out the day before dressed for the beautiful warm day, not intending to stay overnight. He hugged himself with his arms as he stood in the doorway waiting for someone to answer the bell. A young woman answered. "Are you Mrs. Elizabeth Hutchinson?" he asked.

"Oh, no, I'm Jane Andrews. But I think there was an old lady called Mrs. Hutchinson who lived here before we bought the place 3 years ago. Would it be her you're looking for?" she asked, looking rather puzzled. "She was very old. She must have been in her 70s or 80s. She couldn't keep the place up. Left it in rather a ramshackle state I'm afraid. I don't know what happened to her."

David's heart dropped. Perhaps she was dead and he would never know what the real story was behind the dress. To have come so far and have the trail go cold was just too frustrating.

"What would a real detective do under the circumstances?" he asked himself. "I doubt if he would just give up and go home with his tail between his legs at the first set-back."

"Is there anybody else who might know where she had gone afterwards? I would really like to try to find her. I have a question to ask her," David inquired.

"Well, I could ask my husband when he gets back from the barn. He shouldn't be long. It's almost time for him to come in and have his lunch. He starts his day real early so he likes to have his lunch around this time. Come on in. Will you have a cup of coffee while you wait? Come to think of it, he might know because for a while he used to take her mail to her."

David followed her into the house. Good food smells were coming from the kitchen. It was warm and welcoming. He saw a big pot of soup on the stove. Although the farm looked a bit run down in some ways it was clear the young couple was doing their best to fix it up. She served him a coffee in a nice pottery mug with a matching creamer and sugar bowl. The coffee and warm kitchen started to thaw him out again.

Shortly the door opened and a young man in his 30s came in, bundled up in a coat and scarf.

"Bit of a change in the weather today," he said to his wife and then looked up and saw the stranger sitting in his kitchen. He came over to greet him.

"Hi, I'm Ted Andrews," he said, holding out his hand in a friendly, welcoming way. David introduced himself.

"This gentleman's looking for Mrs. Hutchinson, the old lady we bought this place from," said Jane. "Has a question to ask her. I thought you might know where she moved to when she left here."

"Hmm. Let me think. Yes, I remember—Betty. She went into a home. The one on the way out of town on the old highway 11. I used to drop her mail off there when she first moved out. Don't know if she's still alive though. We stopped getting mail for her and I haven't kept in touch. No reason to."

They invited David to stay for lunch and share the soup and some home-made bread. He hesitated and then decided he would accept their warm hospitality. Again, something he wouldn't normally do, but he was on an adventure and that made him more adventuresome. It would be much more pleasant than sitting in another restaurant by himself and the soup smelt so good. Over lunch he told them the story of the ad for the wedding dress and why he was looking for Mrs. Hutchinson.

"That's odd," said Jane. "I can't imagine why a woman of her age would be selling a wedding dress. Now you've got me all curious too. Well I hope you find her and get an answer. It would be a shame if she had died after you've gone to all this trouble to track her down."

"Good luck," they said as he left.

He drove back into town, feeling a little panicky that she might have died and he'd never know the truth, or she might be dying right now or be senile—that would be even worse. Just out of town on Highway 11 he spotted the Seniors' Residence and pulled into the parking lot. At the reception desk he asked if they had a Mrs. Elizabeth Hutchinson living there.

"Oh yes," said the receptionist, "Have you come to visit her? She'll enjoy that. She loves to have visitors, but she's having her after-lunch nap right now. Would you mind coming back in an hour and I'll see if she can see you then?" David relaxed a bit on hearing she was alive and was with it enough to enjoy visitors, but he felt really impatient to wait another hour to meet her. He asked if there was somewhere he might sit and the receptionist showed him to a waiting room with large windows, reasonably comfortable chairs and a coffee table with lots of out-of-date magazines. He flipped through a couple of them and found himself dozing off. He awoke with a start when the receptionist came back to get him.

"She'll see you now," she said. "She didn't recognize your name and she's curious to know who you are and why you want to see her. She's a bit deaf so you might have to speak up a little. Come this way please." She led him down a bright hallway to another sitting room at the other end of the building where a white-haired lady, who looked to be in her eighties, was sitting at a table.

"So, you're my mystery visitor," she said as he came over and shook her hand. "I understand you have a question for me. I am filled with curiosity." She was bright and spry and seemed full of life and interest.

"Yes," he said and introduced himself. "I saw an ad in the *Free Trader* a few years ago that read 'For sale: wedding dress, size 20, never worn.' It piqued my curiosity and stayed with me. I wanted to know the story behind it. Why the dress was never worn. My curiosity and sadness just wouldn't go away and so the other day I decided I would do a little detective work and it has led me to you. I know it's rather nosy of me but I would love to know if you placed that ad and would you be willing to tell me the story behind it?"

"Oh, my goodness," she said with a bright twinkle in her eye. "I would never have guessed that that was what brought me a visitor here. The dress was my mother's. We found it in the attic long after she died when I was starting to pack up to move out of the farm. I don't know why she kept it. My father was a pilot. He died in the war. It was all a bit of a scandal actually back then. Her pregnant and not married, but she certainly wasn't the only young woman during the war years to find herself expecting with no husband. They'd been very much in love and it had all been very whirlwind. The wedding had been planned for his next leave. But it never happened."

"How very sad," David responded, his heart going out to her and her mother.

"Not really," she said. "It might have all been for the best in the long run. So many of the men who came back from the war were never the same again afterwards and made life miserable for those around them. They couldn't help it, poor buggers. They were that messed up by all they'd seen and done. It was particularly hard on some of the young pilots. The attrition rate was horrendous. The life expectancy of those young men was something like three weeks once they finished their training and started flying missions. They watched their buddies being picked off one by one. No, it was probably for the best in the long run. My mother met another young man about 3 years later. He was a farmer and so was needed at home to grow the crops to feed the war effort. He had wanted to go off to fight, as so many young men do. God only knows why. Dreadful business—war. He was a couple of years younger than my biological father and by the time he got it all organized and got through his basic training—infantry, you know—the war was finally over and so he never got to see any actual action. My mother was a big, buxom woman, strong and sturdy. She loved it on the farm—took to it like a duck to water and it was a good place to grow up. Lots of fresh air, fresh home-grown food, physical exercise. And my dad, that's how I always thought of him, was a really good and loving man. He adored my mother. They were really close, although I think she always lived a bit with the fear that something might happen to him and he wouldn't come home one day. It made her fuss a bit too much sometimes but he didn't seem to mind. Seemed to know it was another sign of her love for him. He died a couple of years before her. She was never the same after that. Lost her will to live a bit and was ready to go and join him. She was sure he was waiting for her somewhere nearby and she said she didn't want to keep him waiting any longer. No, it was probably for the best in the long run—for everyone except my biological father, of course. Or maybe even for him too. Who knows? That's why I was surprised when I found the dress. Perhaps she just packed it away and never got around to getting rid of it. I sold it through the *Free Trader*, you know. I wanted to give the money to a charity for unwed mothers, but I couldn't find one. No-one seems to worry about that now. No-one gets married any more it seems and women bring up children on their own all the time with no shame. So I gave it to the Am-Vets, sort of in honour of my biological father who never got to see her wearing it. She didn't wear it when she married my other dad. Just didn't seem right, I guess. Anyway, thanks for coming by. It's nice of you to care and to follow up on it. Not many would bother doing that I don't think. You seem to be a good man. You remind me a bit of my dad."

"Thanks for sharing your story with me," said David, as he took his leave. "I really appreciate it. I can let it go now that I know the truth. I don't have to carry that sadness around with me anymore. I'm glad it all turned out OK for you and your mum."

He walked away down the path feeling much lighter and full of joy that he had followed his urge to find out the truth. As he drove back home the rain stopped and the sun came out again bathing the fall landscape with brilliant colours. He couldn't wait to tell Sophie about his adventure.

The Final Invitation

I hope that the invitations at the end of each story have inspired you to write something. It isn't always easy to shift from intention to action, so congratulations to you if you did. If you didn't then maybe this isn't the right moment for you or it will take something different to inspire you.

Did you write a wedding dress story? I'm sure each person's story would be unique and different. If you would like to send me yours, I would love to read it and maybe I'll pull together a selection and put them online or publish them in another volume—giving you credit of course. So I invite you to send your story to me at slade.imago@gmail.com.

Acknowledgements

Firstly, I would like to thank David for inspiring me to write these stories with his emotional response to and curiosity about the ad in the *Free Trader*. He has been my support and my audience throughout this process and has made valuable suggestions, such as to write a story from the perspective of the wedding dress. He has been my life partner, my teacher and my companion on the fascinating, at times challenging, but mostly joyful journey of relationship. His support of me following my sometimes seemingly crazy dreams and impulses has been steadfast and has allowed me to do many things that have enriched my life.

I would also like to thank my fellow Crones: Carol Kramer, Sue Mautz, Cheryl Dollinger Brown, Barbara Bingham, Maya Kollman and Sylvia Rosenfeld. All are brilliantly wise women who have been invaluable fellow travellers with me on this journey of life. By not writing stories of their own as I originally requested, they spurred me to keep writing myself and then were so encouraging and supportive of all I shared with them right through to the publishing phase. I am also grateful to my friend Theresa Scott who helped me with my early efforts to publish.

My editor, Nikki Ali, was extraordinary in the time and effort she put in word by word and line by line. She corrected spelling and punctuation, engaged deeply with the characters and the stories, and made many wonderful suggestions to improve the narrative. It is thanks to her that I moved from one invitation after the first story to including an invitation after each making the book more of a fully interactive experience for those who want to engage in that way. Thanks also to Nicola Keysselitz, who designed the front cover, which I love.

Finally, my thanks go to my children, Janet, Tara, Emma and Andrew. When I struggled with whether to publish this under my own name versus a nom de plume and realized it wasn't just me it might impact but them also by association, they were all supportive of me going for it, to show myself and be seen as who I am—even if they don't want to read it. Too much information! They have all enriched my life in oh so many ways and contributed to who I am today.